D1756190

Devil Dog's Precious

Dublin Falls Archangel's Warriors MC #8

Ciara St James

Ciara St James

Contents

Acknowledgments & Disclaimer

Graphic Designer- Niki Ellis Designs, LLC

Editor- Maggie Kern @ Ms. K Edits- https://www.facebook.com/

Disclaimer: This book contains sexually explicit scenes. It is intended for audiences 18+. There may be graphic description of sex acts some may find disturbing. There may also be descriptions of physical violence, torture, or abuse. Some strong themes are found in this series. While the characters may not be conventional, they all believe in true love and commitment. The book is a HEA with some twists and turns along the way.

Blurb
Devil Dog:
He never thought his days as a Marine would be
    needed like this.
A young pregnant mother falls practically at his
    feet: beaten, scared, running and then in labor.
Everything about her captivates him in one glance:
    her, her daughter, and now her newborn son.
But she's not free. Her soon-to-be ex isn't done with
    her yet.
Devil is willing to bide his time.
He's determined to free her, then claim her for his
    own, using all his deadly skills.

Ashlee:

Years of abuse have taken their toll.
Running in the past never worked, but with the
    Warriors help, maybe this time it will.
She can't let him hurt her kids, she won't.

A chance meeting with some bikers changes her
    life.
And one of them makes her feel something she's
    never felt
But will she let Devil Dog in or will harsh words
    said in the heat of the moment, ruin them?

What happens when a man is willing to beg, plead, and do anything
to get back his new family and keep them safe? Because one thing is
for sure, he can't live without Devil Dog's Precious

Dublin Falls Warriors

Declan Moran (Terror)- President
Grayson Sumner (Savage)- Vice President
Dominic Vaughn (Menace)- Enforcer
Chase Romero (Ranger)- Sergeant at Arms
Jaxon Quinn (Viper)- Treasurer
Slade Devereaux (Blaze)- Secretary
Logan Priest (Steel)- Road Captain
Mason Durand (Hammer)
James Johnson (Tiny)
Talon Adair (Ghost)
Galen Duchene (Smoke)
Dane Michaelson (Hawk)
Jack Cannon (Devil Dog)
Eric James (Razor)
Quin Thomas (Torch)
Gage Lambert (Storm)
Finn Rafferty (Sniper)
Tyler Bennett (Gunner)
Adam Becker (Blade)
Nick Moretti (Capone)

Chapter 1: Devil Dog

The compound was all set for our annual Labor Day celebration. This one was a little different from our usual celebration. It would be the first multiple day celebration the club had ever thrown. The party would begin on Saturday and run through Monday, Labor Day. We had guests coming from out of town from all our clubs, associate clubs, plus local friends and family.

All three of the other Warriors' chapters would have representatives here, as well as the two Pagan Souls chapters and the Iron Punishers. Sean, Gabe, and Griffin would be coming this time as well. They were the group of ex-military guys called the Dark Patriots who had been introduced to us by Reaper, the president of the Iron Punishers.

Reaper had known them from his time as a Navy SEAL. They were now out and did Black Ops work, among other things. You never knew when it might be handy to know guys like that. In fact, they'd helped us out a few times when we needed it. They were also the guys who had rescued my brother, Ranger's, old lady, Brielle, several years ago from her rapist. They'd become close to the club over the last several months since first meeting them.

As I looked around to see if there was anything else that needed to be done for the celebration, I saw Ashlee with baby Jayce and Angel. She had Angel out on the swings, pushing her with one hand while she held Jayce with the other. I watched as she and Angel both laughed. My heart pounded. She took my breath away every time I saw her. She'd been at the compound for two-and-a-half months, and I'd been thinking about her almost non-stop since the first day she'd come through the club-house door.

She'd called and asked for help from the Warriors. Terror, Harlow, and the other married couples had met her back at the end of March in a baby store in Knoxville when they were all shopping for baby stuff. They'd struck up a conversation with her, and then her abusive husband came along and ended it.

The Warriors knew he would probably take his anger out on his wife again, so they had left her with their phone numbers. She had been shopping with her three-year-old daughter, Angel, and was several months pregnant with her second child at the time. Terror had left Ashlee's husband with a warning. It wasn't until almost three months later that she reached out to Harlow, scared and asking for help.

The reason why was her husband had finally gone too far. He'd slapped Angel. Ashlee fought back and was beaten for her troubles. She was able to knock him out and escape to Dublin Falls where she called Harlow in a panic. When she'd walked through the clubhouse door, she'd struck me mute. Even noticeably beaten and heavily pregnant, she was beautiful and almost ethereal with her blonde hair and green eyes.

Little Angel had been with her, looking like a miniature Ashlee. She'd been named aptly. She was an angel, just like her mother. I knew as I stood there, they were what my life had been missing. I had been restless for the last year and hadn't understood why. I'd been patched into the Warriors which I loved, so it had made no sense to me why I'd been feeling that way about my life. Seeing Ashlee, answered that question for me. I knew right then she would be the main focus of my existence until the day I died. From that moment onward, I made sure I was always there to help her.

She was shy and leery, but who could blame her. We'd found out she'd tried more than once to escape her husband, and he always found her and dragged her back home. Sometimes she had been held like a prisoner for months in the house. Ashlee had also confirmed in so many words that both her children were the products of him raping her.

She'd been kept a virtual prisoner and repeatedly raped by him for four years. The thought made my gut roil. I had wanted to go and hunt his ass down and kill the fucker right then, however, the club had been reluctant to kill him. They didn't automatically jump to that, but would if he didn't stay away from Ashlee and her kids. So far, he hadn't disturbed them. Fortunate for them, but unfortunate for my need to kill him.

We had heard he did come to Dublin Falls a couple of times asking around to see if anyone had seen her. Fortunately, she'd only been to the hospital when she had Jayce and here at the compound. So, no one could tell him anything. We'd taken the car she had arrived in that day back to their house without him knowing how it got there. We'd talked to the police in Dublin Falls and Officer Cane tried to help, but since the beating had occurred in Maryville, it was their jurisdiction.

The police chief in Maryville turned out to be a buddy of her husband's and nothing ever came of the report. Over the subsequent weeks, everyone waited to see if he would do anything or show his face to us. He had to wonder if she'd come to us since Terror and the others had warned him, we would be watching out for her and the kids.

She'd moved into the guesthouse after Viper and Harper moved into their new house. I desperately wished I could be living there with Ashlee and the kids, but I knew I had to be patient. Ashlee wasn't ready for a relationship with anyone. However, when she was, I planned on her being with me. I'd do whatever I had to in order to make that a reality. I often wondered if she had any feelings left for the man she'd married. She had to have loved him at one time in order to have agreed to become his wife. A part of me worried she might miss him, though she never said or did anything to indicate that was true. I shook off those thoughts as I headed over to help her with the kids. Angel was giggling and asking her mother to swing her higher. I slid in behind the swing. Ashlee looked startled to see me. I gave her a wink. "Here, let me help. You have your hands full with little man there. I'll push her and you can watch." She gave me a sweet smile.

"Thanks, Jack," she said softly. At least I'd gotten one thing out of her these past few months—she called me by my given name, Jack, whenever we were alone. She sat down on one of the benches to watch.

It was a hot day. She was dressed in a simple tank and shorts, but on her, they were sexy as hell. She'd lost any weight she'd gained with Jayce quickly and easily. Looking at her, no one would believe she'd birthed two children, let alone one less than three months ago. She was on the shorter side at about five foot four. If I had to guess, she was only about a hundred and twenty-five pounds. She had an hourglass shape with larger breasts, a tiny waist, and generous hips.

She could have been one of those pinup girls from the forties. I found I wanted to run my hands all over her curves. I knew I could feast on her for hours. The fact she had two children didn't bother me at all. Some men would be put off on having kids around who weren't their own, but I saw it as they were Ashlee's and therefore, I wanted them like I wanted her.

She had Jayce asleep in her arms and she was watching me swing Angel. She was smiling which she seemed to do more and more. I cleared my throat to get her attention. "Are you ready for the celebration tomorrow? It should be a lot of fun." She frowned, which set my alarms off. "What's wrong? You seem like you're not happy about the party." She sighed.

"It's not that I'm not excited, I'm just unsure. I know all of you and most of the Punishers plus Bull's guys, but there are so many coming that I don't know. I was thinking maybe I should stay in the house those three days. Besides, it sounds like there will be a lot of drinking and other things going on. I don't think I want to be there for that."

My heart stuttered when she said she would miss it. I wanted her there with me. I wanted her to have fun. She needed some of that in her life. As for the drinking and other things, that would be happening and it would get wild in the evenings after the kids went to bed. There would be sex going on all over the place. I was sure that was what she meant by other things. I'd seen her leave our smaller parties when things began to heat up. I looked around and saw Adam, one of the prospects. I called him over to us.

"I need you to keep an eye on Angel and push her swing." He readily agreed. Ashlee looked at me with a little apprehension in her eyes. I took her arm and helped her stand. "Come with me. I want to talk to you in private." She followed me to the guest house. Inside, she laid Jayce down in his crib and we sat down in the living room. I knew she was nervous because she was fidgeting with her fingers. I laid mine over them. She looked at me.

"Ashlee, tell me why you're nervous about others being here, people being drunk and doing other things?" She shifted her eyes away and then back to mine.

"I'm just not comfortable. It's no big deal. I can stay here at the house, Jack." I scooted closer to her.

"Are you afraid someone will hurt you? Does having drunk men around scare you and if so, why? Why do you leave anytime things get a little heated and sexual at the clubhouse?" I decided to be blunt. She blushed and stood up to pace. I waited patiently. I wasn't about to leave until she talked to me.

"Okay, fine. Yes, I'm afraid of having so many men around. You and the others have all been great to me and my children. But, Jack, that's not what most men are like. There are going to be way too many here for there not to be the other kind. Them getting drunk only makes them worse. It always made my husband worse." She paused. I knew she rarely ever mentioned her husband or her time with him. She continued, "As for the other stuff, it's the sex stuff. I feel uncomfortable seeing people so casually hooking up. I know it makes me a prude in your eyes, but I don't see how people can be so casual about it."

"Precious, you have nothing to worry about. I'd never allow anyone to hurt you. Neither would my brothers, Bull, or Reaper's guys. No matter what, we'll always keep you and your children safe. I agree drinking can bring out certain behaviors in men more easily, and as for sex, most bikers are very casual about it. My brothers who have wives are not now, but before they met their old ladies, they were too. I'd never want you to stay if it makes you uncomfortable, but the bunnies and barflies will always be a part of club life unless every member is taken. It's sex and casual because there are no feelings attached, just a physical relief." She shrugged and looked away, saying nothing.

"It's more than just the sex. Tell me," I demanded. She swung around.

"I don't want to see who is screwing who, okay? I know what the bunnies are for. I know men have needs and they'll get it wherever and from whoever they can. But I don't want to know who is taking which woman to bed one night and then who it is the next time," she spit out. I could see she was a little pissed. I was finding the conversation illuminating. I pushed for more.

"Who does it bother you to see? Is it every one of us or someone in particular?" I prayed she wouldn't say one of my brother's names. It would kill me if she felt something for one of them and not me. She paced farther across the living room. She wasn't looking at me. I stood up and cornered her. She glared at me.

"It doesn't matter, Devil. Drop it. I don't want to talk about this anymore. I need to go get Angel. She needs to come inside." She went to push past me. I wrapped her up in my arms. She tensed and gave me a wary look. I leaned my forehead down to rest on hers.

"Don't ever be afraid of me, Ashlee. And remember, call me Jack. I'd never harm you. And it does matter. Now I'm gonna ask you something and you need to be honest with me." She watched me with wide eyes. I was going to take a chance and see if she might have some kind of feelings for me other than friendship. "Do you leave before things heat up because you don't want to see me with one of the women?" She looked flushed and her eyes held anger. She tried to shove me away, but I didn't move. I stood silent.

She finally hissed. "Yes, I don't want to see you with your fuck buddies! There, are you satisfied? Now let go of me." She shoved my chest again. I smiled and lowered my head to take her mouth. I'd stayed very hands-off with Ashlee. Now I knew I needed to let her know what I wanted. She had to feel something for me if she was pissed about me hooking up with other women. Her lips were so soft underneath mine. I'd never felt anything this soft in my life.

She stood unmoving while I sipped at them gently, kissing them over and over until she sighed and tentatively kissed me back. I wanted to yell for joy. She was tentative but she was participating. I licked at the seam between her lips. She eased her mouth open and I gently slipped my tongue inside to lightly duel with hers.

I angled our heads so I could deepen the kiss just a little. She had put her arms up on my chest. At six foot two, she couldn't wrap them around my neck unless I stooped. I pulled back with a groan.

"Precious, you don't know how good that makes me feel to know it was me." She blinked and then shoved.

"Good? So, you think it's funny that I don't want to see you having sex with all those women. Ha! What? Are you kissing me now, thinking I want to become one of them? I won't ever be a bunny for you or your club. Get out!" She was spitting mad. I never meant that at all. She ducked out of my arms and headed for the front door. I grabbed her before she could get it open. Spinning her around, I trapped her against the wall.

"I don't think it's funny! And I wasn't kissing you, thinking to make you into a fucking bunny! I'm happy because I hope it means you have feelings for me like I do for you. I'd never let one of my brothers touch you, woman! Why would you even think that?" She had tears in her eyes now.

"What feelings? You think I want to have sex with you so I can be a piece of trash like all the others in your bed. I wouldn't ever do that. If I ever again trust a man enough to become involved with him, I want someone who will be with only me. Not a manwhore." I pulled back.

"I don't deny I want to be with you, Ashlee, and yes, sex is involved. But that isn't the extent of my feelings. I'd never treat you like trash. You'd never have to worry about me being with other women if you were mine. I'm no virgin or saint, but I'm not a manwhore either. Have you seen me with any women since you've been here?" I growled. Her opinion of me on one hand kind of hurt, but on the other, I could understand. The biker life was usually full of easy sex. As a biker and former Navy SEAL, I'd had my fair share of casual sex. She shook her head no.

"No, because I make sure to leave before things start to happen. I don't want to see if you're with Jen or Amber, or Sally, or whoever." I slid my hand up her arm to cup her face.

"Maybe you should've stayed around to find out. Because if you had, you would've seen me hooking up with —" She tried to put her hand over my mouth. "None of them. I haven't touched a woman since you came through that clubhouse door two-and-a-half months ago." Her eyes got huge and her mouth dropped open. Her disbelief showed on her face.

"I only want one woman and she's standing in front of me. I'm waiting for her to be ready to be with me, however long that takes." I gave her another soft kiss and then I stood back, pulling the front door open and shutting it quietly behind me without saying another word.

I headed to the clubhouse. I needed a drink.

Once inside, I slid onto a stool at the bar. Nick was the bartender today. He slid me a beer without me even asking. I took a big swig. Viper came over to sit with me and ordered one too. Then he looked at me.

"What's wrong, brother? I saw your face when you walked in. Something happen?" I knew Viper knew how I felt about Ashlee. I sighed.

"I just had sort of an argument with Ashlee. She doesn't want to come to the party. She's nervous about all the men. I reassured her, but she also doesn't like the hooking up that goes on. It took some digging, but I finally got her to admit she doesn't want to see me hooking up with any of the women." Viper shrugged.

"Then why the look on your face? Isn't this what you wanted?" I nodded.

"Yeah, but she then got the wrong idea and thought I wanted to treat her like another bunny. She told me she only wants a man who would be with her exclusively. She called me a manwhore! I told her I wanted to be with her, that I'd never treat her like a bunny or let anyone hurt her. I gave her a kiss, then I left. Shit! How could she think that?" I asked. Viper stared at me and then shook his head.

"You're a dumbass. Of course, she'd be worried. Bikers tend not to be angels. Many of them still fool around on their old ladies even if we don't. Her husband was a controlling, abusive rapist and I'd almost bet she's never been with anyone but him. Or at least she's only been with a couple of men altogether. She's scared. And you drop this bomb on her, kiss her, and then walk off. Damn."

I considered his words. A feeling of shame came over me. I had been a bit of a dumbass and asshole. She had been through hell with her husband and had nothing close to a normal relationship with him. Now I'd gone and acted the way I had. I'd be lucky if she would even talk to me again. I chugged down my beer and stood up.

"I need to go talk to her. Apologize. Thanks." He nodded and grinned. I headed out the door and back to her place. As I crossed the backyard of the clubhouse, I saw Angel was no longer on the playset, and Adam was nowhere in sight. I wondered if he'd taken her to the house. I wanted to talk to Ashlee, but not in front of Angel. Hopefully she was otherwise occupied.

I needed to repair the damage I'd inadvertently caused today. I needed to be with her. She was all I thought about. I didn't see other women anymore. Not since she'd come to the compound. I wanted the big commitment sort of thing with her, not some casual, temporary fling and then move on to the next one. I knocked on her door and waited.

Chapter 2: Ashlee

I stood there stunned as Devil Dog left the house. Did I hear him right? He was interested in me and hadn't been with any of the bunnies since I'd been here. No, I couldn't have heard him right, or maybe he only meant he hadn't been with them. He could be hooking up with women away from the compound. I pressed a hand to my stomach. Any time I thought of Devil Dog with another woman, it made me physically ill.

I didn't know what to do. My life had been so screwed up for the last five years. Alex had ruined my life. I had nowhere to go, no way to care for my children. I was twenty-three years old and felt a hundred. I needed to think. I quickly texted Ms. Marie to see if she could take the kids for a while. She answered immediately and was on my doorstep to get Jayce and Angel in less than five minutes.

She frowned when she saw me and wrapped me up in her arms for a big hug. After she got him and his stuff, she yelled over to the playground telling Angel to come with her. Of course, Angel ran off excitedly. I shut the door and went to my bedroom. I laid myself across the bed.

I wasn't sure how long I had been lying there when I

heard a knock at the door. Ms. Marie must have forgotten something for the kids. I got up wearily and walked to the door. I pulled it open. "What did you—" I came to a halt. Devil Dog was standing on the porch. He was staring at me with a furled brow. I just looked back. I didn't know what to say. He was the one to break the silence.

"I need to talk to you. I'm sorry I just walked off earlier. Please. Just hear me out." I reluctantly nodded and stood back so he could come inside. Once he was inside, he looked around. "Where are Angel and Jayce?" he asked. I walked over to sit down on the couch.

"Ms. Marie has them over at Alannah and Menace's house." He nodded.

"Good. I don't want to do this in front of Angel." My stomach knotted up. What didn't he want to do? Maybe he'd thought about what he said, and he didn't want to be with me at all, or that I shouldn't be here anymore. I swallowed hard. Crazy thoughts began to swirl around in my head. He sat down beside me and took my hands.

"You have to stop looking at me like that, Precious. You're killing me. I'm not gonna hurt you, physically or emotionally. I only meant I wanted us to be able to talk uninterrupted. I'm sorry I sprung that stuff on you and then walked off. I pushed you when I shouldn't have. All I want you to know is you're safe. We'll keep you and the kids safe. I want to have a relationship with you, and not a casual one. I want a committed one, but only when you're ready. I realize you just got out of an abusive relationship with your husband. You need time to get over him. I'm here if you want to talk. Just know, when you're ready, I want to be the one you choose to be with, Ashlee, however long it takes. I'm not now, nor do I intend to be sleeping with other women while I wait. If I need a release, I'll take care of it myself."

He'd truly stunned me. This gorgeous, sexy man wanted to be with me. I didn't know what to say. It seemed too good to be true. As I thought about what he said, I knew I needed to set him straight on a few things. I caressed his face.

"Jack, thank you. I do feel safe with you and your brothers. As for springing this on me too soon, no, you didn't. Any relationship I had with my husband was over a long time ago. The only thing now is I have to completely sever the tie with him. I need to divorce him, but I'm afraid he'll find me and take the kids away if I file the paperwork. I'm afraid he'll decide to take the kids away from me if he finds me or if I file for divorce." I stood and started pacing.

"If we're being honest and open with each other, then there are things you need to know. First, let me explain about Alex." He sat back and nodded. "I met Alex when I was eighteen. I'd started college and he was actually several years older. I met him through a friend at a party. I'd lost my parents by then. My dad to cancer when I was ten and my mom, three months after my eighteenth birthday from a heart issue. So, when I met him, I'd been alone in the world for three months.

"He was charming, nice. We talked about so many things. I was thrilled when he wanted my number. He spent the next few months courting me for a lack of a better word. He never pushed me to have sex and barely kissed me. After four months, I was the one to broach the topic of sex. He claimed he wanted to wait until we got married because he didn't believe in premarital sex. I believed him. At the six-month mark, on my nineteenth birthday, he asked me to marry him. I said yes and we were married at the town hall a month later." I paused as I took a deep breath. This next part was the hard part.

"It was three months into the marriage when he seemed to change. He became super critical. He demanded I stop going to college. Alex didn't want me to leave the house without him. He was getting paranoid I was talking to and seeing other men. That's when he hit me for the first time. The next day I drove off in my car and went to the police station to file a report. Unfortunately, I didn't know he was pals with the police chief. The chief refused to take my report and had me escorted home where Alex was waiting for me. I was locked in the house for a month after that and got an even worse beating." Devil growled at this point. I went to the fridge and got us both bottles of water. I took a drink of mine.

"After a month, he eased up on the house arrest but was still critical, paranoid, and didn't want me to leave the house without him. I tried to refuse to have sex with him, but he wasn't having that." I looked at Devil Dog. "From that point forward, every time we had sex, it was rape. I never was with him willingly again. Luckily, he seemed to not want sex often or maybe he got it elsewhere. Usually, he only wanted to have it when I'd pissed him off about something. He used it as punishment. He refused to allow me to use birth control. I became pregnant with Angel when we'd been married seven months. While I now hated Alex, I loved my child as soon as I knew I was pregnant.

"At first he seemed happy I was pregnant then he started asking me who the father was. Said he knew I was cheating on him. He never stopped the beatings while I carried her, but he was careful to never kick or hit me in the stomach. She was born in February. I tried to run again in April. I got to Kentucky and he found me at a motel. I was forced to leave with him, or he said he'd take Angel. He beat me again when we got home. This went on for months. She was almost a year old when I tried to get away the third time. I thought I'd been smart not taking my car. I got the two of us on a bus and paid cash. Somehow, he was able to track me. I was free for three days before he found us. Again, he threatened to take Angel so I would return."

I sat back down on the couch beside Devil Dog. He wrapped his arm around me and pulled me in tight against his chest. "I stayed and endured until she was a little over two years old. He'd beaten me again and it was the worst yet. I had to go to the hospital which I rarely did because he wouldn't let me. Only when it looked like I was really hurt, would he relent. This time I tried to get away by reaching out to an old friend. When I got with Alex, all my friends seemed to disappear, but I ran into this one in the store and we'd talked. She helped me get away and to a house she had in Georgia. I was away from him for two weeks before he showed up. He dragged me back to Tennessee and shut me up in the house for three months. I never left and he made sure the beatings increased along with his attention in the bedroom. At the end of the three months, I found out I was pregnant with Jayce."

I looked at Devil. I could see the compassion in his eyes and the anger. He went to interject, but I stopped him. "Please, let me get it all out. When I found out, I despaired. How could I get away now with two kids? He didn't pretend to be happy this time. He kept saying I was giving him another damn kid to support and of course, it wasn't even his. My arguments that it couldn't be anyone but him since I'd been a prisoner for three months fell on deaf ears. It wasn't until I met the Warriors that day in the baby store that I had a glimmer of hope. He was infuriated with the club after that day. He ranted and raved about Terror and all of. He accused me of sneaking out and fucking bikers, but he wasn't beating me like he would have which was unusual. At least not until the day he went off on Angel and slapped her. It was the one time he didn't beat me. No way was he touching my children. I just lost it. I don't even remember actually moving and hitting him the first time. After that it was a blur and then I hit him with the statue and knocked him out. That was when I came to Dublin Falls and called Harlow." He raised my face with a finger under my chin and kissed me gently.

When Devil drew back, I sighed. "That's my crappy story. The other thing is, I do have feelings for you, Jack. They scare me because I've never had anything like them even back at the beginning of my relationship with Alex. It has been killing me to think about you with other women at the clubhouse. I want to have a relationship with you, but I'm scared. If it doesn't work out, you could destroy me so easily. I have no feelings for Alex holding me back. However, I'm not really free of him as long as I'm still married. I fear what he'll try to do to the kids. He would be vindictive enough to try and get some kind of custody just to hurt me. I can't ever let him have any visitation or custody of them." I was sobbing a little by the end. The thought of Alex getting his hands on my babies made me sick and so scared.

"Look at me, Ashlee. I swear to God and on my patch, he will not get your kids and you will be free of him. Once this party is over, we'll get the club's lawyer, Dyson, to help you file for divorce. We'll work with him on what are the best things we can do to ensure Alex doesn't get any kind of custody. I think you need to file a restraining order. It only helps your stance, but we'll ask Dyson. And finally, I'm so fucking happy to hear you have feelings for me like I do you. I want a relationship and I promise, I won't destroy you. I see us being together for the rest of our lives, babe."

He leaned down and took my mouth. He was more forceful this time but not hurtful. His enthusiasm was exciting to me. He was seriously devouring me. I gripped the back of his neck to kiss him back. My breath was coming in small pants. After several minutes of both of us kissing each other silly, he broke away.

"We have to stop, babe. I don't want us to go too fast. It's enough I know you want to be with me." I smiled and nodded.

"Okay. I can do that." Devil grinned.

"Good. Now for the last thing. I want you to come to the celebration. I'll make sure you're safe. You need to have some fun, and this is the perfect opportunity. I'd like to be able to let everyone know you're with me and under my protection. Are you alright with me doing this?" he asked with an anxious look on his face. I thought about it for a few minutes. I found I really liked the thought of being Devil's. I smiled.

"I'd like that too. And I'll be sure to attend the festivities over the next three days." I gave him a quick peck on the mouth. He growled and tried to take it further, but I pulled back.

"Remember, we're not going too fast," I teased him. He growled again.

"I'm a dumbass. Ignore what I said in that instance." I laughed. After our talk, he went to get the kids from Ms. Marie while I started getting things out for dinner. Devil Dog ended up spending the remainder of the afternoon and evening with me and the kids. He played with Angel and took care of Jayce including feeding him a bottle and changing his diaper while I cooked dinner.

Once dinner was over, he cleaned up the kitchen and we watched television with Angel until it was time for her bath and bedtime. She insisted Devil watch her in the tub. I washed Jayce in his baby bathtub in there with them. Angel went to bed after Devil read her a story. Jayce was easy to get down. He was overall a low-maintenance baby. I'd put him down at eight in the evening most nights. He'd get up around one and then not again until six the next morning. Back in the living room after the kids were down, I got us each something to drink and sat down on the couch.

"Thank you for the help. I've never had help before. It was nice." He sat down and kissed me.

"I enjoyed it. I'll always help you with them, Precious." I smiled.

"Why do you call me Precious, Jack?" He got a serious look on his face.

"It's because you're precious to me. The most precious thing I've ever had." His words made my eyes well up with tears. Devil kissed me and then sat back. "No crying. Let's watch a movie," he insisted. We watched a movie and he left around ten o'clock after kissing me senseless and telling me to dream about him. I did dream about him. They were highly sexual dreams. I was scared but also excited about starting a relationship with Devil Dog.

Chapter 3: Devil Dog

I was anxious and excited today. Last night it had been hard to sleep because I kept thinking about Ashlee and our talk yesterday. She'd finally agreed to let us explore a relationship. I'd been happy to hear she had no feelings for her husband and only wanted a divorce and to have her kids protected from him. It was those thoughts that stuck with me as we sat in church this morning. We were having it at our usual time in the morning before the party started this afternoon.

One of the big items on the agenda was the acquisition of Mr. Turner's garage in town. The deal had been finalized this week, and we were now in possession of it. The next few weeks we'd get it set up the way we wanted it, reopen the doors to the public, and hopefully find another mechanic. A few applicants had been sent to Viper to interview. He wasn't crazy about them but thought one might be okay. If no one else applied, we'd start with him and see how he did over the next ninety days.

With the sale of the garage now finalized, the custom bike business would be able to expand. Ghost and Blaze were run off their feet with business. They turned away most of it because they could only do so much at a time. He'd spoken to Tiger and Falcon from our Warrior chapter in Gastonia, North Carolina.

They had shared a few months ago their interest and experience in doing custom bike work. They both wanted to patch over to our chapter. Terror had talked to their president, Grinder, about our wish to extend them a patch over. They could then work with us on the custom bikes. Grinder had been sad to lose two of his guys, but he was happy they'd get to do what was a passion for them. Today was their first official day with us. The celebration over the next three days was partially in their honor.

We were also honoring Adam and Nick. This month would be the end of their year as prospects. We were going to patch them in today, but they had no idea we were going to do it a few weeks early if at all. We were about to call them in so they could join the end of the meeting. Torch was asked to go find them. As we sat there waiting, I drifted in my thoughts thinking about Ashlee.

Viper leaned over to whisper, "How did it go yesterday with Ashlee? Did she forgive your dumbass?" he teased me. I shoulder nudged him.

"Yeah, she forgave my dumbass. We got several things out in the open. A couple I want to bring up at the end of the meeting." He grinned and sat back to wait. Torch came back with Adam and Nick in tow. They were both looking nervous. Terror called for everyone to shut up, then he looked at them.

"We wanted to make sure everything was in order for

the party. Did you get everything we told you to get?"

"All set, Pres," they both said. Terror absently nodded and then sighed deeply. He looked at them with such a somber expression. Damn, could that fucker act!

"I'm glad because this next part isn't something I want to do at the same time as we're doing a holiday celebration, but it can't wait." He paused. "Guys, today you need to give us your prospect cuts. We can no longer support you continuing with the Warriors as one. The last year we've watched you both to see if you had what it takes to be a Warrior. Prospects are expected to do anything and everything we ask. It has become clear you two are not prospect material." You could see the disappointment on both their faces. They tried hard to not let it show but it was there.

Terror continued, "So, we need you to both give us your cuts right now. Take them off and put them on the table." He gestured to the end of the long table. They both shrugged them off slowly and then laid them gently down on the table. They didn't say a word as they waited to be dismissed. While they'd been out, Ghost had gotten their new cuts. He had stationed himself in the back corner so they never saw him when they came into the room. He really was like a Ghost and seemed able to disappear in plain sight.

Terror nodded and said, "There's just one more thing and then you can go." Ghost stepped up silently behind them and tapped both of them on the shoulders. They swung around in surprise. He gave them each a nod and then handed each of them another cut. This one had the full rockers on the back and their new road names we'd chosen for them.

Since Nick was one hundred percent Italian, we'd chosen to name him, *Capone*. As for Adam, he'd shown us over the last year he had amazing knife skills. He could do things with a knife we'd never seen so naturally we chose *Blade* as his road name. They both stood there frozen when he handed them the cuts. You could see they'd been expecting to be kicked out, not patched into the club. We all broke out laughing which broke the spell they were under. They quickly donned their new cuts.

"Take a seat, you two. Now, we'll have to find some new prospects soon, so we have some people to do the shit work around here." Terror grumbled. We all agreed. Prospects did the crap no one else wanted to do.

"Anyone with a suggestion see Savage or me. Now, on to the next item of business. The renovations on the second floor of the clubhouse. We've mainly kept it storage and open space since we have had enough room downstairs. A couple of months ago, Viper mentioned the idea that we needed a second place for either families or couples to have personal space. This could be for those visiting or in our case, when one of us has finally nailed down a woman and are waiting for a house to be built. We've had more than one occasion when we have had an overlap at the guesthouse and the extra space was needed. Steel and Hammer have gotten plans drawn up. Construction to build an apartment on the second floor will get underway soon. Since we don't have to start from scratch, they think it'll take a couple of months to finish it. They now have five crews building at any given time. One of those will take on this project." Everyone cheered to hear this. He quieted us all down.

"Any other business we should talk about before we close this meeting and get ready to party?" he asked. I raised my hand. He gave me a nod to go ahead. I stood up.

"A couple of things I want to talk about. First, so you all know, I plan on introducing Ashlee at the celebration as being with me." They all gave cheers. My feelings for her had not been kept a secret from my brothers. "She's nervous about this party. Not only because of announcing we're together but because of all the men who will be here. She's scared of having this many men she doesn't know or trust in the compound." This made everyone get quiet.

Capone spoke up, "Is she scared they'll do something to her or just nervous in general?" I sighed.

"Both. She says not all men are like us and with so many more being here, there's bound to be some that are more like her husband than us. I reassured her all of us would watch out for her and protect her if it became necessary. She was going to stay in the house for the whole three days at first." This caused many of them to groan and the others to protest. I held up my hand.

"I know. I got her to agree to come and have some fun. She needs to relax. The last thing is her husband, Alex." They all sneered. None of us could stand a man who'd abuse a woman or a child. He had done both.

"We're going to talk to Dyson next week about helping her file for divorce." Cheers rang out again. "I convinced her we need to talk to him about filing a restraining order as well. Guys, she's fucking terrified he'll come after her and the kids once she does either of these things. She's worried he'll find some way to get visitation or custody of them. I need to say this right now. If there's any chance he can get either of those, he will have to disappear. She'll never be able to live with him having any kind of access to the kids. I won't fucking allow him to either. I don't expect you guys to have to do anything, just know it will happen and I'll be sure nothing ever blows back on the club." They'd all gotten quiet and were staring at me. Terror stood up.

"Devil, we understand your worries, but I can't allow you to go out on your own and kill this man." I stiffened. I loved the club, but I would take Ashlee and the kids and leave if it was the only way to protect them. I went to speak, and Terror held up his hand to stop me.

"No, listen, before you say you'll leave the club and do it anyway." I guess he knew me well. "What I meant is if he becomes a threat like that, we'll all take care of his ass. She's your woman and we protect our women and children. I'm just glad she agreed to give your dumbass a chance," he teased to lighten the mood. A big smile spread across his face.

The others all cheered and put their reassurances out there while congratulating me on getting a woman they all knew was too damn good for me. I had to agree with them on that one. After that was settled, we wrapped up the meeting. People would soon start to arrive. The party didn't officially start until two this afternoon, but many were driving significant distances. They'd be rolling in all morning and afternoon.

Back out in the common room, the old ladies and kids were waiting for us to get out of church. I saw Ashlee sitting with Harlow. Hunter was up running around with Angel while Harlow was holding Jayce and talking to Ashlee. I headed straight to Ashlee. She smiled when she saw me. I leaned down and took her mouth. I hadn't seen her yet today. She startled and then relaxed into our kiss. I kissed her deeply. When we finally broke apart, everyone was whistling and cheering, even the women. She was blushing and trying to push me away. I laughed.

"Oh no, you don't. You said I could tell everyone we were together. Well, I just did. Get used to it." I leaned down to whisper the last part to her. "I'm a really hands-on kind of guy. I will be showing my woman affection frequently and loudly, Precious." She laughed and then gave me another kiss. Harlow was laughing.

"Ashlee, you didn't tell us about this when you came in this morning. When did this happen? And why would you ever want to be with this mangy cur?" She laughed, throwing smirks at me. I grabbed Harlow in a headlock and rubbed the top of her head. She yelled at me to stop it. We loved teasing each other. I'd been in the Marines for several years with Harlow. She was the whole reason I came to the Warriors and ended up prospecting and then patching in two years ago. She was literally the sister I never had. Sniper had been in the Corp with us too. We had all been in the same Marine sniper unit. Terror walked up grinning.

"If you don't let my wife go, I'll have to beat your ass. Because if I don't, she'll give me hell later for not sticking up for her." Harlow protested and he winked at me while he leaned down to kiss his wife. She kissed him then punched him in the gut. He just laughed harder. "Mean ass woman. I should see if Bull wants you back." She smirked.

"Go ahead. Let's see how long it would take for you to come crawling after me." He smiled.

"About five minutes or less, I think. I doubt you'd get out of the gate. Now settle down, Temptress. Too much excitement will get the baby stirred up." He rubbed his hands across her stomach. She was seven months pregnant with their second baby. She was due in November right before Thanksgiving. They'd found out two months ago, they were going to have a girl this time. They were both thrilled but nothing like Bull. He couldn't wait to have a granddaughter.

We were all talking when Viper came over with Harper. She dropped down on one of the other chairs and sighed. I could see she was looking a little pale. I gave her a worried look.

"Harper, are you okay, sweetheart? You look pale." I looked at Viper. He was standing protectively over her. She sighed.

"I'm okay. It's this, morning sickness. It's kicking my ass again this morning. I hope it's true it disappears after the first trimester. If so, I only have another week to go." The other ladies laughed. They knew it didn't always happen like that. She frowned at them.

"Quiet, bitches, let me live in false hope. I can tell you this, if Viper expects me to do this ten times, he's crazy.

I'm capping him at three kids. If he wants more, he has to carry them." She gave him a stern look.

He just laughed and leaned down to whisper something to her. Whatever he said made her light up and smile. She was nodding her head when he pulled back. All of us talked for a little while longer and then the ladies said they needed to make sure everything was all set one more time, then they would go get ready for the party. Ms. Marie came over to take Jayce and Angel from Ashlee. She gave her a confused look. Ms. Marie smiled.

"Listen, love. You need time to get ready undisturbed. Go with some of the other women and get ready. Make sure you come out and knock the socks off this one." She gestured to me. "Wear that outfit I picked out for you." She winked and headed off with the kids. I looked at Ashlee. She was shaking her head and blushing.

"What outfit is she talking about, Ashlee?" I asked. She shrugged.

"You'll have to wait and see if I wear it. I'm not sure I should." Her response had me wondering what she would be wearing. Knowing Ms. Marie, it would be something good. Harper hustled her to her feet.

"Let me see it. I'll let you know if you should or not. Come on." She gave Viper a kiss and Ashlee gave me one which I was glad to see her do. They headed out of the clubhouse.

I helped take another walk around the compound for Terror. Everything looked ready to go. We had more barbeques set up, a roasting spit and even an inground oven built to roast a pig Hawaiian style. The women had worked hard making lots of different kinds of foods as well as buying others premade at the store. Plus, we'd ordered more shit from the Fallen Angel. With it being this many people and for three days, there was no way we wanted the women to do all the cooking. It was meant for them to have fun as well.

Bikes were coming in a pretty constant stream now. Not everyone would be here all three days, but most would. The next couple of hours were hectic. We had to direct people to the designated parking areas. Those were in the regular lot and then behind the garage. The club had set up port-a-potties scattered around the grounds so if the bathrooms in the clubhouse and houses were occupied, there were still bathrooms for use. Even with all our space, you couldn't host well over a hundred people for three days inside the houses and clubhouse. We'd gone farther back on the grounds and had designated an area for some to camp. Many were going to camp either in tents or campers. Those with old ladies would bring them. There were only a few who did have one. The various clubs would bring their bunnies.

We had the pool area, the playground for the kids, the horseshoe pits, cornhole games and even a volleyball net. One of the bands we hired at the Fallen Angel a lot was going to be paying live music tonight and the other band tomorrow night. This was something new. We usually only played music over some speakers. Huge white open tents had been set up to provide shade to sit under since it was only the beginning of September and the temps were in the high nineties.

The kids were going to be housed in the children's room at the clubhouse at night. There they could all be together, and it would take fewer people to watch them. The place was huge and soundproofed so none of the noise would bother them. For this occasion, we had not only Ms. Marie to watch them but Cindy and Gina who worked for Brielle at her house cleaning business. Cindy had done it numerous times for us, but Gina had recently started to help out. From the daycare, Monica and Paige were going to help out. We had eleven kids right now in the club with Jayce being the youngest. Rowan was the oldest at almost five. Ghost and Wren would be adding their first one to the mix at the end of this month.

It was now just after two o'clock and the place was packed. I was talking to various guys from all of the clubs. I could see Sean, Gabe, and Griffin had made it. I was happy they could finally get back to see us again. In addition to the clubs, we had friends from town and work joining us today. I got called away to help carry some stuff out from the clubhouse and then to help with another job.

Before I knew it, it was three o'clock. I hadn't seen Ashlee anywhere, and I started to search for her. I didn't want her to be out here alone with all these men. She was scared enough. I knew they'd be hitting on her if they saw her. She was beautiful. I looked around but didn't see her. I caught sight of Harper, Brielle, and Wren. I went over to them.

"Hey, ladies, have you seen Ashlee?" They all shook their heads. Harper was smiling.

"No, but believe me, you'll be happy when you do." I looked at her with a questioning look. She must have been referring to the outfit mentioned earlier. Now I was even more anxious to see it. I thanked them and decided to go to the house to see if she was still there. I was cutting through the crowd when I heard whistles and catcalls.

Now I knew the guys were unlikely doing it to the old ladies since it would get them killed. Plus, they all would have on their property cuts. That thought had me wishing I'd gotten Ashlee hers already so they would know she was off-limits. Also, it could have been due to a hot bunny, but again, that didn't seem likely with this crowd. Bunnies were just a regular part of the day. My gut told me they were looking at my woman. I shouldered through another group and that's when I saw her.

I froze. My chest felt like someone had taken a hammer to it. I couldn't catch my breath. Coming toward me a little hesitant but with a brave face on was my Precious. I could hear guys all making comments about how fucking hot this chick was and wondering who she was with. Several I could hear were excited to see she didn't have on a property cut. All this flowed around me as I stared at the vision coming toward me.

It was an Ashlee I didn't recognize. She was always beautiful and sexy, but this was a different Ashlee— a much more dangerous-looking one. She was dressed in an outfit I had never seen nor even known she owned. She had on a slashed, ripped-out top that had strips of skin showing across her shoulders and chest. It was a classic black, form-fitted top that dipped low in the front showing her generous cleavage through the slashed areas. The slashed sleeves were just cap sleeves.

Around her small waist was a black and silver ornate belt through the loops of a pair of tight, leather shorts. While the shorts were tight, they weren't so short as to have her ass hanging out. They molded her like a second skin and showed off her sexy legs.

Her blonde, shoulder-length hair was in its usual bob. It was catching the sun and making it shine. Her eyes had been lined with dark liner and dark shadow applied to the crease which made her green eyes pop. She had on a black and silver choker necklace and silver hoops. Around one wrist was a leather cuff.

Her shoes completed the outfit. She had on a pair of black high heels that were open-toed and the leather crisscrossed all the way up the foot to her ankles where they buckled. I felt myself getting hard just seeing her. I was broken from my trance when one of the guys from our Louisville chapter of the Warriors stepped up to her.

He'd placed a hand on her hip and was talking to her. She stepped away from him and was shaking her head to whatever he was saying. I could see the worry in her eyes. I raced over that way. He was just about to reach for her again when I got to them. I grabbed his hand. He looked at me in surprise. It was Stalker. I leaned into him.

"She's taken, brother. You need to back off." He gave me a surprised look. He looked at her and then back to me.

"I don't see a property cut. If she's taken, why doesn't she have one of those on?" he asked. He wasn't necessarily being smart, but I could see he wasn't wanting to back down either.

"Because it hasn't come yet. I wanted to introduce her to everyone this weekend. However, make no mistake, she's taken. She's mine. Do we have a problem?" I asked him while staring him dead in the eyes. He looked a little undecided. It was at this moment Terror and a few of my other brothers all surrounded me and Ashlee. Stalker's president, Brute, came up. He looked at all of us.

"Is there a problem here?" he asked with a frown.

Terror spoke up, "No problem, Brute. Just a misunderstanding. Ashlee here is taken even if she doesn't have on a property cut yet. Devil Dog is her old man. He was just explaining this to Stalker. It was an honest mistake. We were gonna introduce her to everyone this weekend." Brute nodded his head.

"Why're all of you surrounding her? You think she needs to be protected from us?" Terror shook his head. I could see Ashlee was pale and looking like she wanted to run.

"No, I know she doesn't need to be protected from you guys. She, however, is afraid of men she doesn't know. We told her we'd always make sure she's protected. This is just to show her that we mean it." Brute relaxed and nodded. He looked at Stalker who finally stepped back. Then he turned to me.

"Introduce me to your old lady, Devil Dog. And congratulations, she's gorgeous. Way too good-looking for your ugly ass," he joked. He could see she was still uncertain.

I smiled and gestured to Ashlee. Stalker stood with us.

I introduced her. Brute gave her a smile and called over his old lady to meet her. Once they had exchanged greetings, Stalker stepped up. I saw her stiffen just a tiny bit. He offered her his hand which she took hesitantly.

"I'm sorry if I scared or offended you, Ashlee. That was never my intent. I was just struck by your beauty and hoped to be able to claim your attention for myself. But I see this old dog here got to you first. If you change your mind, I'm Stalker and I'm with the Louisville Warriors." He kissed her hand. She gave him a tentative smile and thanked him. This broke the ice.

People were all coming up to be introduced to her. I knew she didn't know what to do with so many people interested in her, so I wrapped her in my arms. Once the flood was over, I took her over to a quieter area of the yard. I hugged her.

"You did great, babe. I have to say, your fucking outfit almost slayed me, woman. Jesus, give a guy a little warning. I could've had a heart attack right there. You are breathtaking. Don't get me wrong, you're always beautiful and sexy, but this was just a different, fiercer look than I've ever seen you wear."

She smiled and I captured her mouth. I had to taste her. She ran her tongue over my lips which caused me to groan. I devoured her mouth as she pressed against me. I knew she had to feel my erection, but she never said anything or pulled back. I ran a hand down to her ass and squeezed lightly. She moaned. I had to pull away.

"We have to stop, Precious. If we don't, I'm gonna explode. Now behave yourself and let's go mingle. Do you want to get the kids and have them with us for a while?"

"Yes. Please, could we?" I knew they were in the club-house with the others and we went inside to find Angel and Jayce. We were back outside with them when more people came up to be introduced and to talk to us. One of them was Rogue. He was with the same club as Brute and Stalker. He shook his head.

"They were right. She's way too damn good-looking for your ass, Devil Dog." Ashlee just laughed. He looked at the kids. "Who are these two little ones?"

I made introductions. "This is Angel, and this is little Jayce." He shook Angel's hand which she found hilari-ous. He looked at me.

"I didn't know you had an old lady, let alone kids." I stopped him.

"They're Ashlee's kids soon to be mine." She looked surprised while Rogue nodded. We spent over an hour talking to various people. Finally, I took her to sit down in one of the chairs. She'd been standing long enough. "What can I get you, babe? I know you have to be tired from standing and thirsty."

"A Coke, please."

"I'll be right back." I caught the eye of Storm. He came over. "Keep an eye on her until I get back, will you? She's still a bit nervous."

"Don't worry, I'll make sure no one bothers her." He went to sit with her and the kids. I was at one of the nu-merous coolers when Venom from our Gastonia chapter came up. We exchanged greetings. He was nodding to-ward Ashlee and the kids.

"I see you have a handful over there. You didn't have an old lady or kids the last time I saw you. What's up?" I grinned.

"Yeah, I met Ashlee a little over two months ago. She had me at first sight. The kids are hers." I went on to explain her history with Alex and how she'd come to be with us. When I was done, he was frowning and swearing.

"You mean some sonofabitch not only beat his woman, he hit his own kid and caused his wife to go into labor with the second one? That bastard needs to disappear."

I agreed. I looked at him.

"It was worse Venom. He kept her a virtual prisoner, kept dragging her back every time she ran and forced her to have sex with him for years." His face got red. I could see his eyes gleaming in rage.

"That cocksucker! Did you kill him?"

I shook my head.

"Not yet. He's stayed away but she's gonna slap his ass with a restraining order and file for divorce. He's gonna try and get those kids just to hurt her. When it happens, he's dead."

He nodded.

"Let me know when you go after his ass. I'll help. I hate a fucker like that. My sister was with an abusive prick until he just disappeared one day." He winked when he said it and then started to saunter off telling me he'd be over to meet her in a few minutes. I hurried back to them.

"Sorry it took so long. I got caught up talking to Venom."

"That's alright, Devil." When I'd come up, she was laughing at something Storm was saying.

He excused himself after telling Ashlee, "I'll be back in fifteen minutes to get Angel, okay, Ash?"

I gave her a questioning look.

"Angel cajoled him into pushing her on the swings. He's gonna take her over to the playground for a while. I told him he didn't have to do it, but he insisted. He said he'd get Rowan to play and see if any of the other bigger ones want to come. He's on his way to talk to Ms. Marie."

I laughed. Angel was like Rowan. She could twist all of us around her finger. Hell, all the kids could, especially the little girls.

When he came back, he had Ms. Marie and Cindy with him. Cindy was going along to help with the kids who wanted to play. Ms. Marie was here to take Jayce. It was time for him to eat, get changed, and take a nap. Ashlee told her she could do it, but Ms. Marie was having none of that. This left the two of us alone to just talk. It was after five, and the pig should be done soon. The chickens were looking good on the spits. The hamburgers and hot dogs were ready to go down on the grills. Several guys from the various clubs were helping at the barbeque.

I ended up helping the women get the various foods carried outside to the food tables. Anything that had to be cooked today or warmed up had been left in the hands of our bunnies, though it did look like they had recruited a few more to help. Typically, our women would insist on doing this, but we had insisted they not do it for once. This kind of thing is what you had prospects for and the other reason we had bunnies. Just under an hour later, everything was set for us to eat.

Angel had come back to us by then. I got her and Ashlee sat down at one of the tables.

"What do you want to eat, Angel?"

"I want a hot dog, chips, and the fruit."

"I can get her food, Devil," Ashlee insisted.

I shook my head.

"No, you sit still. I'll get food for my ladies." She sat stunned. Looking around, I could see my other brothers waiting on their women and children. The few guys from the other clubs with old ladies seemed to be taking care of them as well. The bunnies were waiting on guys from various clubs and those that didn't have one were getting their own, but only after the women and kids got a chance to get a plate.

I brought Angel her food so she could get started and then I went back to fix plates for Ashlee and me. She had gotten drinks. I came back and sat down our plates, then slid into the seat beside her. She burst out laughing. I looked at her.

"What's so funny?" She gestured to her plate. I looked at it, but I didn't see anything wrong with it. I shrugged.

"Devil, you loaded my plate like yours. I'll never be able to eat even a third of this."

I grinned.

"Eat what you want. Leave the rest. I might want more." She just laughed again and started to eat. When we were done, my plate was bare, and she had maybe eaten a fourth. "Babe, did you eat enough? You need to make sure you do."

She nodded.

"I got more than enough. Maybe later I'll get dessert after this food settles." She gave me a tiny kiss. I was so happy to see her initiating things between us. Yeah, it was a simple kiss, but it meant everything to me.

By the time things had settled down, everyone had eaten—for some of the guys seconds were eaten—the items needing to be kept cool were taken back to the clubhouse where people were welcome to help themselves, it was getting closer to seven o'clock. The band, *Chaos & Corruption*, had shown up to set up for the night. They'd play from seven to midnight. They were playing tonight and then tomorrow night the other band, *Hellfire*, would play. I saw they had a different band member, not their regular bassist. Maybe he was sick and this was his replacement.

Soon the band was playing. They did an eclectic mix of rock, blues, and country. They always made sure it was something you could dance to and interspersed it with slow songs as well. This was why they and *Hellfire* did so well. We kept them on permanent rotation at the Fallen Angel. Both played similar music and did it very well. Their vocalists were top notch.

The kids played around for a little bit then were corralled off to the children's room in the clubhouse. We went to make sure Angel got settled plus she wanted to kiss us goodnight. Ashlee fed Jayce his last bottle. She told me I could join the fun and she'd join me as soon as she was done, but I declined. I wanted to be with her.

Back outside the fun was amping up. No one was to the drunken sex stage, but a lot was happening. The women were up dancing even the bunnies. I got Ashlee to join the other old ladies. She was a little reluctant but soon she was laughing and having fun. She had a great body and could move it really well on the dance floor. I kept getting caught watching her rather than listening to the guys. More than one had tormented me about it.

It was going on ten thirty when I excused myself to run to the bathroom. Ashlee had just taken a break and was going back up to dance with the girls. I came back out a few minutes later to find the band was on break. I looked around trying to find Ashlee. I saw Harlow and a couple of the other wives, but she wasn't with them. I was about to head over to another section of the yard when I heard a woman yelling. I whipped around trying to see where it was coming from and who it was. I saw a couple of my brothers take off toward the band area. I raced after them.

When we got closer, I could see the stand-in bassist had a hold of Ashlee. She was pressed up against the side of their van. She was yelling at him and shoving him. He was looking angry and his hands were gripping her shoulders. I roared and shoved through the crowd ahead of me. Before I could make it to her, Stalker came out of nowhere and grabbed the guy. He tore him away from Ashlee and punched him in the mouth. The rest of the band had made it over to us and stood watching. Ashlee was standing there shaking. I made it to her and took her in my arms. She sobbed.

"Shh, you're okay, babe. I'm here. He can't hurt you. Fuck, I'm sorry I left. I didn't know they'd be taking a break and I didn't think anyone would bother you, Precious." She laid her head down on my chest.

"It wasn't your fault. He just scared me. He wouldn't listen when I told him I wasn't interested, and I was with someone. I told him more than once, Jack," she whispered softly.

By this time most of my brothers, plus a whole lot of others had made it to us. Capone stepped up. "Let me watch her. You go take care of that." He gestured toward the bassist. Stalker now had him pinned down on the ground. The guy was swearing and struggling. I thanked Capone and handed Ashlee over to him. He took her to sit down in a nearby chair. Several of my brothers surrounded her like a wall. When I got over to Stalker, he looked up and grinned.

"Look at the little morsel I caught you, Devil. I can see you're real hungry. Hope this piece of shit will be enough." He snickered as he let go of the guy. The bassist jumped up.

"What the fuck is wrong with you, man? Why'd you come up and punch my ass?" he yelled.

I got up close to him and I answered him, "Because you had your fucking hands on a woman who didn't belong to you. You did that and even though she wasn't interested, and she told you that more than once, you felt like you had the right to ignore her and do it anyway." I could see him gulp. His eyes were shifting around looking at all these pissed bikers staring at him.

"Listen. I didn't mean any harm. She was dancing and she's hot. I saw she didn't have one of those vest things on, so I thought she was available."

I just looked at him.

"That would have been understandable, if you hadn't put your hands on her and ignored her telling you to leave her alone and that she wasn't available. See, she's my old lady and I'm gonna make sure you learn your lesson about how to treat a woman, and when to know that no means fucking no," I growled. He was now pale and sweating.

I dragged him by the back of his neck and walked him over to my ring of brothers. They opened up and there sat my precious. She still looked upset. Her eyes got huge seeing me with the guy who had harassed her. I shoved him to his knees at her feet, then I grabbed his hair and jerked his head back, so he had to look at her.

"Fucking apologize to my woman for laying hands on her, for ignoring her when she said she wasn't interested and was taken, and for scaring her." He looked at her. She sat watching him. I shook him. "Fucking do it."

He stammered, "I-I-I'm sorry I scared you and that I didn't listen to you. I shouldn't have laid my hands on you. I apologize."

She just looked at him, and I could see the fear had receded. She said nothing back. I stepped around him to kiss her.

"I'll be back soon, babe. I just need to take out the trash."
She grasped my arm.

"Don't do anything to get yourself in trouble, Devil.
Please. He's not worth it." I grinned.

"I'm just gonna have some fun with him. Stay with my
brothers." She nodded. I left her with Capone, Blade,
Smoke, and Hawk. The others followed me as I marched
him toward the middle of the backyard. I stopped.

He looked at me expectantly. "Well, can I go now? I
apologized," he said hopefully. I shook my head.

"No, you can't. Did you really think all it would take was
for you to say you were sorry and I'd let you walk out
of here? If so, you really are a dumb shit. Now, you and
I are gonna settle this like two men. You look like a guy
who's in shape, and you obviously know how to fight if
you go around hitting on other men's women. So, here's
the deal. As soon as you put me down on my ass, you
can leave. If you can't, then we fight as long as I want
or until you beg for mercy. Then I'll decide if I'll stop or
not. Deal?"

He was sputtering and trying to look to anyone who
would help him. Everyone stared at him impassively,
even the guys in the band. They may not be a club, but
they knew us well enough to know we handled shit a
certain way. Messing with our women always called for
something to be done. He finally realized no one was
going to help him.

He stood up straight and got into a fighting stance. I
stood with my arms loose by my sides. I knew I could
kill him easily, but that wasn't my intent. I let him make

the first move. He took a swing at my head. I easily ducked it and stood back up straight. I didn't throw a punch.

He came at me again and tried to hit me with a round-house punch. This time I side stepped his swing. He was starting to get a little red in the face. I stayed quiet. The next move he tried was to feint to one side and come in from the other to deliver an uppercut. He ended up falling on his face when I whirled and grabbed the back of his shirt, pushing him off balance. He came up off the ground enraged.

"Why don't you fucking fight, you piece of shit?" he yelled. I stared at him. This caused him to lose all control. He came at me like a lunatic, throwing wild punches, trying to headbutt me and use his legs to swipe mine out from under me. He never succeeded in landing a punch or getting me on the ground.

I grew tired of watching his act like an idiot and wanted to end this. On his next pass, I punched him in the mouth. He screamed out in pain. He was holding his mouth and looking at me in surprise.

"What? Did you think I'd just stand here forever and not fight back?" I proceeded to beat the shit out of him. He had no way to defend himself and I wasn't even trying hard. He fell to the ground, begging me to stop after five minutes. He was bleeding from his mouth, nose, and the cut over his right eye. That eye was swelling shut. I knew I'd severely bruised if not broken a couple of his ribs. His thigh would be sporting a large goose egg from one of my kicks for weeks. I leaned down.

"Don't ever touch a woman when she says no. Never

come around my woman again. Never play with this band when they're playing at the Fallen Angel or at one of our parties or fundraisers. Be thankful I want to get back to my woman and that you bore me." I walked away.

Stalker hauled him up off the ground and was walking him toward the gate. I overheard him say to the shit-head. "You don't know how fucking lucky you are, man. Devil Dog was a goddamn Marine and a sniper to boot! You piss him off again, and he can snipe your ass from a mile away and you'd never see it coming." Stalker took him to a van and a couple of the prospects from Bull's club took him to wherever he wanted to go. They'd be sure to scare his ass about calling the cops. It was his word against mine and I had a lot of witnesses who would swear I never touched him, and I had no marks on me. My knuckles were a little red is all.

The band got back to playing. Lucky for them and us, one of the guys from the Souls in Georgia could play. He turned out to be pretty damn amazing. I went to my woman. She was sitting in the same chair and some of the old ladies were with her. She saw me, jumped up, ran to me, and hugged me. I wrapped her in my arms.

"Oh God, Devil, I was so worried. The guys wouldn't let me watch the fight. I was worried you might get hurt."

I clicked my tongue.

"Babe, you had nothing to worry about and you didn't need to see that. I'm fine and he's left. Now, I want you to relax and let's have more fun. Don't let him ruin the night for you." She finally agreed. The next couple of hours passed with us talking and laughing with a lot of the guests. It was now one in the morning and the band had left and the more amorous pursuits had begun. I took her by the hand and started toward the guest-house. She looked at me.

"Why are we leaving?" I smiled.

"Because I know you don't like seeing this and I want to be alone with you for a bit. Let's go to the house. We can talk or watch television or even a movie. I just want to hold you and be with you." She smiled back.

At the house, we sat down to watch television together. I didn't really care what we watched since I only wanted to be able to hold her. We were about halfway through some movie when she sighed. I looked over at her.

"What's wrong, babe?" She turned and the next thing I knew, she was kissing me. Her lips were passionately devouring mine. I returned her kiss while easing her down on her back on the couch. I hovered over her as we kissed over and over. When we finally pulled apart panting for breath, I laid my head down beside hers.

"Shit, Precious. That just shorted out my brain. Warn a guy. As much as I'm enjoying this, we need to stop. I'm not gonna do something you end up regretting tomor-row." She protested, but I held strong. It was the hardest thing I ever had to do. I knew if we continued, I'd be peeling her clothes off and she wasn't ready for that yet. I helped her to sit up. She was now avoiding my eyes and looked like she was uncomfortable. I took her chin in my hand and turned her face so she had to look at me.

"Don't be upset. Believe me, I want you more than I can say, but you just agreed yesterday to be with me. I don't want to chance rushing things and then you end up hating me. Please, understand. I couldn't stand it if that happened. However, I do want to spend as much time as I can with you to explore our relationship. Can we do that?"

She nodded. I took her back in my arms, and she eventually softened against me.

We watched the next show that came on. By this time, I had stretched out on the couch and had her lying in front of me. I thought about how much I wanted her. I could so easily carry her into the bedroom and make love to her until we both dropped. However, I didn't want to move too fast. She needed to think about things a little more before we went all the way, but not too long. I would die if I didn't have her soon. These were my thoughts as I drifted off to sleep with her in my arms.

Chapter 4: Ashlee

I woke up disoriented. The sun was coming from the wrong direction. I went to sit up and felt arms tighten around me. I gasped and looked to find Devil lying behind me. We were on one of the couches in the living room. He had me wrapped in his arms. Last night came flooding back to me—us watching television and then the kissing and him putting a halt to it. I admit I had been hurt when he did. A part of me wanted to say the hell with it and have him take me, but he was right, we needed to take just a little bit of time. Though not too much because I had been wanting him for months already, and once I made up my mind to give in to being with him, I was eager to be with him all the way, which for me was surprising. He cracked open his eyes and smiled.

"Good morning, Precious. You're awfully nice to sleep with, babe." He gave me a kiss. When I pulled away, he lifted his arm so I could get up, and I stood. I knew I had to look like hell. My makeup would be all over my face and my clothes a wreck. I was trying to tame my hair, but he grabbed my hand.

"You look beautiful, Precious. Why don't you get your shower while I go back to the clubhouse? That way I can get a change of clean clothes. I'll be back to get you once I'm done. Will a half hour be enough time?"

I gave him a grateful smile and nodded.

He got up and stretched. His shirt rode up and I could see his muscular stomach and tats. He had them on his arms as well. I wondered where else he had them. Those thoughts started to lead me to somewhere I shouldn't go. He kissed me and then headed for the door. He made sure to lock it behind him. I raced down the hall to my room.

In the shower, I scrubbed off my smeared makeup. My hair I had washed yesterday, so I wrapped it up, so it would stay out of the water. I scrubbed my body as I thought of Devil Dog. He'd been the star of my fantasies for over two months. As I thought about him, my nipples grew hard and my pussy grew slick with my juices. I eased my hand down between my legs and rubbed my fingers through my folds and across my clit. My insides clenched. I began to slide my fingers up and down, flicking my clit and sometimes thrusting a couple of fingers inside as I imagined it was Devil touching me. It only took me five minutes to come, moaning in the shower.

It wasn't enough but it would have to do. I hurried to finish my shower, get dressed, slap on some makeup, and fix my hair. Since it was in a bob, it was quick and easy to fix. Even with my impromptu hand job, I was done and ready only five minutes late.

Today I had on another sexy outfit the girls had talked me into ordering off of a website a couple of weeks ago. That was where the clothes from yesterday came from. Today I decided to wear a short baby doll dress. It had short sleeves and was cut in the front to show some cleavage without being too trashy. It hit me just above mid-thigh and had a ruffle around the bottom. It was black with tiny peach flowers all over it. I paired it with a pair of wedges that gave me more height. My jewelry was gold and simple. I grabbed my sunglasses and headed out the door. I needed to go check on my kids.

I opened the door to find Devil waiting. He whistled when he saw me. "Damn, babe, I can't take you out there looking like this. I think I like this even more than the outfit you wore yesterday. You stay glued to me." He grabbed me and pulled me close so he could ravish my mouth. When we pulled apart, I felt weak in the knees. He groaned and then took my hand to lead me to the clubhouse. It was early, just after eight, so a lot of people would still be asleep. However, I knew both of my kids were awake and needed to be taken care of. I didn't feel right putting the responsibility on others.

Once in the clubhouse, I went straight to the children's room. Inside, the other moms were there getting their kids. Angel ran over to me for a kiss and hug then she demanded one from Devil. He swung her up in his arms and kissed her all over her face. She giggled. Her father never paid any kind of attention to her, so she loved male attention. Jayce was awake and Ms. Marie was holding him. I went and relieved her.

"Thank you so much, Ms. Marie, for watching them for me. Let me take them. You need a break."

She laughed.

"No need. I love taking care of the kids. I wanted to have a dozen myself and only could have my daughter and then I got Alannah. This keeps me young."

I gave her a hug. I'd taken extra clothes to the clubhouse for the kids yesterday, so they were dressed for the day. We took them out to the common room. Others were starting to wake up and it looked like someone was taking advantage of the food in the fridges to cook breakfast. I got Angel set up with some oatmeal, fruit, and milk. Then I sat down to feed Jayce.

I'd pumped a lot of breast milk the last few days, so he'd have enough for his feedings when I wasn't with him. I took a seat on one of the couches and put a blanket up over me so I could nurse him. I personally didn't care if someone saw me breastfeeding, but some people were very uncomfortable about it.

Torch was amusing Angel at the table. Devil came over and sat down beside me. I glanced up from Jayce. Devil was staring intently at me. "What is it?" I asked. He nodded toward my son.

"Why do you cover yourself when you feed him? Does it make you uncomfortable to have people see you feeding him?" he asked with curiosity.

I had often caught him watching me feed Jayce. I shook my head. "No, it doesn't bother me at all. I found out when I had Angel and did this that some people were very upset about it. Some so much so, they would make rude comments. So, I just started to use the blanket. Alex hated to see me breastfeed her. He said it was ugly and disgusting."

Devil Dog cursed.

"Babe, you don't have to worry about me ever thinking that. Don't change how you would care for your child because of the stupidity of others. Now, don't get me wrong, breasts are beautiful and I love them from a purely sexual standpoint, but they also serve a very real and important purpose. Hopefully one day, you'll be comfortable enough to allow me to see you feed him without a covering." He kissed my ear as he said this. I turned and brushed my lips across his.

"I'll never have an issue with you watching. Have you ever seen a woman breastfeed?" He shook his head no. I lifted the blanket up so he could see underneath it. Jayce was latched on with his eyes closed in contentment and his little hand resting on my breast. I watched Devil's face when he saw it.

He stared in absolute fascination. I didn't feel any kind of embarrassment with Devil. As he watched, I took Jayce and switched him to feed from the other breast. I now had both breasts essentially bare for Devil in a room full of people. He tentatively ran his finger back and forth on Jayce's hand. He looked at me.

"Precious, that is one of the most beautiful things I've ever seen. Thank you," he whispered. His finger accidently grazed my breast and I shivered. He noticed my reaction and rubbed across the other. I looked around to see if anyone saw us. They seemed all too busy eating to notice.

He leaned in and took my lips. His tongue was hot and insistent on gaining entrance into my mouth. I let him. We kissed while my son fed.

He was the one to finally break away. He kissed up to my ear and whispered, "I can't wait until the day I get to see them and you in all your beautiful glory."

I moaned. Thankfully Harlow came over at that time. She was rubbing her round tummy. Terror had Hunter at the table getting breakfast. She sighed as she sat down in the chair next to us. She nodded to Jayce.

"He seems to feed well. Have you been giving Devil Dog lessons in breastfeeding?" she teased us.

He was the one to speak up. "She has. I told her it was a beautiful thing and nothing she should hide if she doesn't want to cover up. People who don't like it can look away or leave. It's natural and beautiful to see a woman do it."

She nodded. I didn't know if she'd breastfed Hunter or not, so I asked her.

"Yeah, I did. Though I admit I covered up but more out of just following what I'd seen others do rather than any thought one way or the other. Some of the others have breastfed and they have been ones who also covered up when they did. I plan to do the same with this one." Our very domestic talk was interrupted with the arrival of more of the bikers and bunnies. Devil excused himself to go talk to one of the guys.

Harlow and I had been there talking while I finished feeding Jayce for maybe five minutes when one of the bunnies came over. She was from one of the other clubs. She was sneering. I looked at her in surprise. She nodded toward me.

"That's disgusting. Why don't you go somewhere private and feed that kid? No one wants to see that shit." Her words pissed me off. I'd just adjusted my top under the blanket. I looked at Harlow, and she nodded. I handed her Jayce and stood up.

"I'm not sure where you're from or where you think you're at, but this is a Warriors' compound. We do what we want in our own home. You'd do well to remember that and have some manners. Breastfeeding is a natural thing. Get over it. If you don't like it, then leave." I threw her a glare. I turned back to Harlow to take Jayce back from her.

The bunny snarled something, then I felt my hair get pulled. I whipped around and slapped her. She pulled back in surprise. She gave a scream of rage and started to step into me. I steeled myself. One thing I could say for my years of beatings, I could take a lot and tolerate pain. Before she touched me, she was yanked back. Devil Dog had grabbed her around the waist and swung her away from me. He was pissed.

"What the fuck do you think you're doing, bunny? How dare you touch an old lady in our club?" he roared. The common room had gotten quiet as others noticed what was going on. I could see Terror and a couple of the brothers plus some bikers from other clubs coming our way fast.

The bunny began to stammer. "I-I was just telling her she should feed her baby somewhere private. She got ugly with me." Devil looked at me just as Terror and a guy who's cut said his name was *Wrath* came up. He looked pissed off. I was thinking she must belong to his club and he wasn't happy with me telling her off. He was the first to speak.

"What in the hell is going on here, Devil Dog? Why'd

you yank one of our bunnies around over here?"

Devil faced him calmly.

"Because she grabbed my old lady by the hair and when she defended herself, she was going to come at her again. No one touches my old lady," he growled. Surprise and then consternation flashed through Wrath's eyes. He looked at the bunny who was trying to look innocent and weepy, then he looked at me. It took everything in me to look at him and maintain eye contact. I hadn't seen him last night.

"What's your name, sweetheart, and what started the fight?" he asked me.

I cleared my throat.

"My name is Ashlee. I was finishing breastfeeding my son when she came over here, telling me I should do it elsewhere. She said it was disgusting for me to do it here. I had myself covered. She couldn't see anything. I pointed out it was rude of her to be acting this way in our home and she could leave if she didn't want to see it. I was about to take my son back from Harlow when she grabbed my hair. So, I slapped her."

He was looking angry now. He looked at Harlow who gave him a single nod. He stepped toward me. Devil had left the bunny and was standing near me. He stepped forward to put himself between me and Wrath.

Wrath smiled at me. "I'm sorry she said that, sweetheart, and that she touched you. I can assure you. She'll cause no more problems this weekend. And as for you breastfeeding, do it wherever you want. It's natural for God's sake." He swung around to now face the bunny.

She looked nervous. I hope he wasn't going to abuse her. She was an unfriendly bitch but didn't deserve to be hit. He shook his head. "Shana, why would you ever say something like that let alone touch an old lady? What is wrong with you?"

She shrugged.

"I didn't know she was anyone's old lady. She's not wearing a property cut, and she was just sitting out here as bold as you please feeding that baby. No one wants to see that. It's disgusting," she whined.

Devil spoke up and addressed Wrath. "You guys weren't here yesterday. I had to address this a few times. Ashlee is my old lady. She hasn't gotten her cut yet because it's not ready. She has two children. Jayce," he pointed to him, "is two-and-a-half months and she has Angel, her daughter." He gestured to Angel sitting at the table with Torch. "She's three. All of them are under my protection. And if my old lady wants to feed our boy in the common room, she can."

My heart jumped hearing him call Jayce his boy. Wrath was nodding his head in agreement. He gestured to one of his guys to come over. When he did, I saw his name was *Ryder* and he was their enforcer. I'd finally seen the back of his cut which proclaimed they were Pagan Souls out of Georgia.

"Get Shana out of here. She can stay in the campgrounds, but I don't want to see her face at the party for the rest of the celebration. She obviously doesn't know how to act or know her place. Have the others teach her?" Ryder took her by the arm and led her away.

I was worried about what the teaching was about. Devil wrapped his arm around my shoulders.

"Don't worry, babe, they won't beat her. They'll have the older bunnies educate her on how she should act. Why don't we get Angel and take her to play?" I agreed.

Wrath stopped him.

"Don't run off. I want to talk to this fascinating creature you've claimed. And I want to meet her little mini-me, Angel. She looks just like one, doesn't she?"

Devil called for Torch to bring Angel over. She came running and smiling, and Devil scooped her up. She looked at the badasses in front of her with curiosity.

Devil made introductions. "Wrath, Storm, Dare, this is Angel. Angel, this is Wrath, Storm and Dare. They were talking to your mommy and wanted to meet you." She gave them a blinding smile and held her hand out for them to all shake. They did so with amused looks on their faces.

Then Devil turned to me.

"Sorry, I forgot to formally introduce you, Precious. This is Wrath. He's the president of the Lake Oconee, Georgia Pagan Souls and this is his VP, also named Storm. His enforcer, Ryder, was the one that escorted Shana away. This other heathen is Dare. He's the VP of the Pagan Souls in Cherokee, North Carolina. Guys, this is my old lady, Ashlee, and her children, Angel and Jayce. They've been with us since the day Jayce was born."

I saw that remark caused a few raised brows. I decided to be truthful about my situation.

"It's true. I came to the Warriors two-and-a-half months ago because they extended an offer of their help if I ever needed it. That day my husband had hit my daughter for the first time and beat me again. I fled and came to them for help. My injuries from the beating caused me to go into labor and Jayce was born that same day. I've been here ever since."

Their faces showed shock and anger. Luckily before I'd explained, Devil had let Angel go with Harlow. She'd taken Jayce with her, too. Wrath looked at me.

"Do you mean to say your husband hit you while you were pregnant?" I nodded. "Fuck! Is he dead?" he asked Devil.

Devil shook his head no.

"No, he's still alive and living in Maryville as far as we know. He's not bothered her, but he might know where she is. She's going to be filing a restraining order and for a divorce next week. He may be triggered by that."

They grunted. Wrath spoke up again, "Call me if you need any help with that piece of trash. It was a pleasure meeting you, Ashlee. I hope we talk again while I'm here."

I agreed and they headed out. I turned to Devil.

"I hope you were okay with me telling them so much about how we met. I just want to be open about my life, and that includes how we came to be in your lives. I hid so much for all those years. I don't want to do that anymore, Jack." He took me into his arms.

"Babe, it's fine. You can tell anyone and everyone how

you came to be here. All I know is I'm damn grateful you did. Now, what do you want to do today?"

I thought about it for a couple of minutes. "Why don't you spend some time with the guys? Relax and talk. I'll spend some time with the kids." He went to protest. "No, it will be good. You can talk all that boring man talk and then we can go swimming in the pool. Angel is anxious to get in it again. I know Harlow was planning to take Hunter. It's almost ten now. How about we meet at the pool at noon?" He finally agreed and walked me to the house.

The next couple of hours I got Jayce to take a nap, Angel played with Hunter while I helped Harlow out with a couple of things at the house. She told me funny stories about Agony and Wrath, especially how Agony always bemoaned the fact he never gets the women before the Warriors do. The time went by quickly.

At noon we were at the pool along with several other people. Most of the old ladies had decided to join us as well as several guests. Mainly it was bunnies, but some guys were hanging around too. I think they were there to look at the women. I hope they knew better than to stare at the old ladies too much. The Warriors tended to be a protective bunch.

Jayce was sitting in his carrier asleep alongside the pool in the shade. Ms. Marie was down as usual to help with the kids. I took Angel into the water. She was learning to swim, mainly because Devil had been working with her. I still made sure she was wearing her floaters. She was splashing and having a good time in the shallow end. I was so focused on her. I didn't notice a guy coming up behind me until he wrapped an arm around my waist. I whipped around. He was a big biker with long dark hair and a beard. He was smiling down at me. I pushed against his chest.

"Excuse me. You have obviously confused me with someone else. Let go," I told him.

He shook his head and smiled even more.

"No, darlin', I've got a hold of the one I want. Now all the old ladies from this club I know, so you must be one of the friends of the club or a bunny. I had to be sure I claimed you before one of these other wolves got a hold of you. I'm Crusher. I'm one of the Souls out of Georgia. What's your name, beautiful?"

I realized two things at that moment. One, he was one of Wrath's guys and obviously had no idea who I was. Two, he was about to be set straight and probably in a hard way because powering across the pool was Devil Dog and his face was filled with anger. I tried to save Crusher.

"Listen, Crusher, you're mistaken. I'm not a friend or a bunny. I'm an old lady. I suggest you go before Devil Dog latches on to you."

He frowned and looked around to see Devil bearing down on us. He jerked away from me and held his hands in the air. He turned to face Devil.

"Whoa, Devil, sorry, man. I had no idea you had gotten an old lady since the last time we met. I didn't know she was taken. Peace, brother."

Devil had stopped right in front of him and narrowed

his eyes. I swam over to him. He hooked his arm around my waist.

"You okay, Precious?" I nodded my head yes. He looked back at Crusher. "Well, now you know. She's my old lady, Ashlee. That little one over there is Angel and the little boy sleeping in the carrier right there is Jayce. They all belong to me. Just so you know who is part of my family and under my protection now. Just a suggestion, Crusher. Before you touch a woman, ask if she's available."

Crusher laughed.

"Okay. I get it. I'll try that. Sorry to have bothered you, darlin'. And Devil, damn, man, what a fine woman you caught. Lucky bastard." He winked at me and swam off. Devil looked at me.

"You know that was all your fault, don't you?" he asked, and I gaped.

"What do you mean it was my fault? What did I do?" I asked, getting a little pissed.

He growled. "You came out here looking like that." He pointed to my swimsuit. It was a two piece, but it wasn't a thong bikini and it was more decent than all of the ones worn by the bunnies.

"What's wrong with my suit?" He ran his hands down my sides into the water where he grabbed my ass cheeks and hoisted me up and against him.

"It shows off this luscious body. How could they not help but look and want you? I could put you in a feedbag and you'd still be beautiful and sexy. I think I need to get my name tattooed where everyone can see it, so they know you're taken." He kissed me. I have to admit, he took my breath away.

The need to breathe is what drove us apart. I panted and laid my head on his chest. "Really? You think that? Well, if I get a tat, then you do too. One that tells all women you're mine. Don't think I haven't seen how these bunnies have been eyeing you, Jack. They want to get with you in the worst way," I taunted back.

He grinned.

"I hadn't noticed, but I don't have a problem getting your name on me, babe. Wherever you want it."

I leaned in to kiss him quickly. "Deal. Let me think about it. Now, let's swim." He spent time working with Angel more on her swimming, then he and I spent time playing in the water. Several guys were now at the pool and the volleyball net went up. I got out of the water. I knew how crazy the Warriors played water volleyball. The others were probably just as crazy. The women took seats along the edge to watch and cheer.

Lunch was served later, and it was just a serve yourself deal set up like a deli—sandwiches, a few sides and lots of different chips. I got Angel her ham sandwich and a few chips. She was happily eating. Harlow came over and handed me something. I looked at it and realized it was a cut. I looked at her.

"It doesn't say who you are with, but it may prevent Devil Dog from killing someone before this weekend is over. I have been toying with this idea. When the prospects start, they get a Prospect cut until they hopefully get their own. Why shouldn't we have a generic one that can be worn by a newly claimed old lady until her own is made? This is what I came up with. What do you think?"

I looked it over. On the front in the place where you'd usually see the woman's road name, it just said *Old Lady.* On the back, the top rocker as I had recently learned is what those patches were, said *Property of* and the bottom one said *Archangel's Warriors.* I looked back at her.

"I think it's perfect. Why haven't you brought it up sooner?"

She sighed. "I was going to have Terror present it next week to the group so they could vote on it, but after what happened last night and then this morning, I told him we should let you wear it for the weekend. He can ask the guys next Saturday to vote. We'll treat it like a demo."

I laughed and agreed. I slipped it on over my bathing suit. When Devil got out of the water to let another team play, he came straight to me. He was eyeing the cut.

"Where did you get that?" he asked with raised eyebrows. I explained what Harlow had told me. He smiled. "I think it's a great idea. It makes a lot of sense. Definitely wear it. Just be sure if they ask whose old lady you are, you say it's me," he teased.

I pretended to think. "Well, you know, with this I could say my old man was one of several of the single Warriors. There's Hawk, Storm, Torch, Capone—" I didn't get any more names out because he had grabbed me and swung me up over his shoulder. He walked off with me like this and asked Harlow to watch the kids as we passed her. She just laughed and gave me a thumbs up.

He carried me out of the pool fencing and over to the guesthouse which sat nearby. Once he had me in the house, he took me down the hall to my room. My heart began to race. He threw me gently down on the bed and crawled up to hover over me.

"Now, what were you saying about telling them you belonged to one of my brothers? Because I can promise you, I'm your old man and I plan for it to stay that way." He took my mouth in a fiery kiss. We licked and sucked at each other's mouths and he bit my bottom lip before soothing it with his tongue. Our tongues had a duel. I was on fire. My nipples were hard and tingling. My pussy was wet and throbbing. God, did I want this man.

I knew we were supposed to be going slow, but I didn't want to. I wanted to feel him inside of me. I moaned and ran a hand down to his crotch. I could feel his hardness pressing against his trunks. I gently squeezed, and he groaned.

"Babe, you can't. I'm holding on by a thread. We're not rushing things, remember?" I looked at him.

"Jack, I'm glad you want to take things slow for my sake, but I don't need or want it. I want to be with you. Do you understand? I've been wanting you as long as you've been wanting me. I ache to feel you inside of me, Jack."

He growled and laid his forehead on mine. "Okay, but not right now. I want to be able to take my time with you. Let's rejoin the party. Tonight, we'll see where you want us to be in regard to this."

I relented because I knew where I would want us to go tonight. I planned to have Jack Cannon in my bed. I wanted to know what it was like to be with a man who really cared about me. I couldn't ever remember having an orgasm with Alex. I'd had some when I pleasured myself. I was so hoping Devil could make me have one.

Devil took me back to the pool, however, this time, I was on my own two feet. People were teasing us about running off. Devil just grinned. So, I took this as my clue and smiled. The rest of the afternoon passed quickly. After pool time was over, some played pool, darts, horseshoes, or even cornhole. Dinnertime was on us in no time. Tonight's dinner was all Italian food—huge trays of lasagna, fettuccine Alfredo, breadsticks, and salad, plus several desserts. We'd made the lasagnas days ago and froze them. The bread was the same. The Alfredo they'd made today in huge commercial kitchen-sized vats in the clubhouse. It had industrial-sized fridges, ovens and stoves. In addition, it had two massive dishwashers and sinks. This warehouse had been used as some kind of business and the industrial kitchen had been here when they bought it. You could feed an army out of that kitchen.

The other band came to set up around six thirty. I went to help get Angel her bath and settled back at the clubhouse. Tonight, they were having a Disney movie marathon for the kids. She was excited. Devil insisted on coming with me. He watched Jayce while I got her ready. The children's room was equipped to handle lots of kids. Besides a huge television that they could watch movies or play videos when they got older, it had several bunk beds stacked along the walls. There were cots and tiny toddler beds as well as cribs. Attached to it was a big bathroom with a shower, separate tub, toilet and dual sinks.

In addition to being soundproof, Devil had told me it could be locked down as a panic room. This made me feel very secure. It was around seven thirty by the time we got away from the kids. *Hellfire* was playing and people were dancing. Devil went to grab us a couple of drinks.

I stood with Menace, Alannah, Ghost, and Wren. I'd donned the cut Harlow had given me. They noticed and asked about it. I explained it while we waited for Devil to get back. They thought it was a good idea. Wren was sitting next to me. She was due at the end of this month. She was big but not huge. She was still gorgeous. She was rubbing her belly.

"Is she stretching and causing you to have Braxton-Hicks yet?"

She nodded her head yes. "She kicks most of the night."

I could tell she was tired.

"Try music. Sometimes it's the lack of movement and sound they miss. So, if you can put on music, it can help to soothe the baby so she doesn't kick as much or as long."

She gave me a surprised look. "Really? Have you done it?" I nodded.

"Yeah, with Jayce. He'd kick all night, so I tried it. He did it for a much shorter amount of time and less vigorously. Angel kicked but not like he did." Devil had walked up during my explanation and had a look of concentration on his face. As he handed me my drink, I asked him what he was thinking about.

"I guess it just struck me how experienced you are from having two kids and wondering how much of it you did alone." The others got quiet.

"Honey, I do have a lot of experience, but it was all trial and error. I was scared to death sometimes, like when Angel would get sick. As for how much I did alone, it was all of it. Alex made it very clear she was my kid and my job to take care of her without it interfering with his life. That was even before I had Angel. Hell, when I went into labor with Angel, he was busy, so I had to call 911 to come and take me to the hospital. He was pissed I ran up an ambulance and hospital bill." My confession had Devil swearing. I ran my hand up his chest to curl along his jaw.

"Honey, it's okay. I made it and I never have to be with him again. It made me tougher. Now, no more talk about depressing things. We're here to have fun, so, let's do it!" The rest of the evening was spent drinking until I felt relaxed but not drunk, dancing with the girls and then slow dancing with Devil. Those were the dances I loved, to be close to him was heavenly.

We partied and talked to various people all night. There were so many of them, they were a blur. It was around one o'clock in the morning when Devil told me he wanted to go back to my house. I was eager to be alone with him. I only hoped when we got there, he'd make love to me. I knew he wanted to give me time to adjust and all, but I didn't need more time. I wanted to be with him. I stood nervously in the living room after he got us back to the house. I was waiting to see what he would do.

Chapter 5: Devil Dog

I had been dying all day. I'd woken up with Ashlee in my arms, then to see her in her dress and then that bathing suit had almost made me lose my mind. The kiss we'd shared in the bedroom this afternoon had frayed my nerves. I wanted her and was trying to go slow, but she said she didn't want that. God, I hoped she was right and wouldn't regret this, because I planned to make love to her tonight. The last few hours watching her body gyrate and sway on the dance floor had sapped my last resistance. She was facing me in the living room looking nervous. I took her in my arms.

"Babe, there's nothing to worry about. We don't have to do anything tonight. You're not ready and that's okay. Do you want to watch television or something?" I was trying to think what we could do besides sex so I could remain with her for longer. She pressed up against me more and slid her hand up my chest as she stood on her toes to reach my mouth. I lowered my head.

I knew I should stop this. It would do nothing to bolster my resistance to her. The touch of her soft lips on mine almost snapped my control. I kissed her with everything in me. I devoured her and only wanted more. Her hands were tracing the muscles on my chest. I fought to bring myself back from the edge and tore myself away from her.

"Ashlee. Stop! We can't do this. It isn't right. We need to think about this. We should have put more thought into this." She froze and I watched as a veil came down over her usually expressive face. She stepped back. I waited for her to say something.

"You need to leave, Jack. Right now. Go!" She sounded upset but also remote. I moved toward her, but she threw up her hand. "No! Don't touch me or say a word. I need you to leave right now. I can't do this." She pushed past me to race down the hall and into her bedroom, slamming the door. I heard the door lock. I hurried down the hall and tried the handle anyway. It was locked. I pounded on it.

"Ashlee, babe, please, talk to me. I'm sorry. What did I do?" I was starting to get worried because all I heard was silence. I pounded on the door again. Still no answer. "Ashlee, if you don't open this door, I'm going to break it down. Do you hear me?" She still didn't answer. I wasn't leaving here until she talked to me. I kicked the handle destroying the lock on the door and shoved it open.

The room was empty. The drapes were blowing around due to the patio glass doors being open. I went straight to them. She wasn't out on the patio as I'd hoped. She had left. I headed to the clubhouse. Maybe she went to get the kids. I was trying to figure out what I'd said that had set her off. I didn't understand.

Most people were still partying, and things were definitely getting hot and heavy. I ignored them and headed to the children's room. I entered quietly. Cindy was up reading a book. She looked at me in surprise. I looked around and didn't see Ashlee. "Did Ashlee come for the kids?" I asked her. She shook her head pointing to where each of them was fast asleep. I thanked her and left.

As I hit the common room, one of the bunnies who I think came with the Souls grabbed my arm. Before I knew what she was up to, she wrapped an arm around my neck and had a leg around my thigh.

"Hello. I've been wanting to get a chance to talk to you all weekend. I'm glad to see you got rid of the taga-long you seemed to have. Come with me. We can have so much fun. She's at home with the kids. She'll never know." I wanted to scream at her, but before I could, she kissed me. Her attack had surprised me, so my reaction time was slower than normal. I was pulling away from her when I heard someone gasp. I looked past the bunny to see Ashlee.

She was staring at me with such a pained and devas-tated look, I almost puked. I'd seen shit like this happen with some of my other brothers and they'd almost lost their old ladies over it. I wasn't about to have that hap-pen. I shoved the bunny away from me. She yelled out and was pissed. I looked at Ashlee.

"It isn't what it looks like, babe. I came here looking for you, and she just—" I didn't get a chance to finish be-cause the bunny jumped in.

"He said he was tired of messing with you and wanted to have a real woman. One that didn't have a couple of kids hanging off her. You interrupted our fun. I promise to send him home when I'm done." She smirked. Ashlee barely glanced my way. She was focused on the bunny.

"Don't let me stop you. He's available and he won't be coming home to me. I don't want him. Have fun." She turned and took off toward the door. I rushed after her only to be slowed down by the crowd and then waylaid by Knight from the Souls.

"Hey Devil, man, what the hell is wrong? I just saw your old lady running out of here like her ass was on fire." I shoved past him.

"Sorry, Knight, I'll have to talk to you later." He nodded. His small delay allowed her to get out the door of the clubhouse. I pushed my way through more people until I came to the door. The yard was still pretty full of people partying, drinking, and fucking. I scanned frantically searching for her. I didn't see her, so I headed to the guest house. I checked it out to find it was empty. I stood there trying to figure out where she had gone.

A part of me was a little concerned someone could grab her in the dark thinking she was available. I rushed over to see if Terror was home. I pounded on the door. It took him a few minutes to answer the door. I could see I probably interrupted them. He stood staring at me with his hair messed up and his jeans unsnapped.

"What's wrong, Devil? You look upset." I grabbed his arm.

"Please tell me Ashlee is here with you guys." He got a worried look on his face. Harlow came up behind him.

"No, she isn't here. We haven't seen her for over an hour. What happened? Why isn't she with you?"

I groaned.

"She got pissed and left the house. I went looking for her at the clubhouse and a bunny got all over me. Ashlee came in and saw it. She took off again. I can't find her. She wasn't at the guesthouse." I explained as quickly as I could. He stepped back.

"Come in. Let me get dressed. We'll find her. Why is it fucking bunnies are always causing shit?" He headed off to get dressed. Harlow stayed with me.

"You'll find her. What set her off in the first place?"

I shrugged.

"I'm not really sure. I wanted to find out and she was gone. Damn it! I just got her to accept we'd be together and now this shit. She told that bunny I was available, and she could have me, Harlow! Jesus Christ!" I rubbed the back of my neck in frustration. Terror came back fully dressed. He had his phone in his hand.

"I texted the guys to meet us at the guesthouse ASAP. Let's go." I hugged Harlow and followed him out the door. As we headed to the guest house, Terror spoke up. "She'll be alright. I can guess what's going through your mind. Fuck! I'm almost at the point of banning bunnies altogether around here. They cause more trouble than anyone can imagine."

I nodded and agreed with him. We made it to the house, and a few were already there. Some were more than a little drunk, others looked like we'd interrupted them mid-sex. When they all arrived, I apologized.

"I'm sorry, brothers. I hate to ruin your night, but I can't find Ashlee." I went on to explain her getting upset, leaving and then finding me with the bunny. Several of the ones who had trouble with a bunny in the past groaned in sympathy.

Terror took over the conversation. "We need to find her. I want us all to take a different part of the compound and look for her. Report to me or Savage via text when you've cleared an area or if you find her. Plan to meet back here in an hour."

They all agreed and in no time, we'd split off to search. I ended up going through the clubhouse and garage areas. I didn't find her. As the minutes dragged by with no text from Terror, my stomach became sicker and sicker. It was forty-five minutes later when I got a call from Terror.

"Did you find her?" I asked quickly. There was a pause.

"Yeah, Hawk found her," he said in a subdued voice.

"Great. Where is she?" I asked quickly. He was quiet. "Terror, where is she?"

He sighed.

"He saw her going into Stalker's tent at the campgrounds. He had his arms around her. She wasn't struggling. Fuck, man, I don't know. Just don't go off."

I felt a flash of rage flow through me. She left me to go to him. What the fuck? I knew which tent was his because he'd shown me yesterday.

I took off running to the campground. When I got there, I could see a few of my brothers headed in my direction. I ignored them and raced to Stalker's tent. I ripped the flap open in time to see Stalker pulling off his shirt and

Ashlee was lying in his sleeping bag. I fucking lost it. He looked up in surprise and then started to protest. I didn't let him. I didn't want to hear it. I tackled him.

We were rolling around punching the hell out of each other. Ashlee was screaming. I was jerked away from him by a couple of my brothers. I was going to kill him. As the anger began to settle, I could hear what Ashlee was screaming.

"What the hell? He came in here like a madman." I swung to look at her. It hurt to see her standing there.

"I fucking came to find my woman, only to find her in another man's bed. You accused me of wanting something with that bunny. Seems like I should have been worried about you being a slut. You sure warmed up fast to being with a man," I growled. All color drained from her face. Savage hissed at me to shut up, but I was too pissed and hurt to think about what I had said.

Stalker got in my face. "You're a fucking dumbass. I never touched her. I found her upset and crying out near the woods. I brought her here. That's all."

I gave a raw laugh.

"Yeah, you have to take your shirt off to talk. I guess I'm the one who can say she's all yours," I spit back. I heard her sobbing, as she pushed out of the tent. Menace threw me a pissed look before I watched him follow her.

Stalker pulled my attention back to him.

"I was taking it off so I could change it. She soaked it with her tears. Here, feel it, asshole. She was sobbing about how you were with some bunny. I was trying to figure out what she was talking about. She basically was collapsing when we got here so I had her lie down. I planned to come find you."

His words and expression sounded like he was being truthful. As I calmed down more, a sick sensation grew and grew in my gut. Shit! Had I just accused her of cheating and called her a slut? Fuck! The guys let go of me. I dropped to my knees.

"Fuck! I screwed up."

Terror nodded. His face looked so serious. "You did. You essentially called your woman a cheating slut, Devil. You fucking crushed her even more. You didn't see her face when she left. You'll be lucky if she ever talks to you again."

I laid my head down on the ground. I wanted to vomit. The next several minutes were a blur. I remember people talking and then someone getting me to my feet. Next thing I knew, I was outside and we were walking. When I finally tuned back in, we were inside of Terror's house. I swung around.

"Why are we here? Is this where Ashlee went?" He shook his head no.

"No, she's not here. She's safe. You need to stay here tonight."

I objected, "Thanks Terror but I need to speak to Ashlee."

He shook his head sadly.

"Devil, leave her alone right now. She's safe."

I persisted, "No, I have to apologize to her."

He sighed and paced away from me and across the room. Several others had followed us inside the house.

"She doesn't want to talk to you, Devil. She told Menace that and he texted me. If you push it, she said she'll leave the compound tonight. We don't want her to do that. You have to stay here. Let her cool down and you do the same. We'll work on getting you with her later in the morning."

I didn't want to, but it looked like some brothers were prepared to stay and keep me here. I gave a very begrudging nod, and Terror showed me to a room. When I went inside, I saw a couple of my brothers standing at the end of the hall.

I laid down. I drifted off to dream of her and the fight. All I could think about was everything would have to be okay in the morning. Right before dawn I finally drifted into a deeper sleep. When I woke up, it was late morning—going on eleven. I jumped out of bed. I dressed and hurried downstairs. Terror was there with Harlow. Harlow was giving me a pissed look. Obviously, she knows about me being an asshole last night.

"Why didn't you wake me?" I scowled.

"Sit down," Terror ordered. I dropped on the couch. "I didn't because for one, you needed sleep. Two, Ashlee still didn't want to see you and three, we needed to figure out how to tell you this."

I looked around. A couple of my brothers had come in the door.

"Tell me what Terror?"

He glanced at the others then back to me. "Ashlee insisted on leaving this morning. She showed up back at the guesthouse early. We didn't know she'd left Menace and Alannah's house. Once we did, someone went to look and found her there. She was packing shit for the three of them. She said she'd had enough of this place and wanted to leave. We tried to get her to stay but she threatened to call the police and tell them we were holding her and her children against their wills. We had to let her go."

I literally screamed and jumped to my feet. Two of the guys had a hand on my shoulders squeezing them. After I pounded the couch, I looked back up.

"Please tell me she didn't go alone. That we know where she is."

He nodded.

"Of course, we wouldn't let her leave without protection. She had us take her to the hotel in town. Storm and Torch are there keeping watch over them now."

I staggered toward the door.

"Which room? I need to see her."

He frowned. "I don't think she'll listen, Devil. Whatever happened last night, it triggered something with her. We talked until we were blue in the face this morning. She wouldn't listen. I guess you have to try. She's in room 212. Let a couple of guys go with you. You shouldn't be riding alone."

I nodded and ran over to the clubhouse to change into clean clothes before I saw her. I brushed my teeth and then ran out to my bike. Capone and Blade were waiting to go with me. We raced out of the compound. All the way to town, I kept playing what Terror said over and over in my mind.

We pulled into the hotel and circled the building until we saw where room 212 was. I parked next to Storm and Torch. They gave me a worried look as I told the guys to wait for me. I headed up to the second floor. I looked until I found it, then I knocked on the door. I heard rustling and then nothing.

"Ashlee, I know you're in there. Let me in. We need to talk. If you don't, I'll get the manager and tell him my suicidal wife won't open the door." There was a stretch of silence then she opened the door. She looked like she hadn't slept all night. The hotel was a nice one and she was in a room that was considered a suite, so the bedroom was separate from the living room. The door appeared to be closed.

She walked away to stand behind the couch which placed it as a barrier between us. I paced as I got my thoughts together. Finally, I began to talk. "Ashlee, babe, I'm fucking sorry. I'm sorry I went off on you and didn't listen. I should've talked to you first. I overreacted. But you need to know you did as well. First, you get mad at me for God knows what and lock yourself in the bedroom only to escape it. I looked for you and unfortunately you found me right after a bunny essentially jumped me. You assumed the worst and took off again! Jesus Christ, what were you thinking?" I asked her. I knew I was getting a little too upset, but it killed me that she would think I'd cheat on her.

She stood there staring at me. The expression on her face was blank and her eyes looked vacant. She was worrying me. Then she spoke. "No need to apologize. You just showed who you really were. I'm glad I didn't sleep with you first. This showed me what I'd forgotten. So, it was good it happened."

I was confused.

"Babe, what are you talking about? What did you forget?"

She gave a humorless laugh.

"That all men really have ugly streaks and they pretend to be one thing when they're another. I thought you were a good man and wanted me. Well, now I know you don't. You called me a slut but what does that make you? Just another manwhore who wants his own way. Go away, Devil. Go away and leave me and my kids alone. I don't need you or want you." Her words tore me apart. I tried to get through to her again.

"I don't want anyone else. I want you. I told you she kissed me. I had no intention of fucking her."

She shook her head.

"Well, you sure weren't going to be fucking me. You kept pushing me to take things slow. I thought it was because you were worried, but now I realize I was wrong. You didn't want me. You were playing a game to protect me or something. When push came to shove, you wouldn't have sex with me, which I find insulting for a manwhore to tell me no when he'll fuck anyone else. What were you afraid of? I'd try to pull something on you and get knocked up so you'd have to take care of me and my kids. After all, I'm useless. I can't even get a job because I have no education. Well, you can rest easy. I'll take care of my kids. I don't need you and I don't need the Warriors. It's time for me to stand on my own two feet and face my life. Thanks for the lesson."

I couldn't stand it. I went across the room toward her. She backed away and the next thing I knew, she had a knife pointed at me. I froze.

"Stay away, Devil. Leave," she hissed.

I backed up. At this point I felt someone coming up behind me. I chanced a glance back to find Ghost and Smoke standing there. They were watching her with leery eyes. I tried one more time.

"Babe, please, we need to talk. I don't understand why you think I don't want you. Please." She shook her head.

"I don't want to talk anymore. Leave or I'm calling the police." I could see there was no getting through to her. She was looking shakier and pale. I slowly backed toward the door.

"Okay, I'm leaving, but we need to talk. Please call me soon so we can." She never said anything. Once we were out the door, she closed it and I heard the locks engaging. I sagged and Ghost grabbed me. I looked at him in despair.

"What do I do?"

He shook his head.

"All you can do is give her time and keep after her. She'll come around."

I hung onto his words as we went back to the compound. I went to the guesthouse to be alone.

It had been almost a week since Ashlee left the compound. She never called anyone. Not even the old ladies had heard from her. She was still at the hotel. I knew this because a couple of brothers took turns keeping an eye on her and following her everywhere she went. I knew she'd been to the police station and a lawyer's office. She'd also gone to a couple of businesses. At first, we had no idea why until it dawned on someone, she must be looking for work.

I knew when she ran from her husband, she'd taken cash he had stashed in the house. I just didn't know how much. I went to the hotel every day and knocked on her door asking to speak to her. Every day she never answered. I called the hotel room and the phone would just ring and ring. I left her flowers and letters. They'd be outside the door torn up the next day. I was at the breaking point.

Today we were having our regular church. Everyone was here except the two keeping watch. We'd covered all the business when Terror looked at me.

"How's it going, brother? Any change?" I knew he was aware nothing had changed. I shook my head.

"No. She still refuses to see or talk to me. I don't know how much longer I can stand this. If she doesn't let me in, I'm gonna fucking storm the place and take her out of there by force," I growled. A couple of the guys chuckled.

Savage jumped in, "I know you're desperate but hold off doing that. There has to be some way to get her to talk to you and come back home."

We sat there trying to brainstorm what I could do when there was a knock at the door. No one typically interrupted church. Capone answered it. Harlow was there looking worried.

"What's wrong, babe?" Terror asked her with a frown on his face.

She looked around and then cleared her throat. "Razor just called me since you guys were in church." My heart skipped. Razor and Storm were watching Ashlee and the kids right now. "He said you should probably get to the hotel. Apparently, Ashlee's husband has showed up and is causing problems." She barely finished before I was up out of my chair and racing toward the door. The others quickly followed.

We were racing out of the compound in a matter of minutes. The whole way there I worried about Alex and what he might do. When we pulled into the parking lot, a crowd was forming. I pushed through it and raced up the steps. This hotel was one where the doors opened to the outside of the building like many motels did. I could hear a voice raised in anger before I saw anyone. Rounding the corner, I saw Ashlee standing behind Storm and Razor. Her husband was standing in front of them. His face was beet red and he was the one yelling.

"It figures. You hooked up with those filthy bikers. What're you doing, Ashlee? Fucking the whole club so they'll keep you and those brats? Well, a judge will love to hear this. I'll make sure you never get to keep those fucking kids. No judge is going to give them to an uneducated, unemployed whore who sleeps with a bunch of bikers. You want a divorce, fine, but then I get the kids. Otherwise, you need to pack your shit and come home now." She looked sick but she wasn't backing down.

"I'm not a whore, Alex. I'm not sleeping with any of the Warriors. You're breaking the temporary restraining order. I'm filing for a divorce and you'll never get your hands on my kids." He laughed.

"Oh yeah? How do you think you can pay for an attorney to fight me, Ashlee? You don't have any money or a job. Face it. You can't win. And when you come crawling back to me, I'll make sure you learn your fucking lesson this time," he snarled. I came up behind him.

"I've heard enough. You need to leave. She's not going back to you ever. She's getting a divorce and her restraining order went into effect this morning. You should go home. I believe someone is looking for you to serve you the papers. And she has the money to get the best lawyer to represent her. No way a judge would grant you anything regarding these kids after they find out how you abused her, held her against her will, and raped her for years."

He looked surprised then he sneered. "Oh, are you the one she's giving it to right now? Well wait. She'll soon be giving it to someone else. She's always been a slut." I could see her face pale as he called her a slut. I shut my eyes silently groaning. I'd called her the same thing last

Sunday.

In the distance, we could hear sirens. He shoved his way past us. By the time the cops got there, he was gone. We explained what had happened. It seemed since he hadn't been served with the notice of the restraining order yet, they couldn't arrest him for breaking it. They left not too long afterward.

The guys had eased away and left me alone with her. At this point, we were in the room. Angel and Jayce were awake. I didn't want to fight in front of them. They'd heard enough from their father. Angel was crying and Ashlee was trying to comfort her. Jayce started to cry. I went over to pick him up. Ashlee jumped up to take him from me. I held on to him.

"I've got him. You calm Angel down." She gave me a reluctant nod. It took almost a half hour for her to get Angel settled. By this time, a few of the old ladies showed up. They told Ashlee they'd take the kids for a while. Before she could protest, they whisked them away.

She kept standing by the couch and wasn't making eye contact. I walked a bit closer but stopped when I saw her step back. "Ashlee, are you afraid of me?" I dreaded her answer.

"No," she said quietly.

"We need to talk about last weekend and then today. I don't know what the hell is happening, babe. One minutes we're kissing, then the next you're storming off, leaving the house and then with Stalker and finally, poof, you leave the damn compound to live in a hotel!

I need to know why. Talk to me. The things you said didn't make sense. This is fucking killing me. I want you to come back home," I pleaded.

She sat down and looked at me. "You don't want me. You made that clear when you pushed me away that night. I was upset so I went to my room and decided I needed air. I didn't want to deal with trying to get past you, so I went out the patio doors. I was upset. I walked a little and then decided to go check on the kids at the clubhouse. That's when I saw you with your friend." She paused and then continued, "I left there and went for a longer walk where I ran into Stalker. He told me it wasn't safe to be out alone and took me back to his campsite since it was the closest. I was upset and we talked, or I guess he talked more than me. Then you came in and went crazy. That's when you made it very clear what you thought of me. I didn't think it was right for me to stick around. It would make things awkward and it's your home not mine. So, I left. This is temporary until I can get a job and a place to stay. That's the end of it." I sighed. This wasn't the end of it by a long shot!

"Babe, I don't know why you think I didn't or don't want you. That has never been the case. As for the incident in the clubhouse, I was telling you the truth. The bunny came at me out of nowhere and honestly stunned me. I was pushing her away when you saw us, but you just acted like you didn't care and left. I went after you and couldn't find you. Do you have any idea how fuck-ing afraid I was? I went to Terror's to see if you were there. He called the others to help me look for you. One of them saw you going into Stalker's tent looking chummy. I admit I went in there ready for a fight and seeing him without a shirt on and you in his sleeping bag set me off. But I was upset. I said a bunch of dumb shit. I didn't mean it."

She stood up to pace. "People always say I didn't mean it when they say things when they're upset, but that's when most tell the truth. And the truth is, you became like Alex in that moment. You called me a slut! Just like he did. You thought I was sleeping with Stalker. I realized all men start out acting all nice and then when you get comfortable, their true colors come out. And it's rich for you to call me a slut. We both know you've been with countless women, Devil. I've been with one man. Who's the slut or whore? So, there's no need for us to keep up the charade. I'm moving on with my life. I need to build something stable for my kids. You need to go do whatever it is you did before I came in the picture. Thank you for coming today but it's not necessary. Also, the club needs to have the guys stop watching and following me around everywhere. I'm not the Warriors' concern. Now, please go. I need to call and get my kids back here." She stood to walk over to her purse. I rushed over and took her in my arms before she knew what to do. I pulled her in tight.

"I was a fucking asshole for saying what I did. But you have to believe me, I want you and only you. I'm not going to give up or go away. You're mine and I plan to prove it. I'll keep as many men on you as I want in order to be sure you and the kids are safe. Alex isn't going to go away, Ashlee. He knows where you are now, and he's pissed. You're not safe." She tried to get away, but I wouldn't let her.

"Devil, let go of me. It's over. Whatever it was we were is

done. Stop making things worse. I need to have a clear head to get my life on track. It doesn't matter what you meant or didn't mean. It wouldn't have worked anyway. Now, please leave." She was about to cry.

I didn't want to leave but I knew if I pushed her more right then, I'd lose her for good. I reluctantly let her go and went to the door. I stopped and looked back.

"I love you, Ashlee, and I'm not giving up. Not ever. Not until the day I die." I left before I broke down and cried like a baby. Outside, a few of my brothers were waiting. They must have seen by my face things hadn't gone well. I heard several of them swear. I got on my bike and took off. They let me go.

I turned off my phone and just rode. It was four hours later when I pulled into the clubhouse. I'd barely shut off my bike when Terror and several of the others came racing out. They all looked grim. I jumped off my bike. "What's wrong?"

Terror spoke first.

"Something happened after you left the hotel. We tried to call you." I pulled out my phone and turned it back on. It lit up with calls and texts. I looked back at him. He continued, "After you left, Storm and Razor stayed behind to watch Ashlee. A half hour later, Ashlee came out. She was headed here to get the kids. The old ladies had brought them back here to give you two time to talk. They were following her when a car came out of nowhere and ran her off the road. They were following her but not right on top of her. Before they knew it, her car rolled."

My heart seized at his words. I rushed at him. "Tell me she's okay! Tell me she's not dead, Terror. Fuck, don't tell me I lost her!" I half screamed, and he grabbed me.

"No, she's alive. She got banged up but luckily nothing serious. We got her checked out. She's resting—"

I interrupted him, "Is she at the hotel?"

He shook his head. "No, she's here. We convinced her it was safest here. If not for herself, she needed to think about the kids. She's at the guesthouse. Harper and Janessa are with her." I went to pass him, headed for the house. He stopped me. "She still doesn't want to see you, Devil. I know you don't want to hear this but leave her alone tonight. If you push, she'll leave. And if she does, I'm convinced Alex will kill her and probably the kids."

I glared at him. "Do we know for sure it was him?" He shook his head.

"No, but who else would it be? I sent a few guys to check out his house. They did a discreet check inside and found it had been trashed and most of his clothes are missing. It looks like he left in a hurry. He's in the wind right now. He could be anywhere."

My gut clenched. I could feel the rage building. I couldn't hold my woman and a psycho was out there waiting to kill her.

I stormed into the clubhouse to the first table I found. I flipped it over and then kicked the chairs all over the place. After that, I sat down and shut my eyes. I stayed this way for several minutes. When I opened them again, the guys were quietly watching me. I sighed.

"Sorry. I just can't take this. She's convinced herself I don't really want her, and I think she's a slut. She told me I sounded like Alex. She said all guys start out nice until they decide to show their true colors. Fuck! In my attempt not to go too fast for her sake, I made her think I really didn't want her and was playing a game. I'm so fucked up right now, I can barely eat or sleep. What do I do if she doesn't forgive me? I can't lose her or those kids. If she leaves for good, I might as well drive my bike off a cliff and get the misery over with." The single guys looked shocked. The married guys all were shaking their heads in understanding. I knew they all felt the same about their old ladies. We'd die for them and would die without them. Menace cleared his throat.

"Just wait until tomorrow to try and talk to her. Take it slow but make sure you see her everyday. Show her you're serious and not like him. Beg, plead, but don't give up. Our women end up putting up with a lot. Our former whoring ways is one thing. Then we can't always tell them what we do. We put them on lockdown or give them a guarded escort at any time. They give up a certain amount of personal freedom to be with us. They're worth everything we do. Make her see that. Protect her from this bastard."

I nodded. We had a few drinks and then I went to my room to sleep. Sleep didn't come easy or quick. I dreamed of her all night.

The next morning, I was up and in the common room by seven o'clock. Most of the guys were still in bed since it was a Sunday morning. I was drinking coffee when

Harlow came through the door. She came straight over to me. She gave me a hug then a smack on the back of the head like the guy on that investigative television show. I rubbed it.

"What was that for?"

She snapped at me, "Because you're a bonehead like the others. I swear guys can fuck up anything. Now, finish your coffee and go see your woman. Don't let her say no."

I kissed her cheek, gulped down my last bit of coffee and headed to the guest house. I stood on the porch a second before I knocked.

It was opened by Ms. Marie. She waved me inside. "Ashlee is still sleeping. Angel just got up and so did Jayce. Why don't you take care of her while I feed him?" she asked kindly. I went to help Angel get her favorite cereal fixed. Within five minutes, she was sitting down to her cereal with a glass of milk and orange juice in front of her. She was chatting up a storm telling me about staying in the hotel and how much she missed everyone. She'd just finished, and I got her hands and face wiped when Ashlee walked into the kitchen. She froze when she saw me.

She was dressed in shorts and a tank. I could see she had a cut along her hairline as well as little nicks on her face, upper chest, arms, and she had a black eye. I went over to her.

"Babe, are you alright? The guys told me what happened. I wanted to come over last night, but they said you were tired. Can I get you anything?" I decided to not mention her not wanting to see me as the reason I didn't come over last night. She looked surprised and then she moved to the fridge.

"I'm fine, Devil. Some scrapes, bruises, and cuts. Nothing I haven't had before. They'll heal. Thanks for checking on me but I'm okay."

I pulled out a chair for her to sit on. I poured her some juice, a cup of coffee with creamer and started on making her some toast. In the morning, this was her go-to meal. She watched as I fixed it.

"I'll always be worried about you, babe. And I had to see with my own eyes you were okay. You're lucky. Your injuries could have been so much worse. The guys said you rolled the car." She nodded.

"Yeah, it was one Harlow had insisted I use. I hope the insurance company pays for it to be fixed. If they don't, I'll pay for the repairs." I looked at her in amazement.

"Do you think we care about the car? It's you we care about. Fuck the car! What you need to do is get better and stay here. Alex is pissed and obviously out to get you."

She cringed, then asked me hesitantly, "Did they find him? I know some of the guys were going to check on him after the wreck."

I realized no one had told her the news. I scooted closer.

"Precious, he wasn't there but they found evidence he'd trashed the place and took a bunch of his clothes. They think he left in a hurry. No one knows where he is. You have to stay here. It's the only way to be sure you and the kids are safe." She flinched when I told her he was gone. She wearily nodded her head in agreement. At least it looked like she'd stay.

She pushed her uneaten toast away. Her gaze was fixed on the window and she seemed a million miles away. Angel came racing back into the room. "Mommy, Ms. Marie is taking me and Jayce to the pool. Where's my suit?" This got her attention. She gave her a wan smile and got up to walk out to the living room.

"Ms. Marie, there's no need for you to take her. I'll take them. Thank you." Marie tried to tell her it was no big deal, but Ashlee insisted. Ms. Marie excused herself. Ashlee took Angel to her room to get her changed into her suit. They were back out within five minutes. Ashlee worked to grab what else she needed while I kept Angel reined in. When she was ready, I took Jayce and carried her bag. She tried to get me to leave, but I ignored her. At the pool, there were a couple of others there already. She settled in. I went to talk to Savage. He nodded toward her.

"How's it going?"

I sighed.

"Well, she hasn't threatened to leave if I didn't, so it's progress, I think. She tried to tell me not to come with them, but I ignored her. She's not really talking but as long as I can be close to her, that's enough for now. I wanted to see if we could get some drinks down here. I hate to leave her." He promised to get some. I went to sit with her. She was getting Jayce settled so she could take Angel into the water. I swung Angel up in my arms.

"Come on, squirt. I'll take you in, but we work on your swimming before we play. Deal?" She nodded. I waded in with her. I could see Ashlee watching us. The next fifteen or so minutes I kept my attention on Angel. When some of the others got in the water, Harper took over working with her. I got out to sit by Ashlee.

"Babe, I can stay with Jayce if you want to get in the water. He's asleep but if he wakes up, I can get him." She shook her head.

"I didn't put on my suit and I can't submerge these cuts in the saltwater." I nodded. I hadn't thought of that. Savage had come back with a big cooler while I was in the pool. I got up and got both of us a drink. She softly thanked me when I handed her a bottle of water.

We sat there not talking for several minutes. All the others were good about sitting away from us so we could talk. I decided to give it another try. I looked at her.

"Ashlee." She looked over at me. "I don't want to fight or anything. I just need to tell you again, I'm sorry for the way I acted and for making you think I didn't want you. That is so far from the truth it's comical. Having you gone for the last week has been hell. I couldn't think, eat or sleep worth a damn. Do you know how many nights I sat outside your hotel?" She shook her head no. "Ever damn night you were there. I couldn't sleep knowing you guys were gone and living there. I know you came back because of the accident and threat from Alex, but I don't want that to be the only reason. Please. Tell me what I need to do or change to make you forgive me and let me back in your life."

She stayed quiet and then whispered quietly, "I don't know if I can. I need to think."

Her words almost crushed me. I nodded. A little while later, I excused myself and went to my room. Inside, I sat down and let the tears gather. I didn't know how long I sat there before there was a knock on the door. I opened it to find Viper standing there. He looked serious.

"I need you to come and take a look at this." I followed him into the common room and then outside. He headed to the gate which was standing partially open with several of the guys standing in front of it. They moved when they saw us. Taped to the gate was a note. It was crudely written and read, *you can hide, but they can't keep you safe forever. I'll get you and you'll pay. Whore.* It was unsigned but it didn't take a genius to guess who left it.

Terror was making sure no one touched it. He looked at me. "We can call the cops. She has a TRO. They should be contacted just so they know she was threatened. They know about the accident, but of course there was no way to say for sure it was him. Maybe they can get prints or something off the note. I'm not sure if he's in the system or not. Or we don't tell the cops and do our own thing and take his ass out when we find him. It's obvious he won't stop now that he knows for sure she's here. It's your call since she's your old lady."

I stared at the note. "We keep the cops out of it. We want the least amount of spotlight on the club so when he comes up missing, we're less likely to be suspects. However, whatever we do, we need to make it look like an accident, so she doesn't have to wait years to have him declared legally dead." The others agreed. I took down the note and pocketed it. "Does she know about this?" They all said no. "Good, keep it between us. I don't want her even more worried."

Back behind the clubhouse, I could hear kids playing. I went back to check it out. Angel was now there with Rowan, Hunter, Kenna, and some of the other bigger kids who could walk. Rowan, as the oldest, was playing mother hen to the smaller ones. The women were sitting down watching them. I saw Ashlee under a shade tree with Jayce. He was lying on the blanket fast asleep. I was about to head over toward some of the others when she gestured to me. I went over to her. "What can I get you, sweetheart?"

She gave me a slight smile. "Could you sit here with me?"

I was a little taken back but eagerly agreed. I sat down beside her.

As we watched the kids play, she started to talk. "That night I was so ready to sleep with you, Jack. I wanted nothing more, but then you pushed me away. Again. I got to thinking maybe you were regretting what you'd said to me. Maybe you didn't really mean it. I got upset and went to the bedroom because it hurt. Then, when I went walking instead and came into the clubhouse, it was like a knife through my heart to see that woman all wrapped around you. It was like my worst nightmare had come to life, and it was like confirmation of the fear I had just been having."

I went to interrupt but she shook her head and held her

hand up.

"Let me finish. I said whatever came out of my head and I have no real idea what I told her. I just knew I had to get out of there before I broke down. When I got outside, I headed for the woods. I was crying by then and must have been making noise, because Stalker found me. He took me to his tent so I could calm down. I cried so much I soaked his poor shirt. He told me to get in the sleeping bag and rest. He was changing his shirt when you came in. You jumped to conclusions and attacked him, Jack. I was stunned and then you were saying so many things and you called me a slut."

I winced recalling I'd said it.

"That hurt even more because you were acting like Alex and talking like him. I couldn't stand it. I thought about it all night and decided I needed to leave. It would've been too painful and awkward to stay and see you with other women to say the least. I'm telling you all this, so you know why I think we will just keep things uncomplicated. I'm staying for the kids. They need to be safe from Alex. But I promise, I won't interfere with you being yourself or with anyone else. I won't be spending much time at the clubhouse, so you don't need to worry about me seeing you with the bunnies and getting jealous. I won't act like that. I hope we can be cordial to each other. Angel really likes you and it would hurt her if you ignored her totally."

I couldn't let her say another word. I dropped down on my knees in front of her and took her hands in mine. "I don't want anyone else. I want us to be together. I will work for the rest of my life to make up for what I said and how I acted if you promise to never think I don't want you or that I'd cheat on you. There's no way I can see you and not want to be with you. And you leaving isn't an option because I'll follow you. Believe this, Ashlee. If you can't and won't take me back and let me love you, then you might as well kill me. Because without the three of you, I have nothing worth living for. I love you, Ashlee."

She gasped and looked at me in shock. "You said you love me. Again," she whispered.

"Of course. How could I not? And I love those two kids. I want to be their father and love them and their mother for the rest of my life. I want you so badly I can't think. You think I don't, well feel this." I grabbed her hand and slid it down to my hardness. She gasped. "I'm like this day and night. I have fought myself for months not to just sweep you up and take you somewhere I could make love to you until we both passed out. But I don't just want sex. I want all the things that go into a relationship and having a family. So, no, we can't just be cordial."

I took her down to the ground and laid over her as I took her mouth. I kissed her over and over as I ground my cock into her pussy covered by those shorts. I wanted to peel them off and fuck her right here. Everything was feeling hazy. My need was consuming me. She broke away from me.

"Jack, we can't. People are watching. Please stop. I'm about to explode." I smiled.

"Now you feel a little of what I feel, babe. I want to bury my cock so deep inside of you that you'll never know where one of us starts and the other ends." She whimpered. I gave her another kiss. "Please spend time with me again. Let me show you I love you and you can trust me. I need you, baby."

She looked at me for several long minutes before she gave me a hesitant, small nod. I breathed a sigh of relief. I'd have to build back her trust, but I would. She was going to be mine. The rest of the afternoon and evening passed quietly. That night, I left them at their doorstep even though it almost killed me. I had work to do. I was going to win back my woman.

Chapter 6: Ashlee

It had been over a week since I'd returned to the compound. Things between Devil Dog and I were going okay. He spent time with me every day. He kissed me and told me he loved me. I still hadn't told him I loved him back. I couldn't do it. Not that I didn't. I knew I did. I just had to be sure I wasn't making a mistake. He'd hurt me with his words and actions that night. A part of me couldn't believe he'd want me. I wasn't anything special. I was an unemployed, uneducated mother of two. He could have any woman he wanted.

I had an appointment today with my new lawyer. The club insisted I switch over to their lawyer, though he cost a fortune. He'd spoken to the first lawyer I'd hired and now I needed to meet with him. He was a big attorney in Knoxville, so I had to go to his offices there. Devil Dog was insisting on going with me. He and three of the other guys would be taking me to the lawyer's office. I wanted to ride on a bike. Devil promised he'd take me on a ride soon, but today he wanted me in a car. He even made the ultimate sacrifice. He drove the car and the others rode their bikes.

We pulled into the parking lot of a plush office building. I could tell those who had offices here were wealthy. He took me up to the fourteenth floor. In the elegant office, Dyson's receptionist took us right back like we were important people and got us set up with drinks. Within five minutes, in came a dapper man in his fifties in a very expensive suit. He smiled and greeted Viper and then introduced himself to me. He sat down.

"Well, Ms. Andrews, I reviewed the case and talked to the original attorney who filed the paperwork for your divorce. I also talked to Devil Dog and Terror earlier this week about what has happened in the last week or so. I want you to tell me about your husband. Just start at the beginning and try not to leave out anything. Even something small can count. We have to establish his character."

I spent the next thirty minutes telling him about Alex and all the times he beat me, kept me locked in the house, raped me, came after me when I ran and the threats he'd made. Then I told him about the day he showed up at the hotel.

He was busy taking notes and asking clarifying questions. When I was done, he sat back. "You definitely have grounds for a divorce. I saw you filed for one and you're asking nothing from him, not even child support or any assets. This will help speed it along. Now, we need to build our case to prove all these things you said. We need to get copies of your medical records from the times you went to the hospital, so I need you to sign this for me to get access to them. Also, I will begin work to extend the restraining order. Right now, it was granted for six months. I'm going to talk to the judge about getting it for two years, if we can. Next, we hire a PI to watch him and gather more information. I know you said he was gone. Good. We can show he's not a good guardian for your kids. He left and no one can find him, especially his wife who is caring for those kids twenty-four seven and has been for years. What I need you to do is to let me know of any and all contact, threats, or unusual occurrences right away. I'll be in contact in a week to update you. Any questions?"

I swallowed. "Yes, this sounds like a lot of work, especially hiring a PI. I need to know what it will likely cost me, and if there's any way I can pay in installments. My husband has all the money. I don't even have a job right now."

He shook his head.

"Don't worry. We'll plan to have him pay all the court fees including mine. And if he doesn't, the club will take care of it."

I protested, "No, Mr. Dyson, I don't want the Warriors billed for this. This is my problem not the club's. I'll find a way to cover it." He glanced at Devil Dog then back to me. He nodded his agreement. We left the office not too long after that.

The ride back was quiet as I thought about what he'd said. I wanted to be free of Alex as soon as possible. My biggest worry was what he would say or do in order to get Angel and Jayce. I couldn't have him get any amount of visitation or custody. Devil interrupted my thoughts.

"You're awful quiet, Ashlee. What are you thinking about?"

I sighed. "I'm scared, Jack. I'm scared Alex will find a way to get visitation or custody of the kids. He can't even be allowed to see them supervised. God knows what he'd do if he got them for any amount of time alone. I can't risk it. I've even thought about trying to find somewhere I could go that's far enough away he couldn't find me. You know, disappear." He frowned at me.

"No. You won't need to leave here, babe. I promise we won't let him get any access to the kids. Trust me. I can't risk losing you. Please don't do something like that." I could hear the worry in his voice. I rubbed my hand up and down his arm.

"I won't. It was just a thought." We finished the last bit of the trip in silence. We pulled into the compound at a little after three. Since today was a weekday, most of the kids were at the farm in daycare. Ms. Marie had taken mine there but had them at the farmhouse. This would allow them to be able to play with the others but not affect the licensing parameters for the number of kids they could have. I planned to clean while they were both gone. It was hard to do when they were here. As we pulled in and parked, I told Devil what I was going to do and why. He shrugged.

"Why don't you have Brielle's people clean it? They do all the other houses."

I threw him an incredulous look. "Jack, they do the houses because the other women mainly work. Besides, I don't have a job. I can't pay them. It's bad enough the club pays for the house, utilities, and my food. Which reminds me, I have applied for a couple of jobs in town. Hopefully something comes from them. I don't have a college education, but I worked from the time I was sixteen until I married Alex. I've been a waitress and a receptionist. They don't pay much but it will be a job."

He walked me to the house and came inside. He sat me down on the couch. "Babe, if you want to work for the sake of working, then fine. But you don't need to get a job. I'll take care of you and the kids." I shook my head no.

"No, you won't, Jack, I plan on carrying my fair share even if we do end up together." He sat up straighter.

"What do you mean, *if* we end up together? We're going to be together, babe. Are you having second thoughts? I thought the last week and some change has been going well. Is something wrong?"

"Jack, they have been. I just said that because in this world unexpected things can happen. That's all I meant." He blew out a relieved breath.

"Well, if you want a job, why don't you talk to Harlow? I heard them talking about the need for another receptionist at the spa. One of their two just quit on them. I don't think she worked full time, but they could tell you for sure." I thought about it for a minute.

"Yeah, but isn't that weird? I mean if I ask, they'll most likely give it to me just because of knowing me. It doesn't seem right." He laughed.

"Babe, nepotism happens all the time. They may give you the job for that reason partially, but believe me, if you don't do the job, they will fire you."

I nodded. I'd ask Harlow about it either later tonight or tomorrow. I told Jack he had to go. He said he'd help clean and I laughed. He finally agreed to go to the garage and then the clubhouse for a while. I promised to meet him there. He said he'd go pick up the kids at five thirty so I didn't need to worry about doing it.

I turned on some loud music and changed into old clothes. For the next two hours I cleaned the house and did a load of laundry. I was startled when my sweeper shut off. I looked around to find Harlow standing in the living room with the cord in her hand.

"What's up Harlow?" She grinned.

"A little bird told me to come talk to you. Said you had something you wanted to ask me." My mind went blank for a minute then I remembered the job.

"Oh, yeah. Right. Devil said you guys were looking for a new receptionist, and I happen to be looking for a job. I wanted to see if it was still open and how you have applicants applying." Her smile got bigger.

"We do need someone three days a week. It's no weekends, set days and it's from eight to five thirty. I wish I'd thought of you. I didn't know you were looking for a job."

"Yes, I've been looking for a job so I can take care of my kids." She laughed.

"Yeah, like you're gonna be allowed to pay for shit. Not with these alpha males you won't. Have you done anything like this before?"

"I've been a waitress and a receptionist before. The receptionist was for a dental office. She seemed eager for me to come down and check out the place. I agreed I'd stop by tomorrow. Then I saw the time.

"Shit, it's six. I was supposed to be at the clubhouse to get the kids from Devil by five thirty." She held up her hand.

"Calm down. He's fine. I just came from there. He was changing Jayce and Angel was running around with Hunter. Terror is watching them." I breathed a sigh of relief. She headed back while I hurried to change my clothes after a quick shower. Cleaning had made me sweaty. It was almost six twenty by the time I entered the clubhouse. I rushed over to Devil Dog.

"I'm sorry I lost track of time. Did Harlow tell you I was coming?" He nodded.

"Babe, it's no big deal. I can handle these two. Did you get all your cleaning done?" I told him I had. We talked with the others for a few minutes then I told them we needed to go eat dinner. I grabbed Devil when I left so he'd come eat with us. Inside, he helped Angel wash her hands while I got Jayce in his baby swing and set the table. I'd been cooking a roast with potatoes, onions and carrots in the slow cooker all day.

We all sat down to eat. Devil was able to talk and tease so naturally with Angel. It made me sad to think her own father never had, and a man we'd known three months was more of a father to her than her biological one was. I was pulled from my musing by Devil.

"Ashlee, are you alright, Precious? You seem so far away." I could see he was concerned. I looked at Angel.

"Can we talk about it after bedtime?" He caught my look and agreed. He cleaned up after dinner. I let Angel watch one of her favorite shows until seven thirty, then it was bath time. As I was helping her, Devil was washing Jayce in his baby tub. I tried to tell him he didn't have to, but he insisted. When Angel was tucked in her bed, he read her a story. By eight fifteen, both were out for the count. Back in the living room Devil had grabbed a soda for him and iced tea for me. I sat down with a sigh. He pulled me close.

"Now, tell me what you were thinking about over dinner."

"I was just watching you with Angel and felt sad that her own father never acted that way with her, yet you've known us for three months and you act more like her father." He gave me a slow, gentle kiss.

"Ash, I'm sorry Alex was such a bastard. But I act like I do with the kids because I care for them like I do their mother. I want to be their father. Do you understand? I say I love you, and I mean it. I know you need time to forgive me and I know those same kinds of feelings will grow one day in you. Please, just give it time." I couldn't let him think like this.

"Jack, I don't need time to have feelings grow. They're already here. I know I haven't said it while you have, but I do love you, Jack. I want us to work out and be together for the rest of our lives. I've just been scared and trying to work through being upset. I want you to be the father Angel and Jayce need."

I'd barely finished and he had me pinned to the arm of the couch and was devouring my mouth. His kiss was a little frantic and oh so hot. He was nipping, sucking, and licking at my mouth while he ran his hands up my ribs to cup my breasts through my shirt and bra. I moaned. I could feel my nipples pebbling. My core was slick from my excitement. I decided right there, I wasn't going to wait. I was going to throw caution to the wind. I needed him.

I was returning his kisses and ran my hands up under his shirt. His skin was hot and hard. I could feel his scars. I knew he had them along with tats from his going without a shirt in the pool and sometimes at the garage. He groaned and broke our kiss long enough to pull off his t-shirt. He started kissing me again. I traced his hard nipples with my fingers. Despite having two kids, I had very little sexual experience. Alex had always taken his pleasure without worrying if I got any. He was always in such a hurry, I never got to explore his body even at the very beginning of our marriage.

I pressed closer to Devil as he laid me back on the couch. His hands had slid under my top and he was tracing along my abdomen and up to the underside of my breasts. He stopped. "Babe, I won't go farther than you're comfortable with. But if you're okay with a little exploring, I have to ask. Can I take off your top and bra?" I swallowed.

I was nervous to have him see my body. Yes, I was slim, and my body was in decent shape, but it wasn't like it was when I was nineteen. I now had a scar from my C-section. It had healed remarkably well but it was still there. He felt my hesitation and started to back away. I grabbed his hand.

"Don't stop. I want you to. I'm just a little insecure with my body. I don't know if you've ever been with a woman who has had kids, but it changes your body and I have a scar, too."

He groaned.

"Precious, how could you think I wouldn't love your body. I've seen you in your bathing suit and, babe, you have nothing to worry about. Even if you think you're not perfect, you are for me. Let me see you, please."

I nodded giving him my consent.

He eased off my top and kissed all over my stomach and upper chest. He did this for a bit before he ran his hand underneath my back to release my bra's clasp. He removed it and flung it across the back of the couch. He was staring down at my breasts. They were bigger than they had been because I was breastfeeding Jayce. After I had Angel and stopped breastfeeding her, my breasts had stayed a C-cup compared to my pre-pregnancy B-cup. Right now, after having Jayce, I was well over a D-cup, so I figured I'd retain most of it with him too. It helped to balance out my more generous hips. I had a curvy figure.

Devil groaned and then took my left breast into his mouth. He sucked and licked it while he plucked at the other one with his fingers. I felt bolts of pleasure shoot from them to my pussy. I was getting wetter. He switched breasts. I was moaning and running my hands up and down his back. He broke away and looked up at me.

"Precious, you're so fucking beautiful." He went back to sucking. That's when it happened. I felt my milk leaking down the front of me. Shit! I pushed at him. I was so damn embarrassed. This never happened before because Alex never was interested in my breasts. Devil didn't let go. Instead, he moaned and sucked harder. I knew he had to be tasting my breast milk.

"Jack, stop. You don't need to keep doing that. I'm sorry. I didn't think this would stimulate my breast milk." He growled and leveled me with an intense look.

"Don't be embarrassed, babe. You taste so sweet. No wonder Jayce loves to have his milk. He might have competition now." He went back to sucking on my nipples. I could feel him swallowing occasionally when he got some of my milk. Now that I knew it didn't bother him, I wasn't grossed out he was drinking it, rather it made me hot. I lifted my hips and ground them into his. I could feel his hardness. I whimpered. He thrust back, rubbing his cock against my pussy through our pants. I couldn't stand it. I pulled him off my breast. He stared up at me in concern.

"We need to stop." He started to pull away. "And take this somewhere more private, Jack. I don't want Angel walking in on us if she happens to wake up." He looked torn. "Please, if you want me, then take me. I don't want us to keep starting and then stopping."

He gave me a quick kiss and stood. He scooped me up in his arms and carried me down the hall to my room. Inside, he locked the door and laid me down on the bed.

"Babe, are you positive? We don't have to do more than this. Not if you're not ready." I took his hand and ran it down to my denim-covered crotch. "I need you, Jack. So much. I've never felt anything close to this. Please, make the ache go away," I pleaded. My pleas must have broken his last restraint. He groaned and started to lick his way down my stomach. When he got to the waistband of my shorts, he unsnapped them and slowly lowered the zipper. He paused to allow me time to object which I didn't. Then he was working them and my panties down my legs until he had them off.

Devil kissed his way up my legs and when he got to my center, he pulled my thighs apart. He looked down at me. I squirmed a little with him looking so closely at such an intimate part of me. He ran his finger across my scar which was just at the top of my pubic bone. He ran a finger down my folds and across my clit. I shuddered and my ass came up off the bed. Devil then bent his head and kissed my scar and licked my swollen folds from top to bottom. I let a small gasp escape. He proceeded to eat my pussy like it was candy.

He licked, sucked and pinched my clit. His tongue thrust in and out of my entrance. I was now moving all over the bed and I found myself gripping his head without realizing I'd done it. He was groaning and panting. I was getting close to what might be an orgasm. I hoped. Then he slid one finger and then a second one inside of me. I moaned. He thrust in and out as he sucked my clit. He kept this up for I don't know how long until suddenly I was hit with an orgasm! It shot through me and was way more intense than anything I'd ever given myself. He lapped up the juices spilling from my body.

When I came down from my high, he raised his head. "You taste so sweet, Precious. Like honey. I could feast on your pretty pussy all day." I moaned.

"Jack, I didn't know it could feel like that." I wasn't

thinking when I said it. He froze.

"Babe, what do you mean you didn't know? Haven't you ever had an orgasm from oral sex before?" I blushed and tried to close my thighs. He wouldn't let me. I took a deep breath. I knew we needed to be honest with each other even if it was embarrassing.

"I've never had oral sex before, Jack. And I've never had an orgasm during sex. I've had some when I've pleasured myself but nothing like what you just gave me." His eyes widened.

"Fuck, you mean that sonofabitch—"

I stopped him. "I don't want to talk about him right now." He nodded his head then he gave me a devilish grin.

"Well, I have some proving to do then, because I know without a doubt, I can get you to orgasm, babe. My question now is, do you want to stop here for the night?" I shook my head no.

"No, I don't. I want you to make love to me, Jack. Show me what it's supposed to be like. Please." He licked his lips and growled. Next thing I knew, he was standing and undoing his jeans. He slid his pants down and stepped out of them. When he straightened up, I could see his erect cock. I gasped. He was way bigger than Alex was. His cock was long and thick with veins running all up and down his shaft. The head of his cock was flared and a dark red almost purple. Devil Dog was watching my face as he stroked his hand up and down a couple of times. I could see cum glistening on the head. I had an overwhelming urge to taste him.

I raised myself up to tentatively run a finger along the head and down his shaft. He shuddered. Then I leaned forward and licked his cum off the head of his cock, and he moaned. I savored the slightly salty, musky taste of him. I found that I liked his taste. He gently pushed my head toward his cock. I knew he wanted me to suck it. I looked up.

"Honey, I need to let you know, I have no idea what to do here. I've never done this." He cursed. I started to draw back when he stopped me.

"I'm not angry with you, babe. Just you know who. Just do what you feel like doing. There is no right or wrong way. I can tell you I like my balls played with. I like lots of licking and sucking and light teeth are fine. You'll know what I really like by my reactions. And I'll tell you if you do something I don't like, okay?" I smiled and nodded.

He took my hand and wrapped it around the base, and he squeezed down. I thought it would be too hard, but he moaned in pleasure. I stroked up and down a few times then took the head into my mouth. From there, I got lost in exploring him. I licked all over the head and shaft. I massaged and then licked his balls.

As I got more confident, I began to take more of him into my mouth. I made sure to suck hard and stroke the base. He was breathing hard and his hips had started to thrust back and forth. "Right there is the spot, babe. So, fucking good. So good. Yeah, that's right, suck me harder," he groaned out. I put more effort into pleasing him. I found I loved the sense of power I was getting from knowing I was giving him pleasure.

I was lost in trying to get him to come when he pulled out of my mouth. I whimpered. He stood there looking at me with his eyes hooded and burning. "Ash, babe, I need to stop before I come in that sexy mouth. I don't want our first time to be like that. Are you ready to take my cock inside that hot little pussy? Are you ready to be fucked until you scream in pleasure?" I moaned and nodded. He grabbed my legs and pulled me to the edge of the bed, so my ass was hanging over the edge. Devil spread my thighs and then I felt the head of his cock pushing against my entrance.

Now I'm no virgin and I've had two kids, but his cock was so big, he was stretching me to the point of it burning. For a moment I worried he wouldn't be able to get inside of me. He slowly worked himself in until he bottomed out. We both groaned in relief. He stayed still, not moving. "What's wrong?" I asked him.

"Nothing. I just want to remember what it was like the first time I got my cock buried inside of you, Precious." He began to thrust in and out. He was careful to go slow and let me get used to him. Soon, I was feeling nothing but tingling and bolts of pleasure.

I thrust my hips back to take him deeper. He growled and then started to thrust harder and deeper. His rhythm picked up. He was now pounding his cock so deep inside I didn't know where he ended, and I started. I was moaning nonstop and thrashing on the bed. He closed his eyes.

"Ahh, babe, you feel so fucking good. Your pussy is so tight and wet. The fire is almost burning me. Give it to me. Show me what you want." I started to thrust up to meet his thrust back even harder and faster. He leaned over and sucked on one breast then the other and slid his hand down to play with my clit. The combination made the jolts and tingles consolidate in my core. I came yelling. I could feel my pussy clamping down on his cock.

I was milking him. I could feel the clasp and release of my inner muscles. He let out a roar and then slammed in and out of me like mad until he came grunting. I could feel the hot splash of his seed bathing my tender walls. He finally stopped jerking and collapsed over top of me. Devil was panting hard. I rubbed his back as I tried to catch my breath.

He slowly raised his head and kissed me. When he broke away from my lips, he eased out of me. I moaned, feeling him scraping my walls. He pulled out and ran his fingers down my folds, then he froze. He looked at me stunned.

"What?" I asked.

"Shit, I forgot a condom, babe. Fuck, I've never done that. Ever. You just drove every other thought out of my head. I meant to protect you. I know you're not ready for another baby yet. Are you close to the middle of your cycle?" I shook my head no. He nodded. "Then we might be safe. But Ash, know this. If you get pregnant, I won't be disappointed." I gasped at his admission.

"What do you mean you won't be disappointed and me not being ready for another baby yet? You sound like you're wanting one." He grinned.

"Precious, I'd love nothing more than for you to have my baby, but you just gave birth three months ago.

Your body needs time to heal. Besides, we've not talked yet about more kids." I looked at him in shock, then a thought struck me. I sat up.

"Jack, I'm not worried about getting pregnant. I'm on birth control. The doctor put me on it after Jayce was born. But I'm not protected from any kind of STDs. Have you—?" He cut me off.

"Ash, you're safe. I've never had sex without a condom. No wonder it felt like you were on fire around me. We all make sure to get checked regularly. I go every six months. My last one was about a week after you came here, and I've been with no one since. I'm clean." I gave a sigh of relief. He went to the bathroom and came back with a wet washcloth. I went to take it and he shook his head. He insisted on cleaning me and then himself. Then he crawled into bed and pulled me into his arms.

"Ashlee, that was indescribable. You made me lose myself like I've never done in my life, and I'm glad you got your release. Did that orgasm meet your expectation?" I laughed.

"Yes, and then some. I had no idea I could feel like that or come that hard."

He kissed down my neck to nip at my shoulder. "Since the topic came up because of the condom fiasco, let's finish talking about kids. You're protected but do you ever want more kids?" he asked me quietly. I stared at him.

"Yes, I do. I've always wanted more kids just not with him. I would love to give you a couple kids of your own if you want them one day. If not, I have Angel and Jayce."

Devil kissed me softly on the lips. "If you're willing to

carry them, I'd love to have more kids. As many as you want. And, babe, we can have them when you're ready. While I'd like you to heal more from having Jayce, if you said you wanted one tomorrow, I'd say yes." I took his mouth. We kissed and held each other until I fell asleep, sated and tired.

Chapter 7: Devil Dog

It had been a week since Ashlee gave herself to me for the first time. I'd never imagined it being like that. I'd had a lot of sex and what I would consider really good sex, but with Ash, it was beyond great. I'd been staying with her at the guesthouse. She had worried that first morning when we woke up to Angel knocking on the door wanting breakfast. Ashlee had panicked, and I calmed her down and opened the door. Angel didn't even bat her eyes at seeing me in her mom's room. She hugged me and asked if I wanted pancakes like her. I'd been waking up every morning since with Ashlee in my arms and having the best sex of my life every night.

I was helping out at the garage today. We were opening it to the public next week, so final touches were being done. Viper had hired a mechanic. He told us in church on Saturday he wasn't in love with the applicant, but he had been the best out of those who had applied, and his references had been good. He would be on a ninety-day probationary period while we evaluated if he met the Warriors' standards. His name was Cody Sanchez. I'd met him. He didn't strike me as being really friendly, but it could have been because he was intimidated.

Ashlee started this week at the spa. She would work

there Tuesday through Thursday. The other reception-ist worked Friday, Saturday and Monday. The spa was closed on Sundays. She was loving it. Harlow had been praising how quickly she caught on to the computer system and the customers loved her. I knew she hadn't gotten the chance to finish college due to her ex. I planned on asking her what she had been studying and if she wanted to go back. I wanted her to have every-thing she ever wanted, including her degree. She'd rid-den with Harlow to the spa since Harlow was going to spend the day going through inventory and catching up on some paperwork.

It was around two when I got a text. Actually, all the guys working with me got one. It was from Ghost. Wren had gone into labor and he'd taken her to the hospital. It seemed their little girl was intent on coming a few days early. She was due on September thirtieth and today was the twenty-sixth. I called Ashlee, and she picked up on the first ring.

Before I could say anything, she burst out excitedly, "Wren's in labor. I'm going to the hospital with Harlow." I laughed.

"I was just calling to tell you the news and see if you wanted to go. I'll meet you there. Be careful. Love you." She told me she loved me too before she hung up.

Me and the guys locked shit up and got on our bikes to head to the hospital. As we rode, I thought about Ashlee and her soon to be ex-husband. He still hadn't shown up which worried me. I almost told her she couldn't take the job at the spa, but I knew she needed to have some kind of work so she felt independent. Besides, we had the spa wired with cameras and alarms.

I'd gotten her to get the tracker implanted on Sunday. We'd had issues before with not being able to find some of the women. I also talked to her about having the kids injected with one. Up to this point, no one had implanted one in any of the club's kids, but it wasn't a bad idea. Smoke had promised to research if it had been used on kids and if so, what ages and if there were risks associated with using it in kids.

We pulled into the hospital twenty minutes later. There were several bikes already in the parking lot as we headed through the doors of the ER. Inside was the bulk of the crew. They said they were checking her and then going to move her hopefully upstairs to the maternity floor. Harlow and Ashlee came in about five minutes after I did. She came over to give me a hug and kiss. Everyone sat in groups chatting while we waited to hear if she was really in labor. Ghost came out thirty minutes later. He looked excited and a little anxious.

"She's definitely in labor. They're moving her right now up to the maternity ward. We can go up there and wait. This is gonna take hours so be prepared." We all laughed. This wasn't our first vigil at the hospital.

We all headed up to the maternity floor's waiting room. Over the next several hours, Wren progressed. At one point, I took Ashlee home so she could take care of the kids and get them into bed. Cindy was watching them at the clubhouse with several of the other kids. We were back at the hospital by eight thirty. From what we found out, Wren had been in labor since around ten this morning and hadn't said anything until sometime after one.

So technically, she'd been in labor ten hours already. Ghost was with her the whole time and the ladies took turns visiting her.

When she went into what they called transition phase, Brielle stayed. She was the closest to Wren. They had endured horrible things together. At eleven-ten p.m., Wren delivered seven-pound two-ounces and twenty-inch-long, Bethany Adair. She had a head full of dark hair with auburn streaks. Not unexpected since Ghost was half Apache and Wren a redhead. Her eyes were bright blue, but we'd know around six months what her permanent color was. Wren had blue/ green eyes and Ghost had green.

All the ladies were going crazy holding her for a couple minutes each. I gave Wren a kiss on the cheek.

"Great job, little momma. Look at Ghost. He's floating around on cloud nine." She laughed and thanked me. We all left by midnight. The hospital knew us and luckily was cool with our tendency to stay past visiting hours. Back at the house, we both showered and fell into bed around one a.m. Tonight, we didn't make love since Ashlee had to get up at six to get the kids ready to go to daycare and herself to work by eight. I would help her get them fed, dressed and down the road so she could get ready. This routine had been working well the last couple of days.

The next day went by quickly. This would be the last day this week that Ash would work, and I would be done tomorrow. We worked on the weekends as needed to fix cars but usually we had our non-member employees do it most of the time. At five-fifteen, I headed over to pick up Ash from the spa. She'd ridden in with me on the bike this morning. As I came up to the door, she came running out. I could see she was upset. I grabbed her up in my arms and hugged her close. "Precious, what's wrong?" She sniffed.

"This was just delivered to me about five minutes ago. I was served, Jack. It's from Alex," she cried.

I opened the envelope. Inside were court papers that stated Alex was countersuing Ashlee for a divorce and custody of the kids. His reason was desertion. He wanted to have one hundred percent custody without visitation rights for Ash and she would have to pay for all his court costs, child support and he'd keep all the assets. She was sobbing and shaking.

"Come on. Calm down so I can get us back to the clubhouse safely. When we get there, we'll call Dyson. I swear to God, Ash, he won't get the kids. I promise on my club." She clung to me for a few minutes. Finally, she got herself enough under control I felt we could make it to the compound. We took off with her clinging to me tightly. I opened the gate with the remote in my pocket and roared through. All of us had one, but we needed to get some more prospects soon. I let her off the bike so I could back it into my spot.

We headed straight into the clubhouse. Ms. Marie and some of the others would be bringing all the kids home any minute. I texted her to ask if she would take the kids to our house and sit with them for a few while we got this ironed out. She replied immediately saying no problem. I swear that woman was a godsend. She was a mother to all of us and a grandmother to all the kids.

Inside, I looked around for Terror. I saw him over by the bar talking to Hawk and Harlow. I led her toward them.

"Terror, we need to use your office to call Dyson." He frowned.

"What happened?"

I handed him the envelope Ashlee had been served. He read it. The frown got worse, and he got an ugly pissed look on his face. He shook his head. "That fucker. Let's go." He took us to his office, and we closed the door. He stayed and was the one to dial Dyson's number.

He was a very well-known and in-demand lawyer, but the club had been one of his best clients when he went into private practice twenty years ago. He'd never forgotten that. We had his private number. He answered on the second ring. "Hey, Terror. What can I do for you?"

Terror was messing with the fax machine as he answered, "Hey, Matt, I'm gonna fax something over to you right now. Ashlee got served at the spa today. It seems her husband wants to play hardball. I want you to read it and tell us what you think. While we're on the topic of that asshole, has the PI found out anything on where he might have gone?"

Dyson sighed.

"Not yet but don't worry, he'll keep looking. Let me go over this and I'll call you tomorrow around seven in the morning with my advice. I assume Devil Dog and Ashlee are with you."

I answered this time. "Yeah, we're both here. Matt, he has her shaken and scared. I want this sonofabitch bur-

CIARA ST JAMES

ied, Matt. He can't get these kids, period."

He reassured me he'd make sure Alex Andrews would be out of Ashlee's life. We signed off with him saying he'd call Terror in the morning. After we hung up, I told Terror, "I'll be here at seven to hear what Matt has to say." Ashlee was sitting in a chair, her face pale. She looked freaked out. Terror hunched down in front of her.

"Hey, Ash, don't worry. We'll make sure he doesn't get any of this shit, okay. You just take care of you and those beautiful kids and let us deal with this. Please."

She finally nodded. When she stood up, I tucked her under my arm and led her from the clubhouse.

Back at the house, we found Ms. Marie had started dinner for us. Ashlee burst into tears when she saw it. She hugged Ms. Marie, sobbing out her thanks. Marie just calmly patted her back and soothed her. She stayed to finish the cooking even though Ash said she could do it. She left us both with hugs and a kiss. We sat down to a great meal of herb chicken breasts, mashed potatoes, and green beans. She'd also whipped up a pudding which Angel loved. It was a deep, rich chocolate one.

I handled the dishes and had her settle down with the kids to watch television with Angel. When it was time for the kids to get ready for bed, I insisted she go soak in the tub while I handled them. She had extra milk pumped so Jayce could be fed at daycare. Marie had brought back what they hadn't used. I warmed it up and fed him. He looked so content when he ate. I loved to watch his little face. He wasn't mine, but honestly, I felt like he was. I'd been with him since the day he was born. Angel was like my own daughter. I loved them.

After they went down, I took a shower and then crawled into bed with Ash to watch a movie. She wasn't really paying much attention to it, so I turned it off halfway through. She looked at me questioningly.

"Babe, talk to me. You're a million miles away. You need to talk." She took a fortifying breath.

"I'm terrified he'll find some way to get the kids, Jack. I could never let him do that and he knows it. He's doing this to punish me, to force me to go back to him. I hate to say it, but if he gets my kids, I will. Not because I don't love you, but because I will do anything to protect my kids."

Her words stabbed me in the chest. She'd go back to him! I was about to snap at her but stopped to think. She'd do it because she'd sacrifice herself to save those she loved. I hugged her tight.

"Ashlee, it will never get to that point. And know if it did, I'd come after all three of you. No way will you be at his mercy again. He would kill your soul. I love the three of you and I can't live without any of you." She sighed and snuggled into my chest. I laid there holding her for a while. I was dragged back from my thoughts by her tongue licking across my left nipple. I looked down at her.

"What do you think you're doing, Precious?" She smiled.

"Nothing. Just tasting this hard, little nub here. It was teasing me and daring me to do it." I laughed.

This led to us teasing and playing with each other over and over until we were both exhausted but sated. She drifted off around eleven. I stayed awake longer thinking about Alex Andrews and where we could bury him. Because I knew in my gut, we'd have to make him disappear before all of this was over. And I had no problem with that solution.

It was finally the weekend. Yesterday, Dyson called back. He advised us to make sure Ashlee was seen in public more, taking care of the kids and he was happy to hear she was working. He also said she should update her filing from simply asking for a divorce and sole custody to wanting half his assets, child support, court costs, and also file a civil suit against him for pain and suffering from his abuse and rapes.

Unfortunately, the hospital records didn't include any tests that would have confirmed she'd ever been raped. Ashlee had been with us and she approved him doing whatever he thought was best. Dyson planned to bury him in threats in the hopes he'd drop it. If he didn't, we would go after his cars, house and business which surprisingly did well.

We were in church this morning. Terror had just informed us he'd been introduced to two possible guys we might want to have prospect for us. One was Jordan Becker, not a relation to our newly patched brother, Blade. The other, Tanner Jamison, was a family friend of Falcon's. Falcon and Tiger had patched over to us a few weeks ago from North Carolina. They told us about them. Blade was willing to sponsor Jordan even if they weren't related. He joked any Becker was a shoo-in while Falcon sponsored Tanner.

No one could join even as a prospect without a sponsor.

The sponsor was then responsible for the prospect's behavior. Everyone approved the nomination of the two of them. Savage had them come in from the common room. Terror ran through the bylaws and expectations of the club. They were issued their prospect cuts. Now we'd see if in a year they were still with us and ready to be a Warrior or be cut loose.

I updated all the guys on the latest shit Alex was pulling with Ashlee. They were almost as upset as I was. Hammer raised his hand to be recognized. Terror gave him the floor. He turned to me.

"Well, brother, Steel and I were wondering if we should start building you and Ashlee a house. It looks like things are going well for you two. Do you want us to get it on the books? We have five full-time crews right now. The residential being built on the west end of town will be done next week. Do you want the slot?"

I sat there thinking. I knew I wanted to be with Ashlee for the rest of my life. We'd need a home of our own with room to grow since we wanted more kids. I just didn't know if she was there yet. As I thought about it, I came to a decision. No matter what I had to do, I would get her to marry me. A house would be needed at some point. I nodded.

"Yeah, I'll take it. Let me talk to Ash about what she would want, and we'll look for a site and get Terror's approval. Can you give me a week?" He nodded. This ended the meeting. I left thinking about talking to her about a house. I wanted to do it today.

I saw Harlow in the common room when we came out. I went over to her. She gave me a hug. She drew back.

"What do you need?" I looked at her in surprise. She laughed. "Cannon, I know you. What can I do for you?" I shrugged.

"I was wondering if you and Terror had plans today. If not, would you be willing to watch Angel and Jayce for a few hours? I need to talk to Ashlee about something and I wanted to take her for a ride to do it." She smiled.

"We're not doing anything but lazing around today. I'd love to keep the kids. What time do you want me to take them?"

I looked at my watch. It was nine thirty already.

"How about in an hour? I'll bring them to the house?"

She agreed. I gave her a hug and kiss. Terror came up mock growling.

"What? One woman isn't enough? You're after mine too." I backed away laughing.

"No way. You can keep her crazy ass. I love her but only as a brother. You have all my sympathy." I ran out of the clubhouse laughing as Harlow waddled after me. She had less than two months to go with her second pregnancy. I yelled I'd see her in an hour and made a beeline for the guest house.

Inside they had just finished breakfast and were getting dressed for the day. I went up to Ashlee and wrapped my arms around her waist. She leaned back into my chest. I kissed her ear and whispered, "Babe, get the kids ready. Harley is going to keep them for us. I want to take you on a ride. Pack up enough stuff for Jayce to be covered for, I'd say four or five hours. Did you pump any milk?"

I'd gotten used to seeing her feed him and pump when she had to leave him.

Honestly, I was fascinated to see her produce milk for him, and I liked when I could get a little taste. The other day she'd pumped, and I made sure she was fully done by sucking the last bit myself. She'd blushed, but I told her it was so she wouldn't hurt. I'd been reading up on babies and breastfeeding. The mom could actually experience severe pain if the milk wasn't regularly expressed or even get an infection. She'd laughed hearing my pious reason and called bullshit.

She gave me a stunned look. "Jack, where are we going? Why? I don't want to burden Harlow—"

I cut her off. "She is happy to do it. They have no plans. I need to talk to you about something serious and I'd like to do it somewhere quiet. Plus, I'm dying for a ride and you haven't been on a long one yet. Now, can you be ready in an hour? Tell me what I can do." She relented and had me pack the diaper bag for Jayce, and grab an extra set of clothes for Angel.

I cleaned the kitchen and got Angel's shoes on. Ash got dressed and put on some light makeup. She wrapped one of my black do-rags around her head to keep her hair from going wild. She was dressed in tight jeans, boots, and a t-shirt which showed off her D-cup breasts. I grew hard just looking at her. I told her to grab her jacket too. I ran over to the clubhouse for a couple of things I wanted to pack in my saddlebags.

Just shy of an hour later, we were on Harlow and Terror's front porch. Terror answered the door and motioned for us to come inside. Ashlee started out apologizing. "I hope this isn't an inconvenience or we're disturbing family time—"

Terror stopped her. "We're happy to do it. One day, we'll hit you up to babysit then we'll be even. How does that sound?" Ash smiled and agreed. She gave the kids' bags and breast milk to Harlow explaining when he ate, and how much to give him. We took off ten minutes later.

She didn't know it, but I'd asked Terror if it was okay for us to go to his property about an hour east of Dublin Falls. He'd said we could go anytime. I knew it had a great lake, and the fall leaves were in full color. For the whole ride she kept looking and exclaiming over the trees. When we got to Terror's place, she looked around in confusion. "What is this place, Jack? Are we allowed to be here?" I helped her off the bike before I got off.

"Precious, it's owned by Terror, so we're allowed here. Come with me, I want to show you something." I took the blanket off my bike and grabbed the bag from my saddlebags. I held her hand as we walked through the woods to the lake. She saw it and gasped.

"Jack, it's gorgeous."

I explained about Terror and Harlow having their wedding here. She was walking on the edge of the water looking at it and the trees while I spread out the blanket and sat down my bag.

Once I was done, I took her around the lake and then through the woods to the bridge. She was enthralled. When we got back to the blanket over an hour later, she was glowing with happiness. We sat down and I tugged her onto my lap. "Do you like it here?" She laughed.

"No, I love it. Wow. I didn't know Terror owned property."

I explained about the others I knew who had property, then I decided to broach the house subject. I cleared my throat. I was feeling a little nervous. What if she flat out said no?

"Ash, I want to talk about the main reason I wanted time alone with you." She grew serious looking and stared at me. "The guys asked me something today, and I told them to go ahead." She was looking puzzled now. "They asked if I wanted to take an open slot they have coming up after next week. It's for a house. I want to have a house built that will be for the four of us and of course more of us down the road. Now, I know this is fast and you may not be ready for it, but I want to at least get them to build it for us. Then we can move in whenever you're ready." I stopped to see what she had to say. She was looking away from me at the lake. My gut clenched.

We sat in silence for almost five minutes. I was about to burst when she answered. "Jack, I don't know what to say. I mean, you're wanting to build a house for us. It makes us a real family if we do that. Are you sure you're ready to take on an instant family?"

I answered her quickly. "Hell yes! I want the three of you now and forever, babe. Always." She smiled.

"Well, then I'd love for us to build a house we can call our own. Staying in the guesthouse has been great, but it isn't mine. I can't freely change things, paint, or other things because I don't know if the next person to use it will be able to stand it. Where would we put the house?"

I kissed her until we were both breathless. When I could talk, I answered her. "I have a spot I like. I'll show you but we can look around and see if there is one, we like more. Now, what kind of house would you like? You see that every single house on the compound is different. No cookie cutter houses for the Warriors. They've all been built based on the preferences of the couple. So, tell me, what would be your dream house, Precious?"

She laughed and took out her cell phone. Surprisingly, we did have coverage out here. She tapped away on it while I waited. She handed me her phone. On it was a picture of a house and not only the picture but the layout of the rooms. I looked back at her. She was looking unsure.

"I've always had this idea in my head of the kind of house I'd like to live in one day. The house where I lived with Alex was what he wanted. Actually, he had it before we got married. I couldn't even change around the furniture unless he approved it. There was never any painting of walls or decorating to my tastes. It was never my home. One day I was online, and I came across this website showing houses and their floor plans. There was what I thought was the perfect house. Like someone had read my mind. This is that house. I'm not saying we build this but it's an idea."

I studied the floor plans and the picture of the house. It had the look of a farmhouse but with a more modern look. It was mainly siding with shutters at all the windows. There as an attached garage and a nice-sized porch in front and back. Looking at the floor plans, my excitement grew. It was made for a good-sized family.

On the first floor, the entire left side was the master suite which included a sitting area, his and her closets, and the bathroom which had dual sinks, a separate shower and tub. When you walked in the front door, you went through a foyer into a great room which had a fireplace and was open to the kitchen and dining room. The rest of the first floor was rounded out by the laundry room and two more bedrooms which shared a full bath and a powder room.

The second floor was much more flexible. In the plans there were two more bedrooms which shared a full bath, a game room with a wet bar, sitting area and a desk-slash-tech area. It had a smaller room for storage and then a large space that could be extra storage or a workshop. With the way it was laid out, you could also easily have it modified to have another bedroom and a full bath. I glanced up to find Ashlee twisting her hands as she watched me look at the house. I handed her back the phone. She started talking before I could say anything.

"Like I said, it was only an idea, Jack. I'm sure we can find something both of us like."

I laid a finger across her lips to stop her talking.

"Babe, I love the house. It's beautiful. I know it would be stunning. I like the modern farmhouse look of it and it has plenty of bedrooms and room for more if we wanted. If this is the one you love too, then why don't we get Hammer and Steel working on getting the actual plans and start building it? The only thing is, do you think we should have them take the bigger workshop space on the second floor and make it into another bedroom with a bath? As it is, we may be tight if we don't stop at four kids. And even if we do, we should have a guest suite or something." Her mouth dropped open.

"Jack, how many kids do you think we're going to have if four isn't enough?" I grinned.

"As many as I can talk you into, babe. Besides, it could be for guests like I said. Or office space. I work on cars mainly for the club, so I don't need an office at home. What about you? You said you were going to college when you met Alex. What were you studying?" She squirmed at the last part and sighed.

"I was in school to become a web designer. I kick myself for letting him make me quit. When I graduated high school, I'd taken enough dual credit classes, so I almost had my associate degree. That combined with the year I took after high school, left me needing just a little over a year to get my bachelor's and being able to work. I could be earning a lot more to support me and the kids if I had."

"Ashlee, you can't look back and say I should've.... You did what at the time sounded like the best thing. As for supporting you and the kids, I want to do that, but I know you want to be able to have your independence and security. Why don't you go back and finish it? It would be perfect for you. You could work from home and still have financial means." She gave me a surprised look.

"Jack, how can I go back to school? I have two small children and I'm working. How would that work? Not to mention if we build this house, a house to keep up."

"You would have to probably stop the job at the spa, but they wouldn't hold it against you. Janessa worked for us originally at the Fallen Angel while she was finishing nursing school. Savage supported her through finishing it. I'd do the same. The kids can go to the daycare like they do now when you work. When you need study time, I'm here and if I was on a run or something, there are numerous others who would help. As for the house, I can do laundry and cook well enough not to kill us. And Brielle will get Cindy to add our house to the cleaning schedule like they do for the other old ladies. They work and no one expects them to also carry all the house burden too. I think you should do it. Go to the college and find out what you would have to do to restart. Shit, Ash, you're only twenty-three years old. You have so much life to live. You need to start living it." She launched herself into my arms. We laid there and kissed for what felt like forever. This led to me making love to her there beside the lake and then riding back home with her wrapped around me. It had been a perfect day.

Chapter 8: Ashlee

I was super excited. It was just over a week since Devil had asked me about building our house and we'd agreed upon the plan. The club's construction company was going to begin by the end of the week to grade and prep the homesite we'd picked out. On top of it, I'd gotten my courage up and contacted the college about how hard it would be to restart my program and what all was needed. I was pleasantly surprised at how easy and quick I could do it. A lot of the classes I could take online, so essentially those classes started all the time.

As for those I'd have to do on campus, I could see when they were offered and take those as well. I couldn't wait to tell Devil what I'd discovered. He was really pushing that I consider going back to school. If I started soon and went straight through pulling a full-time course load, I could be done by next Christmas which was like fourteen months away!

Today was the first of my three days a week at the spa. I did like the job, but I could do more. In my spare time, I'd played around with the spa's webpage redesigning it. I thought it could do with an updated look. It still ran with the old one which had only been updated to reflect the new name. I knew Smoke was the MC's computer guru, but he didn't spend time on designing web pages, apparently.

I was waiting for Harlow to come back from lunch with Terror to show her what I'd been working on for the past week. My talk with Devil had ignited my passion again. I was helping a customer with directions to the bathroom when the front door chimed. I got her sent on her way and turned around to greet the newest customer. I froze. Standing there was Alex. I felt my gut tighten in anxiety.

He had his pissed-off face on. I felt instantly unsafe. I shifted so I was now standing with the counter between us. As I casually sat down, I pushed the silent alarm under the desk. It would send an alert to the clubhouse and someone would come right away. Only problem is they were ten minutes away, and Alex could do a lot of damage in ten minutes. I knew this from experience. I tried to remain calm and look unaffected by his appearance. I took a deep breath. "What are you doing here, Alex?"

My calm demeanor seemed to piss him off more. His face got red and his mouth tightened. "What am I doing here? What she asks? You could tell me why my whore of a wife is living with a bunch of fucking bikers and keeping my kids from me. You could tell me why she is suing me for divorce and demanding child support, give her half my assets, pay court costs, and a bunch of other bullshit! Ashlee, you can't be stupid enough to think you're going to get away with this. I promise you, you won't. If you stop this nonsense now and come home, I'll go easy on you. Eventually, I'll forgive you. So, get your purse and let's go get the kids. Where are you hid-ing them while you waste your time here rather than taking care of them?" he sneered.

I could feel something welling up inside of me, and for once, it wasn't fear. It was anger. I wasn't going to let Alex run my life or make me miserable anymore. I deserved more. I deserved Devil. I laughed. He looked shocked at my response. I stared him straight in the eyes.

"Alex, I'm not going anywhere with you and neither are my kids. They're somewhere safe while I'm at work. I plan to stay with those 'filthy' bikers as you call them because they're more decent human beings than you've ever thought of being in your whole miserable life. You honestly think I'd come back to you to be beaten, kept hostage, and raped? Really? How stupid does that make you to think I would ever do that? I'm divorcing you, Alex, and I'm going to make sure you never have a chance to harm my kids. And I'm entitled to some of those assets and money for the years of pain and suffering you put me through. Oh, and by the way, you're violating the restraining order which says you can't come within a hundred yards of me or the kids. You're going to go to jail. And it's all on tape." I pointed to the security camera in the corner.

He was now almost purple with suppressed rage. He was clenching his fists and I could see he wanted to hit me, but he was smart enough to not do it. He took a deep breath and sneered. "You think you're so smart don't you, Ashlee. But you're just a dumb whore like all women. You think that biker you're hooked up with is gonna stick around long? He'll use you for a while and then dump your ass. Then where will you and the kids live? You'll come crawling back to me, begging me to take you back."

I laughed at him again. "Alex, I wouldn't come back to you if you were the last man on Earth and I was dying from starvation. I'd give up my kids so they could be taken care of by someone else, but I'd never come back to you. And that biker isn't going to dump my ass. He loves me and I love him. Now, why don't you leave? Or stay so the cops won't have to look far to arrest you." I said the last part because I heard bikes coming and I'd just seen a cop car pull into the parking lot. I guess the club had called the police when they saw who was in here on the camera. Devil had explained they recorded it and if they got an alarm, they'd know to go and check to see who or what was the issue.

The door chimed. Alex turned to look as the officer came in the door. I recognized him. It was Officer Cane. He'd been to the hospital to see me when I first came here—the day Jayce was born. He was the one who had tried to help me get Alex arrested. He was also the one who suggested the restraining order. Behind him was his partner, Officer Kennedy. Kennedy was the one who'd had a thing for Harper. Kennedy stayed by the door while Cane approached me and Alex.

"Hello, Ms. Andrews. We got a call you needed assistance." I nodded. He turned to Alex. "Sir, you're Alex Andrews, I believe. I need to inform you that you are in violation of a restraining order filed by Ms. Andrews which prohibits you from being within one hundred yards of her. From what I see, your five feet away. You'll have to come to the police station with us." Officer Cane was calm and polite, but I knew from our prior discussion, he had nothing but contempt for Alex. At that moment, the door chimed and in came several of the club members with Devil Dog in the lead. He headed straight to me. When he reached me behind the counter, he took me in his arms. I saw Alex's face get even more pissed.

"Babe, are you alright? Did he touch you? Hurt you?" He was running his hands all over me like he was feeling for injuries. I shook my head.

"No, honey, I'm fine." He turned to look at Alex. Officer Cane was putting the handcuffs on him and reading him his Miranda rights when Devil had asked those questions.

Alex heard them and he suddenly exploded in violence. He tried to jerk away from Officer Cane toward the counter. He screamed, "You fucking bitch! You'll be sorry." He looked at Devil Dog. "You're the fucking biker she's screwing. Well, have fun. She'll come back to me. I told her you'd get tired of her soon. I can't wait to see her crawling back begging."

Officer Cane had grabbed him, and Kennedy was now assisting him to get Alex out of the store. He was struggling with them as they placed him in the back of the squad car. As they pulled away, my legs gave out. Devil caught me and helped me into the chair.

I looked around and saw Savage, Ghost, Capone, and Blade with Devil. "Thank you, guys, for getting here so fast and for calling the police." They all nodded. Devil blew out a relieved breath.

"Babe, I almost shit when Smoke said the alarm went off and he saw Alex on the security cameras. What did he want, if I need to even ask?"

I repeated what he said and what I'd said back. The guys were all pissed at Alex but laughed and congratulated me on my comebacks to him.

Harlow came strolling in with Terror and looked around at everyone in surprise. The guys filled them in on what they had missed. Both were pissed. Harlow said Alex was lucky she wasn't there, or she'd have shot his ass. Then she got a thoughtful look on her face.

Terror saw it. "What's come into the devious mind of yours, woman?" She smiled and looked at me.

"I think this week when Ashlee is done working here, she should have Ranger put her through the concealed carry course. All the rest of us have ours, she needs to join too. After all, she's an old lady now." All the guys were enthusiastic about the idea. I looked at Devil. I knew some of the women carried guns.

"Precious, all of us carry and have permits to do so. A couple of years ago, we started to have the women go through the training to get their CCW permit as well. You should really do it. It's just a precaution and not just because of Alex. Ranger is certified to do the training. I'd like for you to take it."

I thought over his request. I personally had no issue with guns like some people. I'd just never had the opportunity to learn to use one. I could remember my dad having them when I was growing up. I nodded.

"I'd like that. I'll do it whenever Ranger has the time." This seemed to please him. I looked at the clock. It was now two o'clock. Alex wouldn't be getting out of jail tonight. "Jack, there's no need to stay. Go back to the compound. And the guys can go, too. Alex won't be getting out of jail tonight."

"No, babe, I'll stay here," he argued.

Harlow, I think helped seal the deal when she said, "Go, Devil Dog, I'm staying and will bring her home." She was one of Devil's best friends and a trained sniper, so I knew he trusted her.

He gave me a kiss and said, "I'll see you at home, Ashlee. Everyone else followed him out the door. Once they were gone, Harlow turned to me.

"Girl, I know you have to be a wreck after that. Take a few minutes in the back. I'll cover the desk. And Ashlee, it's a really good idea to take the class. Most of us like to go shooting as you know. You've not gone before but now you should. It's fun. Did you know Alannah used to compete in shooting competitions?" I shook my head in amazement. These women really were badass biker chicks. She promised to tell me more after my break.

After I returned from my break, she regaled me with stories of which other old ladies had used their guns to defend themselves or others. I'd had no idea. Heck, even Ms. Marie could shoot. The time passed quickly, and I was headed home with Harlow at five thirty in no time. The spa was actually open until seven o'clock, but the last customers were rung up by their esthetician or masseuse.

As we pulled into the compound, Devil Dog was waiting with Jayce bundled in his arms and Angel hanging onto his leg. As soon as the car was stopped, he let her run over to greet us.

I got hugs and kisses from her and then a big kiss from my man that curled my toes. He told me to come into the clubhouse first. I was curious, so I followed him. Inside, Angel ran over to play with Rowan. I took Jayce from Devil. He sat me down with Terror, Savage, and Smoke. "Babe, I just got a call from Officer Cane. He wanted me to let you know they're charging Alex with violating the restraining order. Since this was the first time, it's most likely the judge will charge him a civil penalty and maybe a bond which would be around twenty-five hundred dollars that the court keeps for the length of the TRO. Now, they could decide to keep him for it, but Cane thought it wasn't likely on a first offense. What he's also trying to do is charge Alex with resisting arrest for the way he jerked away when he was trying to handcuff him. If he can get this to stick, then this would be a Class B misdemeanor and they could incarcerate him for up to six months and fine him up to five hundred dollars. He's not sure if he can get the DA to sign off on the resisting arrest but he'll try. He also said he'll let me know the outcome right away. He knows Alex is dangerous. Cane's actually a decent guy."

I sat there shaking. Alex would be mad enough about them arresting him and maybe fining him, but if they actually jailed him, he'd be furious. I shivered. Devil Dog wrapped an arm around me. "What are you thinking babe?" I sighed.

"He's going to be pissed period. But if they actually do put him in jail for a while, he's going to be super furious. He'll be even more dangerous when he gets out. He will come after me. I have no doubt. I want to take the CCW class as soon as possible."

He promised to talk to Ranger as soon as he came home from the range, then he looked at Smoke and nodded.

Smoke looked at me. "Ashlee, I talked to my source about the tracker and using it on the kids and babies. He said they've not done any testing so he can't be sure, but we've done it on pregnant women without issue. The reason it hasn't been studied is technically this capability doesn't exist out on the market yet. Most people say this is still years away from being possible, but through my contacts, I was able to access experimental ones. We've been serving as test subjects for the development of them. All this means is, you and the others will need to weigh the benefits and risks to implanting them or not in the kids." His news wasn't what I wanted to hear, but it did give me something to think about. Under regular circumstances, I'd probably outright say no, but Alex posed such a risk to not only me but the kids that I had to consider it.

I scanned Smoke's face. He was calm and his expression neutral, but I knew he was way more than he seemed. "Smoke, how is it you had access to something like this? It sounds like something the government would be working on. And if so, how did you get your hands on them?" I knew I'd probably asked too much by the exchanged glances between Terror, Savage, and Smoke. I was about to apologize when Smoke shocked me by answering.

"I wasn't always in the MC, Ashlee. Prior to coming to the Warriors, I worked for a government agency. I won't say which one. I made a lot of contacts and friends while

I was there. Occasionally, I still help them out. So, when we started having concerns about the club's old ladies, I contacted them to see if they had any ideas. They told me about the chips and how they were experimenting with them. They're not advertising that they're testing them. Their first round of test subjects were military personnel. We've essentially become their second wave of test subjects. However, no one in the first group has had any adverse effects. The reason this is thought to be impossible for several more years, is the GPS ability would need a power source so it can constantly transmit. Up until now, no one had been able to develop one as small as what is in the one we have implanted. I shouldn't be telling you this, but you are family and I know you'd never talk about it outside of the MC." His revelation surprised me.

"I swear, I'll never talk about it with anyone. Thank you for telling me."

Not long afterward, we went to the house so I could fix dinner. It was a typical night, but I was glad when the kids were down for the evening. Devil and I took our showers and were now lying in bed. He stared at me saying not a word. "What are you thinking?" he asked.

"I'm thinking about what Smoke said about the chips. I'm torn. I don't want to do anything that could harm the kids, but with Alex being in the picture, I feel like I might need to do it. He would take them if he could get his hands on them just to punish me. What do you think?"

He sighed. "I'm torn too. I don't think they'll pose any kind of risk, but we can't be positive. I agree, if Alex could get his hands on the kids, he'd do it. While we have them essentially always with someone from the MC, the chance is lower but not impossible. Shit can happen. Let's think about it over the next few days and then talk more."

I agreed with him. Then I decided to tell him about what I'd found out at the college and to show him the spa website I'd developed. I sat up and grabbed my tablet off the nightstand. He raised his eyebrows.

"I want to tell you something and then show you something. First, I contacted the college to find out what it would involve for me to go back and complete my degree in web design. I have to say, I was pleasantly surprised. It takes very little to restart—a few forms, a fee and they have my transcripts, so no need to get those. Most of the classes can be taken online with only a few which would need to be taken on campus. If I go straight through carrying a full-time course load, I could be done in fourteen months." He leaned over and gave me a kiss.

"Precious, that's great news. Did you fill out the paperwork?"

I laughed. "Jack, I just found out. Don't you think we should talk more about it?"

He shook his head. "No, I think you should just do it. Get it started and we'll make sure everything else gets handled. And the fact many of them can be done online is great. You can work when Jayce naps and while they go to daycare." I sat there with my heart pounding. I could really do this, and he'd support me. I hugged him.

"Thank you. I'll do it. I can't tell you how much this means to me. For you to support it means everything."

He smiled. "Babe, I'll support you in anything and everything you want to do."

After I got myself back under control, I brought up the current spa website and handed him the laptop. He looked at it then at me in puzzlement. I explained, "This is the spa's current webpage. From what I understand, it has been the same for several years. The only real changes were to the name after you guys bought it and adding the new services offered. Now, here is the new one I designed which I'm going to show Harlow to see what she thinks. I think the site needs updating and it could be made to be more interactive." I opened the new website. Devil was scrutinizing it closely. He clicked around, opened things, and explored the dropdowns. He was playing around for maybe ten minutes before he stopped and looked at me.

"Ashlee, this is incredible! You have to show it to Harlow and the rest of the guys. Hell, babe, we need you to look at all our businesses and redesign the websites. This is beautiful and so user friendly."

I smiled.

"You really think so? You're not just saying it because I'm your woman," I teased.

He growled. "No. But if you don't believe me, let me show it to the guys at church on Saturday. See what they think. You can go ahead and show it to Harlow too."

I was happy with his response. I was feeling such a

sense of accomplishment. I put the laptop aside and crawled on top of Devil. He gave me a sexy smirk. I kissed him and then licked his nipples. His hands began to wander over my body. We finished out the evening by making love. Every time he touched me. I experienced the most mind-numbing pleasure. I drifted off thinking about how happy I was.

Saturday came sooner than I'd expected. It was three days after showing Devil Dog the website, and the days had sped by. I'd heard from Devil that Officer Cane said Alex hadn't been put in jail and got off with only a fine. I was disappointed he didn't get jail time. I was now on alert for him and one of the guys was staying with me when I worked at the spa. Mainly it would be one of the prospects, Tanner or Jordan.

This morning I was out in the common room with the other women while the guys were in church. Harlow was telling them all about my new website and how Devil was showing it to the guys this morning in church. I was nervous. I found myself holding Jayce and pacing. They tried to reassure me everything would be fine. They had looked at my proposed new website and exclaimed over it. I couldn't seem to settle. It was almost an hour and a half later when the guys came out. I looked at their faces trying to judge their thoughts. Of course, they were all proficient at looking neutral. Terror, Smoke, Devil Dog, Savage, and several others came over to our table and sat down. Terror looked at me and started to shake his head. My heart sank. They didn't like it.

"Ashlee, I have to tell you, I'm disappointed. I'm disappointed that you have this kind of talent and hadn't told us about it before now. And that you never got to complete your degree. Hell, we could've had all our websites redone with your beautiful ideas already. This is truly impressive, darlin'. We all loved it. Even old Smoke here was impressed." He was smiling now and so were the others. They were singing praises for my design. I felt my face break out into a huge smile.

"You guys really like it?"

He nodded. "Yeah, we do. So now, work up a quote for redesigning not only the spa's website, but the main club one, the garage's, the bike business, the Fallen Angel, the daycare, the tattoo shop, the construction and the range's websites. We'll review and approve it in church, then you can get to work on the others."

I protested, "Terror, you guys don't need to pay me to redesign any of them. If you really like what I did, I'm more than happy to do the others."

"No, you won't. If we went with someone else, we'd have to pay them. Why would we do less for you? This is your work. You deserve to get paid."

I sighed. "This is one way I can repay you for all you've done for me and my kids. You've essentially provided for every one of our needs for the last three months."

He was still shaking his head no. "That was because we wanted to help, and we never expected repayment. Besides, you're Devil Dog's old lady. Of course, we'd help. We knew almost right away how the wind blew with him when it came to you." His words truly stunned me.

I looked at Devil. He was nodding his head in agreement, but I really didn't want to charge them.

Terror cleared his throat. "Devil Dog said you wouldn't want to be paid, so here is the other option, but know you have to pick one or the other. If you won't charge us to redesign all our websites, then you have to let the club pay for your schooling."

I sat there frozen. Had I heard him correctly? The club was willing to pay for my college. I'd been planning to apply for financial aid.

"Terror, that is very generous of you guys, but with tuition, books and other fees, the rest of my program is going to cost several thousands of dollars. I can't have you do that."

He was back to shaking his head. "It's one or the other. You choose."

I sat there thinking. I could see he was serious. I thought about what others would actually charge for those redesigns. I figured Smoke or someone would look into it to see if the quote I gave them was appropriate. Them paying for the remainder of my degree would be cheaper than the other. I nodded.

"Okay, I'll take the second option. And thank you so very much."

He smiled and gave me a peck on the cheek. "You're more than welcome, Ash," Terror said. I could feel the urge to go design. As others drifted away or grabbed drinks, Smoke sat down next to me.

"Ashlee, I had no idea you had such mad design skills. Do you have any skills with other things pertaining to computers?"

I shrugged.

"I've played around with writing programs, but I've never taken classes or anything. Why?"

"I might need help with some things, and I was wondering if you could help me. Most of the people around here aren't super computer literate. If you're willing, how about I show you sometime and we'll see? It would be nice to have another mind to work with once in a while."

I readily agreed. He seemed happy with my answer.

Devil gave me a hug and a kiss. "Babe, they're not lying. They went crazy when they saw it in church. I told them you're going back to school to finish your program. That's when the topic of paying you came up. I told them you wouldn't want to be paid, so Viper suggested paying for your schooling instead. All agreed you had to pick one or the other. I bet you picked the degree because it would be cheaper, didn't you?" He gave me a knowing look. I blushed and then nodded. He laughed.

I overheard the guys talking about having a ride tomorrow for everyone. I turned to Devil. "Where are you and the guys going on your ride tomorrow?" He gave me an odd look.

"Not sure just yet if we'll go toward Reaper's club or down to Agony's in Cherokee. Do you have a preference?"

I shook my head.

"It doesn't matter to me. It's you guys who are going. I think you should decide."

He started to laugh.

"Ash, babe, you're coming too. It'll be the guys and the old ladies, not just the guys." I began to sputter. I'd never gone on a ride with the club.

"I-I can't, Devil. Someone needs to stay behind and take care of the kids. Ms. Marie can't do it alone." Ghost sat down and interrupted our conversation. He must have overheard our discussion.

"It won't just be Ms. Marie. She's gonna get Cindy, Paige, and Monica to help plus both of the prospects will be left here to help and keep an eye on them. So, you have to come with us. You'll have fun."

I gave both of them an absent nod. I was thinking of what I needed to do to get ready. I'd have to pump breast milk for Jayce. As I was thinking, Devil distracted me.

"Babe, don't worry, we'll get everything set. Let's take Angel outside to play on the playground and maybe swim in the pool since it is still warm. Then we'll do any prep we need for the ride later."

The rest of the day was a blur of fun with several of the kids outside on the playground and in the pool. Angel loved living here. She had playmates which she didn't have at our old house. Alex wouldn't allow me to take her places to socialize with other children. By bedtime, she was exhausted. I'd taken time in the afternoon to pump milk for Jayce and to get things ready for tomorrow's ride. I was looking forward to going on the ride.

Chapter 9: Devil Dog

I was awake early this morning. I had to admit I was more excited to go on a ride with the club than usual. It was all due to the fact Ashlee was finally going on it with us. In the past three months, the club had ridden like this a few times, but Ashlee had never asked to go, and I had no right then to insist. However, now that she was officially my old lady, she'd be going with us. To ride for several hours with her wrapped around me would be heaven. We planned to leave at nine, so everyone was supposed to be at the clubhouse with the kids by eight thirty. We'd get them situated and then head out.

Angel was up and full of energy by seven. Jayce had gotten up at six to eat and then he went back to sleep. I told Ashlee to rest for a bit longer and I'd take care of Angel. In the kitchen, I made her favorite blueberry pancakes for breakfast. When she was done, I helped her get cleaned up and dressed for the day. When she was all situated, I cleaned the kitchen and was getting ready to go take a shower. Angel was busy watching her favorite cartoon and singing along to the songs. I was standing there watching her sing and dance, when Ashlee came out of the bedroom. She stopped and looked shaken as she watched Angel. I hurried over to her.

"Precious, what's wrong?"

She had tears in her eyes when she looked at me. I wrapped her up in my arms.

"I was just reminded of the day Alex slapped Angel. This is the show she was watching and even the song she was singing. He had watched her and had such a look of anger on his face. You were standing there watching her, but you were looking at her with love and amusement. It just struck me how different two men can be." I gave her a kiss.

"Babe, I'd never lay a hand on her, Jayce, or any of our children when we have them. I'd never do that to you either. He never loved you, if he could hurt you. He only wanted to possess and control. Forget about him. Let's enjoy the day. I'm gonna take a quick shower. She's all set. Do you need me to do anything else?"

She shook her head no.

In our room I got ready as fast as I could. She'd had a shower and was dressed. When I came out, she had gotten Jayce up and dressed. The kids' things were set by the front door. All we had to do was grab them on the way out and get the milk in the fridge.

We were walking across the compound to the clubhouse with the kids and all their paraphernalia by eight twenty. When we got inside, it looked like all the couples were there. Since Bethany was just over two weeks old, Wren would be riding mainly in the car with Harlow since she was eight months pregnant. Her little girl would be here in about a month. Wren said she'd drive the SUV since we were leaving the prospects behind. She didn't want any of the brothers to have to give up the chance to ride their bikes.

Ms. Marie, Monica, Cindy, and Paige were there waiting to take the kids from us. We were all getting ready to head out to the bikes when I caught Viper's attention and he nodded. I whistled to get everyone's attention.

"Before we go on the ride, we need to do something first." The guys knew what I was up to, but the women all exchanged puzzled looks. "We can't go on this ride unless everyone is properly attired. Babe, you need something else on if you're going on the bike." She was now frowning. Viper slipped the bag to me. I held it out. "You need a proper cover up. Here, put this on, Precious."

She took the bag and opened it. She gasped and looked at me then back at the bag as she pulled out her gift. It was her leather property cut. It had finally come in the other day and I'd wanted to present it to her in front of the club. She slipped it on. On the back it said *Property of Devil Dog* and on the front was her club name, *Precious*. It filled me with such satisfaction and pride to see my name on her back. She flung herself in my arms kissing me over and over as the others laughed and cheered.

Angel was clapping seeing her mommy so happy. When Ashlee calmed down, I told Angel to come over to us. She skipped over to me. I handed her a small bag. She opened it to find her own cut which said *Property of the Warriors* and her club name was *Our Angel*. She jumped up and down in excitement and put it on her. I had a feeling we wouldn't be able to get her out of it at bedtime.

Despite this interlude, we were on the road by nine as planned. Ashlee had been watching and learning from the other old ladies. She was dressed in jeans, sturdy boots, and a long-sleeved shirt. She also had brought along a jacket, as the temp would drop toward evening. Her hair was covered by the do-rag and then her helmet. She had her cut on and slipped on her sunglasses. She looked badass and sexy as hell.

When she swung on behind me, I reached back and pulled her against me tight and tugged her arms around me tighter. I looked over my shoulder to be sure she was set. She kissed me and then whispered, "You're sure getting laid tonight to thank you for my cut." I laughed.

We all took off. Terror and our road captain, Steel, had decided we'd head down to Cherokee and the surrounding area. Fall was in full bloom and the trees were beautiful. Cherokee would be breathtaking to see high up in the mountains with all those trees. It took us over an hour to get there because we took our time riding the back roads and enjoying the scenery. As we pulled into town, we were met by a few of the Pagan Souls. Terror had made sure to let Agony know we'd be riding through his territory. We followed them back to their clubhouse.

When we pulled in, Agony and his guys were there to greet us. He was grinning and laughing as we got off our bikes. The last time we'd been here, he'd taken us to the Harrah casino in town. I looked up and jerked in surprise. There stood Wrath and his guys from the Pagan Souls Lake Oconee Chapter. Lake Oconee was about three and a half hours away. We turned to greet them.

Agony was explaining how Wrath and the guys had come over for a meeting with them. It was pure luck we'd decided to visit at the same time. We followed all of them inside. We were given drinks, and the ladies shown to the bathrooms. As we sat down, Terror casually asked them, "What were you all meeting about, or should I not ask?"

Agony and Wrath both got serious looks on their faces. They glanced around to see where the old ladies had gone and then back to us.

"Do you guys remember the Steel Outlaws you had a run-in with at the poker run for the hospital in May?" Agony asked.

We all nodded. They had tried to cause trouble when one of their guys had tried to get handsy with Harper. We'd run them off.

"Well, they're stirring shit up down here. We've heard through the grapevine that they intend to move their businesses further north. They want to take it through Cherokee, with the ultimate goal of getting through eastern Tennessee to Virginia. They're in the same kind of businesses as the Black Savages and Satan's Bastards were—drugs, guns, and prostitution. We know in order to make it a more profitable venture, they need to be able to move through Dublin Falls. We met yesterday about it and then you called. I thought it would be better if we told you in person," Wrath added.

I could see all my brothers exchanging looks. We'd eliminated two rival clubs in the past year who had been targeting us for a few years. Now it looked like we would probably be acquiring a new enemy if they got the opportunity. I knew this was all the information we'd get with the women here. Terror, Agony and Wrath all agreed to set up a conference call with us when we got back to our compound so we could discuss it freely.

After a brief rest and everyone getting a chance to use the bathroom and grab something to drink, Agony insisted we were having a barbeque. The next hour or so was filled with the food getting situated. The guys could do the grilling, but sides were the issue. Agony had said he had planned to go to the store for those. The women told him they'd make them if he had or would get the ingredients. He put a prospect and a couple of their bunnies at their disposal. By one o'clock we were busy grilling and the ladies had whipped up several sides and even desserts. They were patiently showing the bunnies how to get things pulled together.

The Soul's bunnies seemed to be appreciative of the instruction and the fact our women weren't treating them like shit. By the time we had the chicken, hamburgers, and smoked sausage grilled, they had baked beans, macaroni salad, a vegetable plate, and street corn made. For dessert they made something called a fruit trifle, a berry cobbler and another thing they said was summer dessert tacos. Apparently, someone had frozen a ton of different berries and they figured different ways to make use of them. Agony, Wrath, their guys and even the bunnies were filled with nothing but praise.

Everyone ate too much while we talked and laughed. It was about two thirty when Agony suggested we hit Harrah's. Most of the women had been there but not Ashlee. She told us she'd never been to a casino. That decided it.

Everyone headed over for a couple of hours of fun. She had a great time just playing different games. She even won a little money. We wrapped it up and headed back home around five. This time of year, it was almost dark, so we couldn't enjoy the trees, but we did enjoy the ride and the wind in our faces. We hit the compound after six that evening.

All the kids were at the clubhouse. The bigger ones, mainly those cognizant like Rowan, Angel, Hunter, and Kenna were entranced in a Disney movie. The others were too little, so they were being held or pushed in the baby swings. Angel ran over to kiss and hug us before running back to the movie.

Ashlee headed over to get Jayce. He had been napping in one of the cribs. It was almost time for his evening feeding. We usually got both of ours down around eight. It startled me when I had that thought. *Ours.* I loved the ring of it. We ended up letting Angel finish the movie. Dinner had already been prepared at the clubhouse, so she was set. After everyone was thanked, hugged, and kissed, we took them home.

Back at the house, Angel insisted I help her with her bath. We ended up playing with her toys a bit, while Ashlee bathed Jayce and got him settled in his crib. She'd breastfeed him before we left the clubhouse. Once Angel was out of the tub and dressed in her pajamas, I read her a bedtime story about puppies. She was out like a light by eight fifteen. When I came out of her room, Ashlee was sitting on the couch with a glass of wine for herself and a beer for me.

I sat down beside her and kissed her neck. "Thank you,

babe." She smiled and nodded. "Did you enjoy today?" I asked. She smiled even more.

"I loved it, Jack. The ride and seeing all those trees were awesome. And the casino was a lot of fun too. I had such a good time. Thank you for taking me." I pulled her onto my lap.

"Any time, babe. I'm glad you enjoyed it. I want you to get to do things you were never allowed to do before—like sit down and have a glass of wine, go to a casino, finish college. I just want you to share them with me."

She took my face between her hands and leaned down to latch onto my mouth. She slipped her tongue inside. I could taste the wine she'd just drank. I grabbed the back of her head to bring her in tighter and I devoured her mouth. When we broke apart, she was flushed pink and breathing heavily. I was a little breathless myself.

Ashlee stood up off my lap and held out her hand. "Let's go to bed. I told you earlier you'd be getting laid for that gorgeous cut you gave me. I can't wait any longer," she taunted with a sexy smirk on her face. I took her hand and stood up. As we passed the coffee table, I grabbed her glass of wine to take with us.

In the bedroom, she led me to the bathroom where she began to strip. She did it slowly, peeling off item after item to reveal her sexy body. As she did, I took off my clothes. In no time, we were both naked. Her eyes were roaming all over my body. She had a hungry look in her eyes. My cock was already hard from seeing her strip and the heated look in her eyes.

I growled. She laughed as I started to stalk her around

the bathroom. She tried to get to the door, but I caught her. I swung her up in my arms and took her mouth. She ran her hands all over my shoulders and chest as we kissed. I sat her down reluctantly so I could turn on the shower. As the water got warm, I ran my hands up and down her body.

"Babe, you're so fucking sexy. I love being able to touch you, taste you, look at you, and make love to you. You have no idea how happy you've made me."

She sighed happily.

"Jack, you've done all those things and more for me. I don't know what I did to deserve to find someone like you. You love me and the kids."

I pulled her with me to the shower. Hot water sprayed down on us. I started to wash her hair. "That's no surprise, Precious. The three of you are so damn easy to love. Now, let me show you how much I love you." She sighed as I proceeded to wash her from head to toe. As I rinsed her, I'd lick and suck all over her gorgeous body. Her slick skin felt so soft under my hands. She was trying to wash me, but I kept interfering with her ability to get it done. I'd suck on her nipples or run my fingers through her folds. She was wet with excitement. Finally, she grabbed my hand.

"Stop, so I can get you finished. Then you can do whatever you want."

I held still while she finished bathing me, though it was almost more than I could stand. After we dried off, I carried her to the bed.

Her pale, sexy body was framed by the dark

CIARA ST JAMES

sheets on our bed. I crawled on it to taste her sweet pussy, but she stopped me with a hand on my shoulder. I looked at her in concern. We'd made love several times so far, but I'd been going slow. Oral sex for both of us and missionary sex had been the limit. I planned to go farther tonight, if she'd let me.

"What's wrong, Precious? Don't you want me to go down on you?"

She smiled. "I'd love for you to do it. But first, I want to taste you, Jack. I want that gorgeous cock in my mouth. Because if I let you go first, you'll not let me get my mouth on you."

I groaned. She was right. After eating her sweet, addictive pussy, I'd want to fuck her. I nodded my consent and laid down on my back.

She pushed my legs apart and crawled in between them. Her small, soft hands caressed my inner thighs and then up to my balls. She played with them, rubbing and pulling lightly on my sac. Then she encircled my cock with one of her hands. She couldn't reach clear around it, but she tried.

She stroked up and down a couple of times. Just that much touching had me aching to come. She looked up to catch my eyes. When she did, she slowly lowered herself to take me in her mouth. She never broke eye contact while she engulfed my cock. It was so hot to have her look at me while she had me in her mouth. She proceeded to drive me to the edge of fucking sanity.

She played with my balls as she sucked me. Her suction was perfect, and she was taking more of me than she'd ever done. She broke away to lick down my shaft to my balls. She took them into her mouth and gently sucked on them, rolling them around like marbles. Her tongue would lash around them while she sucked. I closed my eyes and moaned.

She let go of my balls and worked her way back up to take my cock back in her mouth. This time she took me so deep, she gagged. But unlike previous times where she'd backed off, she pushed forward. The head of my aching cock slipped down her throat. She swallowed over and over. The pressure of her throat squeezing down on my sensitive head caused me to groan and my hips involuntarily thrust deeper. I knew now that her air was cut off. I tried to back off, when she shook her head no. She held me deep in her throat, swallowing over and over until she had to take a breath.

"Jesus, Ashlee, that was perfect, babe. It felt so good. Just don't do anything you don't want to do or aren't comfortable doing just to please me," I told her. She smiled and deep throated me again. I got caught up in the pleasure and didn't realize I'd grabbed her head and was pushing her down on my cock as I thrust up. When I did, I stopped.

"Precious, I'm so sorry, babe. I got carried away and didn't realize what I was doing. Are you okay?" She licked down my shaft and back up.

"I'm fine, Jack. I'm glad you got lost in the pleasure of what I was doing. I liked it. Show me what you want. Use my mouth to bring you pleasure."

Her words caught me off guard and caused me to lose a little more of my control. She engulfed my cock again, and I took over control of her movements. I held onto her hair and pushed her down and thrust up in an increasingly deeper and faster rhythm. When I hit the back of her throat, I'd hold myself there until she needed to come up for air. She'd swallow and swallow. As she moved up and down, she maintained tight suction and teased with her tongue when she could. All too soon, I could feel the tingling moving up to my balls. I took my hands off her head.

"Babe, you're going to have to stop. I'm close," I warned her. She tightened her grip on the base of my cock and increased her up and down movements. So far, I'd never come in her mouth. We'd always stopped before it got to that point. I hadn't asked her if coming in her mouth was something she wanted. I knew from her, that I was the only guy she'd gone down on.

As she kept working me, my hips began to thrust again. I knew I was about to come. I gave her one last warning, "I'm coming, babe." She kept sucking and working me. The tingling centered in my balls and then shot up my cock. I came, yelling as I fired off shot after shot of my cum down her throat. She took every drop and never stopped sucking and swallowing. When I'd stopped coming, she gently licked up my length and around the head before sitting back on her heels to look at me.

"Fuck, Ash, that was amazing. I never expected you to do that, babe. Most women don't like a guy to come in their mouths. What did you think of it? Be honest. I never want you to do it just to please me."

She smiled and crawled up my body kissing me all over as she went.

"Jack, I didn't know what to expect. But honestly, your cum wasn't unpleasant to taste. It was a little salty and musky. I found it super-hot to have you come in my mouth and me be able to swallow it. I'll never mind doing that." Her words went through me. She was perfect. I loved getting head and having a woman suck me to release. But as I said, most women wouldn't do it.

I pulled her the rest of the way up my body and kissed her. I could taste a faint hint of my cum in her mouth. We spent a couple of minutes ravishing each other's mouths over and over. As she pulled back, I flipped her on her back and hovered over her. She had given a little shriek when I did it. I looked down into her eyes.

"Now it's my turn. I want to taste that beautiful pussy." I slid down to her center and spread her thighs. She was neatly trimmed and only had a small patch of hair above her clit. The rest of her was smooth. I muzzled her patch with my nose before flicking her clit with my tongue. She jerked and moaned. I ran my tongue down and back up her folds gathering the honey she'd generated while she sucked my cock. She was soaking wet already.

I moaned as I tasted her. She was so sweet, and I loved her flavor. I dove into her pussy, licking, lapping, and sucking on her folds, clit and even working her entrance with my stiffened tongue. I was thrusting it in and out mimicking my cock thrusting in and out of her pussy. She was pushing herself harder down on my face. I slid a finger through her juices, coating it. I slipped one into her entrance and thrust several times. She was breathing heavily, and her hips were jerking off the bed. I took the lubricated finger and circled around her asshole. She froze as I rubbed across it. I stopped.

"Babe, what's wrong? Don't you like that? Or is it something else?" I didn't know if Alex had ever engaged in anything anal with Ashlee. She was tense and not looking at me. I eased back away from her.

"I- I..." she stuttered then closed her eyes.

Shit! I didn't want to make her uncomfortable or remember something terrible. I tried to comfort her.

"It's alright, babe. You don't have to say anything. I'll just be sure not to engage in anything anal. Okay?" I liked anal play and sex, but I'd never want it or do it if Ashlee wasn't comfortable with it. She opened her eyes and I saw tears.

I moved up to take her in my arms. Sex was forgotten as I comforted her. As I held her, she started to talk. She spoke so low I had to lean closer to hear her. "I'm not sure if I'd like it or not. Alex never played with me there." I nodded. No surprise, he hadn't gone down on her or done much of anything other than ram it in and get himself off.

She continued, "There were a few times when he was really pissed at me, that he shoved a dildo he bought in there. No warning, no lubrication, nothing. It hurt so much, Jack. He did it to punish me. I would hurt and bleed for a couple of days after he'd do it. When he was being mean, he'd torment me telling me he'd be using it again. I know people say it's pleasurable, but if it's anything like what he did to me, I don't see it."

Her explanation infuriated me. It was bad enough he'd

raped her vaginally for years, but to basically rape her anally with a toy as punishment was even sicker. I wanted to kill him with my bare hands even more.

"Ash, we don't ever have to do anything anal. Yes, many women do find it pleasurable if it's done right. If the man takes his time and prepares her properly, it can be really good. But don't worry about it. Thank you for telling me, babe."

She shook her head. "No, Jack, I don't want us to just rule it out without discussing it. Do you enjoy performing it? Do you like just play or having actual anal sex?"

I sighed.

"Babe, yes, I've done it and I've done actual anal sex. Did I enjoy it? Yes, I did because my partner did. But I don't have to have it." She was watching me as I explained. She scooted closer to me.

"Then I want to know if I would like it too, if the man I'm with prepares me and does it gently. I want you to feel free to try it. I was just caught off guard. Please, go back to what you were doing and show me."

I tried to protest, but she was insistent. I knew during our talk she had become unexcited. I needed to build her back up. I planned to get her off and then I was going to fuck my woman until she was boneless.

I went back to pleasuring her. I sucked and worked her breasts before moving back down to her pussy. There I started my feast over. She soon was back to squirming and her wetness was glistening in the light. She seemed to be lost in the pleasure. I slipped off the bed and grabbed a bottle out of my drawer.

I'd recently put a bottle of lube in there in case we ever did engage in anal sex or used toys. Her eyes got big, but she didn't protest. I slicked up my finger, so she could see what I was doing. Then I got between her legs and slowly slid toward her asshole.

When I reached it, I rubbed all around it for a bit, so she could get used to my touch and relax. Once I felt her relax, I pressed just the tiniest bit of the tip inside. She tensed.

"Precious, if it becomes too much, tell me to stop. It helps if you try to push down as I push inside. Try to relax." She nodded. I kept licking and sucking her clit, as I worked my finger in a bit more, then pulled it back. As I did this, I'd advance it a little farther each time. She hissed a couple of times. When she did, I'd stop to let her get used to it. She didn't tell me to stop altogether, so I kept advancing. I was careful to go slow and only incrementally go deeper. Finally, I had my whole finger buried in her ass. She was clamped so tight on my finger, I thought she might cut off my blood flow.

Then I attacked her pussy with my mouth with gusto. I sucked her hard clit and thrust my other fingers in and out of her pussy, while I gently worked the other finger in and out of her ass. As the tempo increased, she began to bear down on my fingers, and she moaned. Her head thrashed on the pillow and her hands clenched the sheets.

There was an expression of pleasure on her face not pain. Seeing her lost in pleasure made me harder and horny. I kept working her two holes until she grabbed my hair, pulling on it as she came screaming out her release. Her pussy and ass clenched down hard on my fingers. Her juices flowed out coating my tongue and fingers. I lapped every bit of it up. When she finally collapsed from her orgasm, I removed my fingers. I sat back and grabbed a tissue to wipe my digits.

She looked totally sated. She looked down and then her breath caught. Her eyes locked onto my cock which was standing at attention. It was red, and the veins were standing out. I needed to bury it inside of her so fucking bad. My cum was glistening all over the head where it had leaked from my slit.

"Jack, fuck me, honey. I want you to fill me up. Show me what you want." She broke me with those words.

I growled.

"Get on your hands and knees. I want to do you from behind, babe." She scrambled onto her hands and knees. I'd never taken her in this position. I pulled her so she was on the edge of the bed. I stood and grabbed her hips, lining my cock up with her pretty pink entrance. I pushed inside in one continuous stroke until I was buried up to my balls. I groaned, and she moaned. She was so hot, wet, and tight that I knew I wouldn't last.

I started powering in and out. As I went faster, she began to push back to meet my thrusts. She was gripping me so hard. I wanted to pound into her, but she wasn't ready for that kind of sex.

Or I thought not until she panted, "Jack, I need it harder, deeper please. I need to come, baby." This pushed me over the edge. I gripped her hips harder and pounded in and out of her going faster and deeper. She was moaning and crying out.

"Oh God, more. Give me more." I thrust harder and then I was slamming in and out of her. My breath was ragged, and I could feel my orgasm racing up my legs to my cock. I wanted her to come with me.

"Babe, I'm close." She whimpered and slid her hand to her clit. I thrust a few times more, then she clamped down hard on me as she screamed her release into her pillow. She was bucking and thrusting back into me. I grunted and yelled as I came. My hot seed filled her pussy. I kept thrusting as I praised her.

"You're so fucking incredible. Nothing has ever been this good. So perfect." We slowly floated down until I had to pull out because I had softened, and she had collapsed onto her chest on the bed. I rubbed her back to sooth her. She rolled over and kissed me.

"Jack, that was amazing. All of it. God, I love you. Never be afraid to teach me things. I loved it once I got comfortable."

I chuckled. She was slipping off to sleep, but I insisted we clean up first. When we were done, we both dropped in the bed and were asleep as soon as our heads hit the pillows.

Chapter 10: Ashlee

The club was decorated in a pink, purple, and teal explosion. The guys joked this was the Warrior's new colors. We were holding a joint birthday party for Kenna, who just turned two and Rowan, who was turning five tomorrow, the twenty-first of October.

In addition, we were on contraction watch. Harlow had been having Braxton-Hicks contractions for the past few days. She still had four weeks until her due date, but there was always a chance she could go early. Rowan told her she wanted the baby to be born on her birthday. Harlow had laughed and told her she'd try.

Alannah had done her baking magic and created a gorgeous Disney Princesses cake for the girls. From what I understood, all the guys had been busy the last few weeks shopping for little girl stuff. This included the single guys. Devil had bounced his ideas off me when he was deciding on his gifts.

The party would start at one o'clock. The food wasn't going to be your typical hotdogs. No, it was going to be the girls' two favorite types of food. In Rowan's case, she loved Mexican and Kenna, even at two, was partial to Chinese. To say the feast would be eclectic was an understatement. However, with so many great cooks, they were able to do all the cooking. I could cook well, but they were great. Ms. Marie had been teaching her many recipes and secrets to me along with some of the others.

It was ten o'clock, and the guys had just gotten out of church not too long ago. We were waiting for Bull and some of his guys to come in for the party. He liked to say all the Warrior kids were his grandkids. All of them called him grandpa. He loved it.

I also knew he was anxious to have his real granddaughter get here. She was going to be such a poor little thing when she got old enough to date. Just imagine, an older brother, Lord knows how many pseudo brothers, a million biker uncles, her dad, and grandpa who were both club presidents. She'd be lucky if she was allowed to go on a date when she turned seventy!

I was setting another one of the tables when Devil Dog came in with Jayce. He was helping to watch him and keep Angel entertained outside with the other bigger kids. He came over and gave me a kiss. I got lost in it until someone cleared their throat. I broke away to find Bull standing there with a big grin on his face. I laughed and blushed. He shook his head.

"I can see another good woman has been brainwashed. Shit, if I'd known what would happen when I allowed that no good Terror to have my little girl..." He gave a tortured sigh while winking at me. I laughed. I could see Terror was coming up behind him. He'd said it so he could hear it.

Terror jumped in just like Bull knew he would. "Let me? You didn't let me have her. You tried to warn me away and I wouldn't listen. Now look what you got in return, a grandson and a granddaughter. You should be thanking me for taking that crazy woman off your hands," he joked.

Harlow had come up behind Terror and punched him in the kidney. He acted like it hurt harder than it did and swung around like he was surprised to see her. She smirked at him.

"Oh, really? Crazy, am I? Yeah, I'm crazy for letting you talk me into another baby. One who lays on her mother's bladder day and night. I'll remember this the next time you start talking about having another baby," she growled. Terror just smiled.

"About that Harlow, I think once we have this one, we should wait six months and start on the next one. What do you think?" he teased her.

She hissed at him. "Don't make me neuter you right here, Terror. We'll wait at least a year or more, mister."

He laughed.

Bull perked up.

"A year you say?"

She frowned. "Don't get any ideas, Dad. I said a year or more. We talked about having three, but we'll see. Now, you guys have a choice. Decorating and cooking duty or babysitting. Which will it be?"

Bull had all but his prospects with him. Most of his guys went out to help with the kids, while a few stayed inside to decorate and gopher for the ladies. Devil took the babysitters outside with him and Jayce.

When one o'clock got here, the food was ready, and the few kids from the daycare Rowan was friends with had arrived with their parents. We had the kids playing games at first, followed by food. After they ate and played outside on the playground more, we had cake and ice cream. After we'd cleaned up the mess, Rowan and Kenna opened their gifts, which had been weighing down a whole table.

It was an explosion of cute clothes, shoes, toys, movies, and even jewelry. As we sat watching the fun, Devil hugged me. "Babe, I've been meaning to ask, when is Angel's birthday? We need to make sure we give her a party."

I got choked up. "Her birthday is in February."

He nodded. "What day? I need to make sure I don't forget it."

I laughed. "I don't think you have to worry about forgetting it, Jack. She was born on February fourteenth, Valentine's Day."

He laughed. "I think I can remember that. When is your birthday?"

I was uncomfortable talking about it. I hadn't celebrated my birthday since meeting Alex.

"It's January eighteenth. I'll be twenty-four. When is yours?"

He chuckled. "April first. I was an April Fool's baby. I'll be thirty-two."

We watched as the kids settled down in the common

room to watch a movie before their friends left. I told Devil I needed to get something from the house. He said he'd go get it, but I told him to stay and enjoy the *Little Mermaid.* He laughed and smacked my ass. He was holding Jayce who'd fallen asleep. I hurried to the house. I needed to replenish the diapers at the clubhouse. We kept some there for all the babies.

I had grabbed another stack when my cell phone rang. I pulled it out of my pocket. It was a number I didn't know. I answered it. "Hello, this is Ashlee." The voice that came over it was the last one I expected to hear.

"Well, if it isn't my whore of a wife. Still hanging with and banging a bunch of bikers, I suppose. Do you really think you're going to get away from me, Ashlee? I own you. I own those kids. I'll never grant you a fucking divorce. Bring your ass and those kids back home now, or you'll regret it. I can make your life hell. You have until the end of the week, Ashlee. Call off the lawyer, tell those bikers you want nothing to do with them and get your ass home." He hung up.

I sank down on the couch. My mind was whirling. I was having trouble catching my breath. I was only half aware of Devil Dog sitting down out of nowhere and talking to me. It wasn't until he lightly shook me that I snapped back into focus.

"Ash, what's wrong? You didn't come back to the party, so I came to find you. You look like you've seen a ghost. You're shaking, babe."

I grasped his arm.

"Alex called me, Jack. He has my new phone number

CIARA ST JAMES

somehow!"

He got an angry look on his face. "What did he say, Ashlee?"

I jumped up to pace. I felt cold inside and like I could pass out. I haltingly told Devil what he'd said. He jumped up swearing. He came over and took me in his strong arms.

"Precious, he's not going to get any of you back. You're mine. I take care of what's mine. And make no mistake, you, Angel, and Jayce are mine. He can make all the threats he wants. We'll get you a new number or have Smoke block his number. You can't let him rattle you. He wants you afraid and worried. Don't give him the satisfaction."

I nodded as he held me. I knew it was a mind game for Alex. We spent a little while just in each other's arms, before I told him we needed to head back to the clubhouse.

When we got there, the parents of the daycare kids had left with their kids. All who were left were part of the club. Devil Dog headed us toward the tables where Terror, Bull, Demon, Savage and their old ladies were sitting. The kids were still watching movies. Savage looked up with a smile and then it died on his face.

"What's wrong? We thought the two of you slipped off for some alone time, but your faces sure don't look like it."

Devil's jaw tightened. "I wish. Ashlee got a call. Alex somehow found out what her new cell number is, and he called her with a bunch of demands and threats. He's

186

given her until the end of this week to return to him. We need to make sure he can't get his hands on her or the kids. They're safe at the daycare with the precautions there. I'm worried about the spa. We need to have more than one guy watching when she's working. I also want Smoke to get her a new number." All of them were nodding. Bull leaned forward in his seat.

"This is the husband, right? The one she's divorcing and has a restraining order against?"

I nodded.

Devil spoke up. "He came to the spa almost two weeks ago. He violated the TRO, and we had him arrested. Not that it did any good. He's been lying low since then. He's trying to get custody of the kids. He can't ever be allowed to even have supervised visitation with them, Bull. The things he did to her for years is sickening. You have no idea."

Bull was looking at me.

"Listen, sweetheart, Harlow and Terror told me you have an abusive husband, and that's it. I don't need to know any more than that. We'll make sure he doesn't get your kids."

I had tears in my eyes. I thought they deserved to know what kind of man they were up against.

"Don't underestimate him. He kept me essentially a prisoner for over four years. I wasn't allowed to have friends and rarely allowed to leave the house. I tried to escape more than once, and he always found me and brought me back. In those four years, he repeatedly beat and raped me. The last time he beat me was the first time he laid a hand on Angel. That's when I came here."

Bull's face was flushed red. I could see Demon's face was as well. Bull looked at Devil and Terror.

"I want church now."

Terror nodded and got up to tell the other guys. I glanced at Devil in alarm. He rubbed my back.

"Babe, there's nothing to worry about. Bull is our charter president. He just wants to talk to us. I'll be back."

They all headed toward the meeting room while I sat there watching them go, wondering what Bull was going to say to them. Would he want me to leave? I nervously waited to find out my fate.

Devil Dog:

We all filed into the room. Most of the guys were looking at each other with questions in their eyes. Bull had held church with us before, but usually only when it was something very serious. We all sat down as Terror and Bull sat at the head of the table together. Terror started things off.

"I know we had church this morning, but Bull wanted to speak to all of us. So, give him your undivided attention. Bull, the floor is yours."

Bull gave him a chin lift and stood.

"I just learned more about Devil Dog's old lady, Ashlee, and her situation. Devil, tell my guys what's going on with her husband and what she just told me."

I quickly brought his guys up to speed. They were all

muttering and swearing by the time I was done. If there was one thing Warriors detested, it was men who hurt women and children.

Bull whistled to get everyone to quiet back down. "Now, I called this meeting to discuss this. Because I believe we need to be prepared to end this man in a permanent way. His type typically doesn't just give up and go away. He's gone after her every time she's left him in the past. He's possessive and probably obsessed with her. I know you guys will have security on her. That's good. But I think you need to be prepared to put his ass down if he continues to come after her. I mean, for Christ's sake, he held her captive, beat and raped her for years. Were her little ones the result…" He stopped and looked at me.

I knew what he wanted to ask. I looked around the table. "Yes, both Angel and Jayce are the result of him raping her. She hasn't willingly shared his bed in over four years, and the shit he did is sick. I have no plans to let him live. It just has to be done at the right time and in the right way, so nothing blows back on us or her."

Bull pounded the table. "That motherfucker is a dead man walking! No woman should have that happen to her, much less at the hands of her husband. A man who should love, cherish, and protect her. You have one strong old lady, Devil Dog. Any chance we'll have a wedding as soon as this bastard is gone?" He winked and grinned.

I knew he was trying to lighten the mood. I grinned back. "As a matter of fact, I'm planning to ask her soon. Nothing says she can't be engaged while she waits for her first husband to become her ex-husband or better yet make her a widow." All the guys laughed.

Bull smiled. "Good. Let me know if you guys need any help from my guys. We'll be happy to do security or anything else. And, since I have you all here, Terror told me about the Steel Outlaws stirring things up in North Carolina." He went on to tell his guys what we'd found out about them. You could see the concern on their faces. Bull reassured us.

"I'm gonna check into some resources I have to see what I can find out. Terror said he's gonna talk to the Dark Patriots—Sean, Gabe, and Griffin's group. If they are planning to take over any or all of the Bastards or Savage's old territory, we need to know and be ahead of them, if possible. Everyone, you need to keep your eyes and ears open. They could already have someone around here feeding them information or watching you." We talked a bit longer and then he and Terror dismissed everyone to rejoin the celebration.

Back in the common room, Ashlee raced over to me as soon as we came into the room. "Is everything alright?"

I reassured her, "Everything is fine, babe. Bull wanted to talk about security and the information we found out about the Steel Outlaws from the Pagan's. He does this every once in a while." I didn't tell her that one of the security topics was her and the kids. I didn't want her to worry. She gave a sigh.

"I was afraid that he wanted me to leave because of Alex." Her words stunned me.

"Precious, why in the world would you think something like that?"

She shrugged and nervously twisted her fingers.

"Because I'm bringing trouble to the club. Alex will bother you guys and it's because of me."

I pulled her tight against my chest and tipped up her chin so she could look me in the eye.

"Ash, Bull nor any of the others would ever think of asking you and the kids to leave. Even if you weren't my old lady, we'd protect you. But the fact is, you're my woman and those are now my kids. This club and all the other Warrior chapters will protect you and our kids. So put that thought out of your mind." I could see her relax. I took her pouty lips. She kissed me back eagerly and with a hunger to match my own. We broke apart only when it was no longer possible to go without a breath.

We went to rejoin the others. Jayce had woken up and was fussing. She sat down and threw a blanket over her so she could feed him. I knew it was so others wouldn't be uncomfortable, mainly the Hunter's Creek guys. I wasn't sure if they'd seen a woman breastfeed before. They had no old ladies yet in their chapter. I saw a few of them throwing her surprised and even fascinated looks. I didn't think any of them would be offended to see a woman openly breastfeeding.

As soon as she was done, I took Jayce to burp him and then change his diaper. Payne came over to watch me. "You look comfortable doing that. Did you have experience with kids before Ashlee?"

I shook my head. "Other than the ones here, no. Why?"

Payne shrugged. He was the enforcer for Bull's chapter.

"Just wondering. I see every time I come here how happy you guys are. More and more of you are finding old ladies. It gives me hope that there is someone out there for me. Honestly, I'm tired of the easy sex with bunnies and barflies." I gave him a knowing look.

"I know what you mean. I was feeling the same and then I met Ashlee. As soon as she walked through that door, I knew she was the one. And no other woman so much as made me look."

He smiled then gestured to Jayce. "And her kids?"

I laughed.

"I love them, too. I love them as if they were mine. I consider them mine. We're having a house built on the compound right now. I'll show it to you. We plan to have a few more kids, so it is a big one." He looked eager to see it. Once I was done with Jayce, I gave Ash the baby while I went to get the house plans. We spread them out and more Hunters Creek's guys came over to look at them. They seemed to like it and even had a couple of good suggestions. After looking at the plans, I walked them out to see the site.

It had been graded and markers set, so they could start pouring the foundation once the blocks were laid. Ours was going to have a basement. Hammer and Steel said barring problems like unexpected delays, with a dedicated team, they'd finish the house by the end of February. It was hard to believe we could be in our very own house in just four months.

By the time we were done walking the homesite, it was going on six o'clock. Bull and his guys would stay the night and head back tomorrow. Ashlee and I stayed and relaxed with everyone at the clubhouse until seven thirty. That's when Ashlee said she was going to take the kids back to the house to get ready for bed. I'd risen to go with her when she shook her head.

"Honey, stay and visit with your brothers. You don't get to see them often. Enjoy and come home later. I can get them down. Please. I want you to relax."

I reluctantly nodded. I gave Angel her kiss and hug, kissed little Jayce and then my woman. She took them out the door. I sank back into my chair. Bull was nodding in approval.

"That's the way you should be. I always helped Harlow's mom when I was home. I had some of the best times with Harley when we were getting her ready for bed. The number of books I read that girl. And some of them over and over."

I laughed. "Angel is the same way. She loves her stories and my different voices. Though some of them I've read so many times, I think I could do them from memory."

Terror sat down and pulled Harlow onto his lap. She protested saying she was too heavy. He just grinned.

"Yeah, like you weigh that much. I can handle you." She laughed and then flinched, her hand going to her stomach. Bull sat up straight.

"What's wrong, baby girl?"

"Nothing, Dad. I've been having false labor pains for the last few days. They hurt but are false contractions. One just decided to hit me. I can't wait to actually go into real labor. I know I'm only thirty-six weeks but I'm ready. Dr. Hunter says I can have her anytime starting now without it causing problems with her breathing or other things. She might be a little smaller but that's it."

"Well, just be sure to take care of yourself. I'm anxiously waiting for the call to tell me she's on her way." She kissed his cheek.

Demon piped in, "Yeah, I want to see my niece. I wonder if she'll be as big of a pain in the ass as her mother?" Harlow flipped him the bird. Demon laughed at her and made kissy noises at her. Terror didn't blink. He knew Demon was like a brother to Harlow like I was, so he had nothing to worry about. I winked at Demon.

"I'm eager to meet my niece, too." Harlow was my best friend. A lot of people, mainly guys, thought it was weird for a guy to have a woman as his best friend and it be totally platonic. But that was the case with us. Sure, Harlow was beautiful, and I could appreciate that, but she'd never attracted me in a romantic way.

We teased her for a little bit longer until she said she was going to head to their house with Hunter. Terror was going to go with her, however, like Ashlee, Harlow insisted he stay and enjoy the others' company. She had Ms. Marie come with her to help get Hunter ready for bed. This late in her pregnancy, he was a little bit of a handful and she had to be tired. He promised they'd be there soon.

When Bull and his guys visited, he and Demon stayed at the house with Terror and Harlow. The rest stayed at the clubhouse. I looked at my watch. It was now after eight. The door opened and in came our club bunnies.

They would be busy tonight with all the extra single guys. I stayed until nine when the single guys began to pay more attention to the bunnies. All the married couples were leaving, so I said my goodnights and headed to the guest house.

I made sure I was quiet when I entered the house. I took my boots off inside the front door and went down the hall to our bedroom. Inside, Ashlee was lying on the bed freshly showered and, in a camisole and short set. That was her preferred night clothes. She'd confessed she'd rather go without any, but with Angel, she had to keep something on in case she came to the room in the middle of the night. I went over to the bed and gave her a kiss.

"Ash, let me take my shower, then I'll join you." She smiled.

"Hurry. I'll be waiting."

I rushed into the bathroom. Under ten minutes, I was done and strolling back into the bedroom. She'd turned off the lights and lit several candles. She was still lying on the bed, but now she was naked. The candlelight made her skin glow. She had such flawless skin that was a pale, cream color. Her nipples were a pale pinkish brown, and they were standing at attention. When she saw me standing in the doorway of the bathroom admiring her, she ran her hands down her body and then crooked her finger for me to come to her. I growled and charged across the bedroom to crawl up on the bed.

"Damn, babe, I didn't think you could get any more beautiful, but candles on your skin is gorgeous. I want to taste all this creamy flesh you have spread out here for me. I'm in the mood to feast." I kissed her mouth briefly then began my journey down her delectable body. I kissed and licked from her mouth to her ear, then down her neck. I stopped to nibble and lick her collarbone before working down to her breasts. There I spent several minutes lavishing attention on both of her gorgeous breasts with my mouth and hands. She was moaning and moving herself restlessly all over the bed.

When I was done with her breasts, I kissed and licked her skin down to her bellybutton where I teased it with the tip of my tongue. The skin below it was baby soft, and it led to my nirvana. I kissed along her C-section scar. With her skin being so pale, you could only see it as a faint pink scar. Soon it would be white and blend in with her other skin. Below it was her core. Her pussy was pale pink and glistening in the candlelight. My playing had turned her on. Ashlee raised her hips and pushed them toward my face.

"Please, Jack. Don't stop. I need you."

I pulled her hips off the bed more and buried my face in her sweet pussy. I kissed her clit and then sucked on it. She moaned. From there I worked to drive her up and over the edge into an orgasm. My goal every time I made love to her was to make sure she got at least two orgasms. I licked, sucked, nibbled, stroked, and fingered her folds, clit, and entrance until she came, wailing out her first release. She put her fist to her mouth to muffle it. I drew back.

"Babe, don't stifle your sounds or responses. No one will hear us. Hearing you getting so much pleasure from what I'm doing brings me pleasure. Now, why don't you give me that sweet mouth."

I crawled up to push a couple of pillows under her head then I straddled her head. "Suck my cock, Precious. It's dying for some attention from that hot, talented mouth of yours."

She laughed. Ashlee gripped me with one hand and began to massage my balls with the other as she sucked me into her mouth. In no time she had me ready to lose my mind.

She was sucking, licking, and nibbling all up and down my cock in between deep throating me and playing with my balls. I could feel my orgasm building. I didn't want to come in her mouth this time. I pulled back.

"No, not in your mouth. I need to be inside of you." I rolled off her and laid down on my back beside her. "Get on top, babe. I want you to ride me. I'm at your mercy." She rolled over and straddled my waist, then rubbed her wet pussy up and down my throbbing length. I groaned.

She kept teasing me until I grabbed her hips and lifted her up. The head of my cock was now rubbing her entrance and making her moan. "I need this pussy now." As I said it, I thrust my cock hard into her in one stroke. She whimpered and circled her hips with me buried to the max inside of her. This made me groan again.

She placed her hands on my chest and lifted herself up and then back down. As she got the feel for being in control of the speed and depth of my thrusts, she sped up. She was riding my cock faster and faster and coming down harder and harder. It drove my cock deep into her hot, tight pussy. Soon, I couldn't prevent myself from grasping her hips and helping to lift her up and then to slam her back down. She was panting and moaning with her head thrown back. Her eyes were closed, and a look of ecstasy was on her face. She was riding me like she was possessed.

I could feel the cum boiling in my balls. Bolts of lightning were shooting from my feet, up my legs and into my sac. I was close to shooting my load, and it felt like it was going to be a big one. I pulled her down, so I could reach her breasts. I sucked one into my mouth and bit down on her nipple as she continued to ride me.

As I did that, I also pinched her clit. She came screaming. Her ride got erratic, but she kept riding me as she came. Her muscles were milking my cock like a hundred mouths were sucking me dry. I roared and grunted as my load splashed inside of her pussy, coating her walls with my burning seed. I kept thrusting, mindlessly until my cock stopped jerking and she'd collapsed onto my chest. Then I switched to a slow, gentle glide in and out, while we caught our breaths and I went soft.

As I pulled out and opened up a gap between her chest and mine, I felt wetness. I looked down, and she wailed.

"Oh shit. I'm sorry, honey. Let me get a washcloth." I stopped her movements. Her breasts were leaking milk, and it had gotten all over my chest. I could tell she was embarrassed, but I also could see she was now feeling discomfort. Our play had caused her to release her milk and her breasts were hard. She'd told me once when they got like that, she had to either feed Jayce or pump them to relieve the pain and pressure.

I positioned her on her back and leaned over her. "Let me help you out here, baby." I lowered my head and pulled one of her nipples and the surrounding areolas into my mouth. Once it was in there, I began to suck. Her milk flowed into my mouth. I'd tasted her milk before, but never like this or this much. It was sweet and I drank it down. Some might be grossed out by this, but I wasn't. It kind of turned me on. She was moaning as I sucked and sucked. When her milk began to lessen, I moved over to her other nipple and sucked that breast. While I was finishing the second one, she stiffened and then shook as she had an orgasm from my attention.

I broke away and smiled at her. She had a sated look on her face. Tasting her milk and sucking her dry had reignited my arousal. My cock was hard again. I kneeled down and spread her thighs wide. She looked at me in surprise and then awe as she glanced down to see my hard cock. I lifted her hips and thrust inside of her.

Her inner tissues were swollen and if possible, even tighter. I thrust and thrust getting lost in the feel of her surrounding my cock. I wasn't sure how long I did this before she whimpered out another orgasm and I came groaning and spilling my cum again. I leaned over her, gliding in and out. I didn't want to lose our connection yet. I kissed her all over her face and chest. "God, I love you, Ashlee. You're perfect, baby. So perfect, sexy, gorgeous and mine. I want us to spend the rest of our lives together. Is that what you want?"

She gave me a startled look. "Of course, I do, Jack. I love you. I want to be with you until the day I die. Never doubt that." I gave her a hard kiss on her mouth.

"Good, then Ashlee, will you marry me?"

She gasped and her eyes searched mine. I held my breath. She reached up and took my face between her hands and drew my mouth down to hers. She gave me a hungry kiss. When she pulled back, she was smiling.

"I'd love to marry you, Jack Cannon."

I gave a whoop which made her laugh. I slowly pulled out of her body. I got off the bed and went to my cut in the closet. From the inside pocket, I took out a small box. I came back to the bed and sat down next to her. She'd sat up against the headboard. I opened the box. Inside, glittering in the candlelight, was an engagement ring. I'd bought it right after she'd agreed to be my old lady. I'd been waiting for the right time to give it to her. She cried out and put her hand over her mouth.

It had a central round diamond surrounded by small round deep blue sapphires which were surrounded by small round diamonds. The lady at the store had said this was an engagement ring with a double halo. The diamonds also ran halfway down the sides of the band. They were set in platinum. In total, the diamonds were one and a half carats and the sapphires were a half carat. I took it out of the box and raised an eyebrow. She held out her left hand. I could see she was shaking. I held her hand gently and slid it on her ring finger. It fit perfectly and looked beautiful on her delicate hand. I kissed the ring and then her.

"Precious, you just made me the happiest man alive. Thank you." She had tears in her eyes now. "What's wrong baby?" She shook her head.

"Nothing. Everything is perfect. I've never been this happy. I love you, Jack."

We spent a few minutes just kissing, snuggling, and looking at the ring on her finger. Finally, we got up and cleaned ourselves so we could get some sleep. I fell asleep happily holding my fiancée in my arms.

Chapter 11: Devil Dog

The next morning, we lazed around the house with the kids. We were in no hurry to leave our little family cocoon. It wasn't until noon that we finally gathered the kids and went to the clubhouse to see what the others were doing. Ashlee had said not to say anything about us getting engaged. At first, I was upset she didn't want to tell anyone until she told me why. She wanted to see how long it took for someone to notice her ring. We hadn't mentioned to Angel we were engaged. I was interested to see her response when she found out. As a three-year-old, she wasn't really paying attention to anything like a ring on her mom's finger.

Angel skipped ahead of us as we headed over to the clubhouse. She was excited to see everyone like always. I was carrying Jayce and holding Ash's hand when we entered. Angel had already spotted Rowan and had made a beeline for her. Most everyone seemed to be there including Bull and his guys. I figured they'd leave early afternoon to get back before nightfall. It was a three-hour drive back to Hunter's Creek for them.

Sherry came over to snatch Jayce away. Her and Tiny's boy, Sam, was almost two years old. I could see the gleam in her eye which I took to mean she wanted another one and Jayce was the youngest until Harlow's baby girl made her appearance.

I seated Ashlee at the table with Viking, Trish, Regan, Steel, Hammer, Ranger, Brielle, Harper, and Viper. Harper would be the next one to have one after Harlow. She was due at the end of March with their first baby. They'd found out last week they were going to have a boy. Neither had cared what they were having, but I knew Viper was thrilled to have a son first. He'd said something about having a son first so he could look after his younger siblings, especially if he had a sister or sisters. He liked to tease Harper they were going to have ten kids.

After Ashlee was seated, I went to grab both of us a bottle of water. She liked the flavored ones since she told me plain water held no appeal for her. I grabbed one that was peach and took them back to the table. She was chatting with Regan about something to do with the hospital and its website. She'd been busy working on revamping all our websites. I handed her the water. She thanked me and gave me a quick peck on the mouth.

I was asking Steel and Hammer about the guys laying the cement blocks for the basement this week. Ashlee pulled out her phone to show Regan something. Suddenly, Regan gasped and grabbed Ashlee's hand. She was staring at the hand with the engagement ring on it. She looked up at Ash.

"When did you get this and why didn't you say anything?"

Ashlee grinned. "I got it last night, and I wanted to see how long it would take for someone to notice. I was about to burst."

Regan tugged her into a hug. The guys and other old ladies at the table began to congratulate us. This attracted the others to come over and see what the commotion was about. Soon everyone was surrounding us. They were congratulating us and laughing. Angel wandered over to her mother.

"Mommy, what's wrong? Why is everyone so happy and loud?" Ash looked at me. I pulled Angel up onto my lap and then pulled Ashlee's hand toward us. I pointed to her ring.

"Do you know what this is sweetie?"

She said, "A ring."

"Yes, it's a ring but it's also a special one. This is called an engagement ring. I gave it to your mommy because I want to marry her. When you marry someone, it means you want to live with them forever. I want to marry your mommy and live with all of you forever. What do you think of that?" I was nervous to hear what she thought. She was three, so I was trying to make it simple enough for her to understand, though she was a bright kid like Rowan.

She was quiet for a couple of minutes. Her little forehead was furled in thought. She finally looked up at me. "Does this mean you'll be our daddy now?" I nodded. "Then we won't be going to live with my old daddy again?" I shook my head.

"No, honey, you won't ever live with him again. Are you happy I'm gonna marry your mommy and be your new daddy?"

She smiled and flung her arms around my neck. "I love you. I'm happy. Can I call you daddy now?" Her question made my heart flutter. I glanced at Ashlee. She was smiling with tears in her eyes. She gave me a nod.

"Yeah, Angel you can call me daddy if you want. If not, Devil or Jack is okay. Whatever you want." She hugged me tighter.

"I want to call you daddy. You're nice not like the other one. He was mean to Mommy, and he hit her. You won't hit us."

Her observations made me want to cry. She knew abuse at three. "No, honey, I won't ever hit your mommy or you or your brother. I promise." She gave me a kiss on the cheek and pulled away to hop down.

"I have to go tell my brother you're our new daddy!" She went over to Sherry and started talking to Jayce like he could understand her. Several of the women had tears in their eyes. Hell, I could feel them wanting to well up in mine. Ashlee was now crying and smiling. I pulled her out of her chair and onto my lap so I could hug and kiss her. Terror called for everyone to have a drink. The whole bunch along with the Hunter's Creek's guys toasted us.

The next couple of hours passed in a blur of conversations. Bull and his guys headed out around two. We saw them off with wishes to have a safe trip. When we got back inside the clubhouse, the ladies drew Ashlee away to talk about a wedding. We hadn't discussed when we wanted to get married. I needed to talk to her. I wanted to do it as soon as we could, which meant we had to get

Alex out of her life. I looked at Terror.

"We need to get Alex out of the picture as soon as possible. Either she's divorced from him or he's gone. You know my preference. I don't want to wait forever to marry her. If I could, I'd make her Ashlee Dawn Cannon tomorrow. I'm gonna talk to her and get her preparing for the wedding even if we don't have a date yet. I need to talk to Dyson tomorrow and see where we are on the divorce."

Terror nodded. "I agree. We'll find out the status of the filing and then decide what and when. I don't think he'll go quietly or permanently either. Not without our help. I'm so glad to see you two so happy. I knew you'd be asking her soon."

I nodded. "Yeah, I've had it for weeks waiting for what I thought was the right time. Last night it was right."

The other guys all chimed in. The rest of the day and evening passed quickly with our family. That night, I again fell asleep with my arms around the woman I loved with our children sleeping safely down the hall.

It was Halloween. The older kids were excited and so were the adults. Since we didn't let people freely into the compound and we had no close neighbors, we were taking the kids trick or treating in town. We'd keep the spa open like some of the other stores and give out our candy there.

The weather wasn't too cold, so even little Jayce would be going. The women had found all the kids costumes, even the babies. We planned to go as a large group. The guys with old ladies would be with their wives and kids with a couple extra guys for additional security. The prospects were back at the compound. We had fourteen guys, nine women and twelve kids in our group.

Harlow insisted she was coming, so Terror ordered Capone to drive one of the SUVs and follow us around in case she got tired or if one of the kids needed it. Ms. Marie, and some of the employees at the spa were giving out the candy for us. Storm and Torch had agreed to watch over them.

Angel was so excited to go. Ashlee explained that Alex had never let her take her before, but she'd always watched all the kids out the window doing it. Her costume was that of the blonde princess, Elsa, from the movie *Frozen.* She had naturally blond hair like her mommy, and it hung to the middle of her back. The costume looked exactly like what she wore in the movies. It was the blue winter dress with white fur around the neck. What made it even more fantastic is Ashlee had made it for her!

I had no idea she could sew and do it so well. She'd confessed she learned it from her mom and that she used to make a lot of her own clothes, particularly dresses. The other women were so impressed, they begged her to do their kids' costumes next year. They said they'd pay her for doing them. I could tell it pleased her they loved it so much. I knew she hadn't had any positive reinforcement of her talents until she came to us. I planned for her to get a whole lot more.

We were working our way through one of the bigger and nicer neighborhoods. This one alone would bring the kids in a nice haul and exhaust them. We started at one end and we're working our way to the other. We were over halfway through. The kids were getting a huge amount of candy. I could see a lot of rationing and bikers eating candy for a while.

We were crossing one of the streets when a dark car came darting out of the driveway of a darkened house. The headlights flared on suddenly which blinded me. I heard the engine rev and then the car was headed right for us. Ashlee, the kids and I had been straggling at the end of the group because Angel's shoe had come untied and we stopped so I could tie it. I'd told the others to keep going and we'd catch up.

I yelled at Ashlee to run while I grabbed Angel. I raced toward the opposite sidewalk with her in my arms. Ashlee was running with Jayce. I could hear the women screaming and the guys yelling. I came up behind Ashlee and wrapped her in my arms as best as I could with Angel already in them. Jayce got tucked into my chest with his sister, as I dove to the ground and rolled with them. The car went roaring by, barely missing us. I laid there for a minute trying to process what had just happened. It was the cries of Angel, Ashlee, and Jayce that shook me back to awareness. I'd landed on my back so as not to crush them, but I did have to roll with them. I couldn't pull Ashlee in close enough. Now I was worried I'd hurt them.

Hands were helping Ashlee up and then Angel. Jayce was screaming in her arms. I could see blood running down Ashlee's face from a laceration at her hairline. Regan was taking Jayce away from Ashlee so she could check him out. She was a nurse practitioner after all. Janessa was looking Angel over while Ghost checked on

Ashlee. He had her sitting down on the curb. Terror came over to see if I needed any help. I told him I was fine. I stood up and hovered protectively over my family.

"Are they okay?" I asked anxiously. Janessa, Regan, and Ghost all looked at me.

"I think they are, but let's get them back to the compound so we can check them out better," Regan said. Ghost and Janessa were nodding in agreement with the plan.

I looked around for our car. It was idling at the curb with Harlow sitting in the front passenger seat looking pale. I asked Regan and Janessa to carry the kids to the car and I swept Ashlee up into my arms and carried her myself. We'd brought several vehicles to transport all of us. The others were parked back where we'd started trick or treating. The rest of our group headed that way to retrieve them, so they could head back too. Ashlee, Angel, Jayce, Ghost, Regan, and I rode in the SUV with Harlow and Capone. Ashlee was now holding Jayce and rocking back and forth. I tried to talk to her to see if she was okay, but she just stared off and stayed silent. She was starting to worry me.

We made it back to the compound in record time. Someone must have called them to say we were coming and why. Jordan was waiting at the gate with his gun and Tanner at the door to the clubhouse armed as well. They always were but kept them out of sight. Not tonight.

The others were right behind us pulling in as we got my family through the door into the well-lit common room. Ms. Marie was somehow here, and she had out the large medical kit we had. We took them to the couches.

Ashlee was following some commands but kind of like a robot. She was clutching Jayce to her chest, and she had latched onto Angel's hand and wouldn't let go. Angel had calmed down and so had Jayce.

I crouched down in front of her. "Babe, I need you to let go of the kids so they can be checked out. You need to be checked, too." She didn't do anything. I gently grasped her shoulders and gave her a tiny shake. She looked at me dully.

"Precious, give me the kids. They're safe. Let us check them out. Please, baby." She relaxed her arms and Regan took Jayce while Janessa took Angel. This left Ghost once again with Ashlee. He started to check her head and arms. As he worked, I started to notice other things. Besides the laceration to the forehead, she had scrapped her cheek, her shirt was ripped, and her arm was bleeding, and so was her leg, all on the one side.

I was torn between trying to check on all of them at the same time. Luckily, they kept them all in the same general area. As Ghost worked, I tore myself away to check on Jayce and Angel. Regan looked up at me.

"As far as I can see, Devil, he doesn't have a mark on him. You and Ashlee protected him. I don't think he needs to go to the hospital." I breathed a sigh of relief. I went over to Janessa next. She smiled.

"She seems to be fine, Devil. Like Jayce, there's not a mark on her or any indication she hit her head." This was another relief. Finally, I could go back to Ghost. He'd cut Ashlee's sleeve and her pant leg to look at her wounds. Her arm had a deep cut with dirt and debris in it. It looked like it needed stitches. Her leg was more like road rash than a laceration, so it would only need to be cleaned. Ghost gestured for me to come to him.

"Devil, from what I can see, physically it's her head laceration, her arm laceration and the road rash to her leg. I felt her head, and she doesn't have any lumps indicating she hit her head. She didn't flinch when I palpated the other areas of her body other than her ribs a little on that same side. I think they may be bruised. My worry is she seems to be in shock and not snapping back yet. I don't think she needs to go to the hospital, but she needs to be treated now. I need to get an IV in her for fluids and as a precaution put her on oxygen. Also, I want to make sure she has adequate blood flowing to all her vital organs. I'm gonna administer her a vasoconstrictor. Her blood pressure is too low. If she doesn't show improvement within an hour, we need to take her to the ER." His assessment made my heart race.

I knew people could go into shock and die, though usually it was due to blood loss. Could they die from just shock? "Do whatever you think is best." He nodded and already had an IV kit out. Regan and Janessa came over. Regan was drawing up medication while Janessa had covered her with a blanket, elevated her feet, and put her on a small portable oxygen machine Ghost had. Ghost had the IV in and had hung a bag of fluids within two minutes.

Ash remained pale and clammy. Ghost said her pulse was rapid but weak and her blood pressure was low. I could see the concern on all three faces. I shook my head.

"Don't wait an hour. I can see you guys are worried. Let's

take her now." They nodded. Ms. Marie got the kids in the car. Since we were going, I'd feel better if they were checked too just to be safe. Within five minutes, we were on our way. As we raced there, I held Ashlee. She was in and out of awareness and shaking in my arms. I kissed her.

"You're gonna be fine, babe. I promise. Hang in there for me. Please."

Ghost skidded to a stop outside the ER. Janessa must have called ahead because we were met at the door. They swept all three of them to the back. Janessa went with them. They'd let her back there and tell her stuff since she worked in their ER.

Twenty minutes later, she came back out. She reassured me they were testing all three. It still seemed like the kids had come out without a scratch. Ashlee, on the other hand, was in shock and they weren't sure yet if it was only psychological or something more. Maybe an internal injury we couldn't see. I paced the waiting room. Most of the club had followed, though some had to stay behind to help with the other kids.

Terror had come with Harlow. I tried to get her to go home, but she refused. At the hour-and-a-half mark, the nurse came out to say the kids were fine and they would be releasing them, but they were still checking out Ash. When they brought out the kids, Jayce was crying, and Angel looked scared and tired.

Alannah said she'd take them back to the compound. I thanked her profusely. Jayce was probably hungry, so I told her he had breast milk at home in the fridge. Menace helped her take them after I held and kissed both of them. Angel protested and wanted to stay and take care of her mommy. I talked her into leaving with only a few tears falling down her face.

Janessa kept checking for me and I paced even more. At the three-hour mark I was about to tear the ER apart if they didn't let me see her or tell me something. Finally, out came Dr. Schramm. Janessa and Regan worked with him. He called for Ashlee's family and I stepped forward with the club behind me. He greeted those he knew and then he looked at me. "Ashlee is in stable condition right now. Thanks to the quick thinking someone had to treat her with the fluids, a vasoconstrictor, and O2. We stitched her lacerations and cleaned her road rash. We also ran several tests. It appears when she hit the pavement, she took a powerful hit to her left lower abdomen. This caused her to injure her spleen resulting in bleeding. This is what caused her to go into shock." His words struck me with fear. I knew people have died due to internal bleeding from their spleen.

He continued, "Thankfully, it looks like we may not need to do surgery. The injury while worrisome isn't severe. I think it can heal on its own with enough rest. We'll put her in ICU tonight and monitor her. If the bleeding increases or she gets worse, we'll need to take her into surgery to remove her spleen. She's not with it enough to make decisions due to the pain medications I have her on. Are you the one who will be making those decisions if she can't?" He was looking at me.

I nodded. "Yes, I'm her fiancé. I'll sign whatever you need if it becomes necessary. Can I see her?"

He nodded. "Just for a few minutes. Once she gets to the

ICU, you can see her one at a time. Just don't tire her out."

I thanked him.

He took me back with him. She was lying in one of those awful beds with tubes and machines hooked all over her. She seemed to be out of it. I looked at the doctor.

"She's sedated. The pain from the trauma finally started to kick in so I have her on a pain drip. She might open her eyes if you talk to her but don't expect her to talk much." He left me with her.

I sat down and took her hand. "Precious, it's Jack. Babe, I need you to open those beautiful eyes and look at me, so I know you're alright. You scared the shit out of me. I'm so damn sorry I couldn't keep you from getting hurt. Fuck, babe, I'm scared." I felt her fingers move and when I looked up, she had cracked her eyes open. She was looking at me. I stood up. "Hi, babe." She tried to talk. I leaned down so I could hear her.

"Not your fault. Don't worry. Love you," she whispered. I closed my eyes then opened them to kiss her.

"I know it is, but we'll talk later. Right now, you concentrate on getting well. The kids are both fine. Not one scratch. I love you, Ashlee. So fucking much, babe." She gave me a tiny smile and then slipped back into dreamland. I sat there for a few minutes until a nurse came to have me leave so they could move her to the ICU. I went back to the waiting room.

The club was still there waiting for me. I explained what the doctor had told me. A part of me was relieved she didn't need surgery but another worried it could go wrong, and I'd lose her if they didn't just go ahead and remove her spleen. Janessa took us up to the ICU waiting room and then me to the nurses' station. The charge nurse reassured me she'd come get me as soon as Ashlee was brought up and they got her situated. I knew I wasn't going anywhere with her in here.

As we waited, I looked at Terror. "We need to find out who was driving that car. It doesn't feel like an accident. The driver headed straight for us. There's no way he couldn't see us. My gut says it was Alex. I need to find out for sure."

He nodded. "I already talked to Smoke and asked him to get on finding any cameras that might be in the area to see if they caught anything. What you need to do is take care of Ashlee and yourself. We'll make sure the kids are alright. I assume you're planning to stay tonight." I gave him a look. He just grinned and held up his hands in surrender.

"I know, dumb question. What I want to know is do you want some guards? If you're right about the driver, it was intentional, and the person might try again."

He did have a good point, and I'd like to think I could keep her safe, but even I might fall asleep or have to use the bathroom.

"Have one guy stand guard outside her room if you will. I'll be her main guard and he can back me up." Terror agreed. Everyone got ready to leave now that they knew what her status was. They would be back in the morning. When they left, Blaze was left behind as the guard.

"Thank you, brother, for staying. I appreciate it." He

shrugged.

"You would do the same thing if it was me and my old lady. It's what we do. We protect our own. Now, why don't you go and relax. I'll be outside."

I did as he suggested entering the room to sit at her bedside. She was still sedated, so I watched her sleep and prayed she'd be alright. Throughout the night, her nurse would come in and check on her, administer meds, or assess her. They didn't put up a fuss about me staying or Blaze in the hallway. The Warriors had done this several times when something happened to one of our family members.

It was early the next morning when a different doctor came in to see Ashlee. He explained they were going to do another MRI to see if the bleeding had stopped or not. If not, they would go ahead with the surgery. I escorted them to the x-ray department and stood outside while they checked her out. Not long after we returned to her room, the doctor came in.

Ashlee had woken up somewhat. "Good news, the MRI shows the bleeding has stopped. We'll want to keep you a couple of days to be sure it doesn't restart. You'll need to take it easy for a few weeks until you completely heal. If you do that, you should be back to normal, Ms. Andrews."

"Thank you, doctor. That's good news," Ashlee told him.

"Yes, it is. Thank you," I added. Relief was coursing through me. She wasn't out of the woods yet, but it looked like she soon would be. He waved off our thanks as he left to continue his rounds.

"Babe, how are you feeling?" I asked her worriedly. She seemed to be in pain.

"I'm okay, Jack. I feel like my whole body is one big bruise and the pain in my lower stomach and back are the worst." I pointed to her call button.

"Call the nurse so they can give you more pain meds." She shook her head no.

"Not yet. I don't like how they knock me out. I want to talk to you first. What happened with the car that almost hit us? Did anyone find out who it was? Was it Alex? Are the kids okay?" I had to stop her. I could see her getting more and more upset.

"Slow down, Ash. First, the kids are fine, and the club is taking care of them for us. Second, we don't know if it was Alex or not. Third, Smoke is working to see if he can find cameras nearby that may have caught something. All I'm worried about right now is you getting better. You could have died from this, Precious. I can't live without you." She took my hand as I leaned down to kiss her. She really had become the center of my life, her and the kids.

After we talked, she did call the nurse for more pain meds and drifted off soon after it was administered. Around ten o'clock, Terror showed up. I went to talk to him while another brother, Hawk, stood sentry. Terror took me to an empty conference room. After I told him how she was doing, he updated me on what they had found.

"We've determined the car didn't belong to the owner of the house it came barreling out of. Smoke found out the guy who does live there wasn't even home last night. The car ended up parking there right after we got to the neighborhood and started our walk through it from the other end. Smoke did some other checking and says he found footage showing the same car had sat outside of the compound yesterday. It had to have seen us all leave. He probably followed us looking for an opportunity. Smoke's gonna look back further to see if it has staked us out before or not. The only thing we can't determine is if it was Alex. The windows are too dark, and conveniently it has no license plates we can have run. I can't say with certainty it was him, Devil Dog, but my gut thinks it was just like you do. I sent guys to his house to see what they can find out."

I paced the room. I could feel the anger rushing through my veins. Terror sat silent and let me pace. Finally, I calmed down enough to speak. "I want to know the second they find something. It had to be him, Terror. There's no one else who would have reason to go after her and the kids. Alex Andrews is enough of a sick bastard. He'd want to kill her and his own kids rather than let them go. She didn't comply with his order to come back to him by the end of last week. This has to be in retaliation for not doing it. We'll catch him, then he's a dead man." Terror nodded his head in agreement. We went back to her room.

Throughout the day, members and old ladies came to see her. They updated us on the kids. Both were too young to be allowed in the ICU. Ashlee was worried because Jayce would now have to be on formula. Even if she could pump, her milk would be full of pain meds and that wouldn't be good for him. Being away from them stressed her out. I hoped the time in here was short. Otherwise, she might go crazy and me along with her.

Chapter 12: Ashlee

It was hard to believe it was almost two weeks to the day since the Halloween incident. I'd ended up spending five days in the hospital which almost drove me insane. Devil had stayed with me the whole time, never letting me out of his sight. Even being back at the compound for over a week, he was hovering. This morning I finally threatened him if he didn't go work at the garage. He'd done it, though reluctantly. He was calling every hour checking on me.

I was spending time working on the websites and watching the kids. It was the only thing Devil would allow me to do. I couldn't lift more than Jayce, so someone was always with me to help. Today it was Ms. Marie. She and I were talking about what ideas I had for our wedding. It was still unreal for me to think of marrying Devil Dog. I wanted to marry him more than anything, but I couldn't until Alex was out of the picture.

"Think positive and go ahead with these wedding plans, dear. The shit with Alex will work itself out. You know the Warriors will make sure of it. Now, let's see how much of Devil's money we can spend." She said with glee. I laughed. She did lift my spirits, even if I didn't plan to bankrupt him with a huge, expensive wedding.

Harlow had stopped by to see how I was doing. She was due in four days and I could tell she was miserable. She was lying on my couch with her feet propped up as we all three talked about weddings.

I looked at them. "Now don't you dare laugh, but I always imagined a princess wedding. Like in the movies Angel loves. The big dress with lots of sparkle, fancy setting with lots of lights, candles, tulle, and flowers. The colors would be sapphire and midnight blue with pops of fuchsia mainly in the flowers. And of course, the tiara," I joked. They were both staring at me. "What," I asked? Harlow grinned.

"I love it! We haven't had anything like a princess wedding yet or in those colors. We could do so much with those. If that's what you want, then let's do it!" I held up a hand.

"Harlow, don't you think I should ask Devil what he wants?" She shook her head.

"No. Because he'll say he wants whatever makes you happy. They all do. He loves you, so I say have the wedding of your dreams." Ms. Marie was nodding in agreement. I felt excitement bubbling up. When I'd married Alex, we'd gone to the courthouse. This time I wanted the real thing. This would be forever after all.

We'd been looking at things online for over an hour when I noticed Harlow had grimaced again. I stopped. "Harlow, are you in labor?" I knew the signs having had two myself. She gave a slow nod.

"Yeah, I think it's for real this time and not those damn Braxton-Hicks ones. Maybe I should call Terror." I laughed.

"Do you think? He'll go nuts if you don't. So, call him already then we'll get you to the hospital." She pulled out her phone. Terror had gone into town to check on the bar. Hunter was playing with Angel in the living room, so we could keep an eye on them. While Harlow talked to Terror, who was apparently a little anxious, I got the kids settled with a snack. I knew Ghost was at the garage on the compound working on bikes as usual, so I called him. I had all the club members programmed in my phone courtesy of Devil. Ghost picked up on the second ring.

"Hey, Ashlee, what can I do for you, sweetheart? Are you doing okay?" They all had been checking on my health constantly.

"Ghost, I'm fine. But we're pretty sure Harlow is in labor. Can you come to the guesthouse and check her? She called Terror so he should be headed back home." He sounded more serious.

"I'll be there in five. Tell her to lie down and put up her feet if she hasn't already." He clicked off the phone before I could say anything else. I turned to her.

"Ghost is coming. It sounds like Terror is returning. Have you timed them?" She nodded.

"They're coming every six minutes." I sighed in relief.

"Okay, we have time. Once they get to under five minutes, we need to be at the hospital because you're definitely dilating and effacing by then. It could go quick or slow. Depends upon you." Ms. Marie was sitting with her holding her hand. I heard a knock and I called out. Ghost came through the door with his medical bag. He went to Harlow and started to assess her and ask questions. Sometimes I thought he was wasted as a custom bike builder. He should have been a doctor. I thought I heard the faint roar of bikes, but I couldn't be sure. Harlow had just had another contraction when Terror followed by Devil Dog came bursting through the door. He ran right over to her. Devil came to me. I gave him a kiss. After we parted, he glanced at Harlow.

"How is she doing?" I told him what I knew. Terror was calling Tanner, one of the prospects, to bring one of the club's SUVs to the guest house. He also ordered him to stop at his house and grab the bag in the front entry closet. It was Harlow's go bag for the hospital. As we waited, Ghost kept Terror calm. Usually, I saw him as this larger than life, stoic guy. But when it came to Harlow or Hunter, he showed more of his soft side. He really loved them.

In less than five minutes, Tanner was at the door. Terror insisted on carrying Harlow out to the car. I assured her, me and Ms. Marie would look after Hunter. I looked at Devil Dog. He was one of Harlow's best friends and I could see he was anxious.

"Honey, go with them. I know you want to be there. I'll stay here with Hunter and you can keep me updated." I could see he was torn but I pushed him toward the door.

He gave me a big kiss and whispered, "thank you babe," before he ran out the door to get his bike. The next few hours seemed to crawl by. All of the club had been notified and a lot of them were at the hospital. Some stayed behind to watch kids like me and Ms. Marie.

Devil kept me updated and said Bull was called and should be there soon. Hunter asked a few times for his mom and dad, but we were able to distract him. Dinner time came and we all ate. The last update was Harlow was at eight centimeters and seventy-five percent effaced. Baby Moran should be here before midnight easily.

By eight thirty all three kids were bathed and in bed asleep. Hunter thought it was cool to get to sleep over. He got along really well with Angel. He was sleeping in her room with her. I told Ms. Marie she could go home and rest. I sat down on the couch to relax and worked on my designs to distract myself. I wished I could be there, but I knew someone had to stay with the kids. Harlow was the one I was closest too out of all the ladies, even though all of them were friendly and accepted me into the club.

It was almost ten when Devil called to say she had the baby. Terror was now the proud father of a little girl. They had decided to name her Emerson Rose Moran. She weighed six-pound twelve ounces and was nineteen and a half inches long. He also said she had auburn peach fuzz for hair and her eyes were bright blue. The hair definitely came from Harlow. The eyes, if they became more violet, would be hers too rather than Terror's blue. He promised to be home soon.

As I waited, I thought about what the club had found out since my accident. Or should I say what wasn't happening. From what Devil had told me, the club had staked out Alex's house and business. He hadn't been home, and the store was closed. The sign said for renovations, but no one had been seen coming or going. They were sure he was the one to try and run us down. So was I. The question now was, where did he go? They had some kind of programs looking for him that Smoke wrote. I needed to talk to him and learn more about these types of programs he used.

I got up to make a hot cup of tea when my phone rang. I grabbed it thinking it must be Devil again. I didn't look to check. After I said hello, Alex's voice came over the phone.

"So, you think you can defy me, bitch. You still haven't learned your lesson. You're my wife. You'll stay my wife. No judge is going to tell me I have to give you up. Just remember Ashlee, things could have been different if you'd listened. Now it will be your fault." He hung up. I was shaking. It was then that Devil came through the front door. His entrance startled me, and I yelled out, dropping my cup of tea. He rushed over to me.

"Babe, I didn't mean to scare you. Are you alright?" I shook my head no. He was now looking at me worriedly.

"No, I'm not. Alex just called me again, Jack. He's making threats." His jaw clenched and he bit out,

"What did the bastard say?" I repeated it for him. His face darkened. He led me to the couch and told me to sit. He was pulling out his phone. I tried to stop him. "Don't bother anyone tonight. We just had Emerson, and everyone is tired and happy. I don't want to dampen the good mood." He paused.

"Okay, I won't tell Terror yet, but I will let Savage know and Smoke. Savage is our VP, he's in charge when Terror is gone. They need to know, babe." I agreed. He started calling.

Within ten minutes I had Savage, Smoke, and Viper in the house. They sat down and asked me to tell them word for word what Alex said. As I did, Smoke was messing around with my phone and a laptop he brought. I scooted over to watch after I told them what he'd said. "What are you doing, Smoke?" He smiled.

"I didn't think he'd call again because we changed your phone number. Obviously, he's finding out some way, so it's likely he'll call again. I want to be able to trace it when he does. I've set it up on CCSS7. If he calls again, I can track his location based on his mobile phone's mast triangulation. I've been running programs looking into his usual electronic footprint. So far he's been careful not to trip it." I nodded in understanding. Viper, Devil, and Savage were looking at us frowning. Savage was the one to speak.

"Ashlee, do you understand all that shit he was saying?" I shrugged.

"Sure. He's gonna use the network interchange service which is like a broker between mobile phone networks. When Alex makes a call or texts using this, he can track his location, read his texts and record and listen to his phone calls. The other is looking for him to do other things online like use a bank card, his social security number, or other identification markers. He's not taking money out to register at hotels or anything. At least not under his real name. Right Smoke?" Smoke was grinning. He looked at Devil.

"Are you sure you want her because I think I'm in

love? She speaks my language." He looked at me and winked. "Run away with me, woman. We're soulmates," he teased. Devil growled.

"Get your geek mind off my woman. She's smart, sexy, gorgeous and all mine." Smoke laughed.

After all of us stopped laughing, we got serious again. I told all of them. "Alex is up to something. He's not going to let this go. I'm just not sure what he's going to try next. Don't underestimate him. He either knew things I didn't, or he had help because he found me every time I ran. And I was careful to not use cards, my real name, or anything else he could have used to trace me, but he still found me." Smoke chimed in.

"Is he computer savvy?" I shook my head.

"Not that I ever saw. If his laptop gave him trouble, he'd give it to me to figure it out. He had no patience for it." Savage looked at Devil.

"Then he has help. What about the Police Chief in Mary-ville, that you said he's friends with? It might be better if we staked him out. He might lead us to Alex." Devil and Smoke agreed. It was after midnight when they left vowing, they'd find him.

I wearily jumped in the shower. Devil got in and washed me before carrying me and tucking me in bed. He kissed me. "Babe, you need to get some sleep. Relax and I'll be back. I just want to wash myself." I nodded. That was the last thing I remember.

The following morning, I woke up to find the bed

empty. I looked at the clock. It was eight! Jayce should have gotten up for his feedings twice by now and Angel should be up asking for her breakfast. I jumped out of bed, throwing on some clothes to race to their rooms. Both were empty but I could hear voices coming from the kitchen. I walked in to find Angel and Hunter finishing their breakfast. Devil had Jayce on his lap as he talked to Angel. He looked up and smiled when he saw me. I went and gave Angel, Hunter, and Jayce a kiss then Devil. "Good morning. Why didn't you wake me up, Jack?"

"Because you needed the sleep, babe. You're still healing from the accident. Plus, you watched Hunter most of the day and was up late talking to the guys. You needed it. Why don't you finish getting ready and I'll get these monsters wiped down and dressed? Ms. Marie is going to get all three of them in about thirty minutes. We're going to the hospital so you can see Emerson."

I was thrilled to go see her and Emerson. "You're sure you don't need help with these three?" He just made shooing motions toward me. I took the hint. I went and washed my face, put on light makeup, and tamed my hair into its usual shoulder-length bob.

I slipped into jeans, boots, and a top. I was just putting in my earrings when Devil came in with the kids, so I could give them a kiss. I kissed them and went out to see them off with Ms. Marie. After they left, I grabbed my jacket and do-rag, so I could ride on the bike. I knew that was what we'd be taking to the hospital.

When we got to the hospital, I almost ran to the maternity floor. We had to sign in and get electronic armbands. We got to Harlow's room and knocked. Terror called for us to come in. Sitting in bed looking much too good for someone who'd had a baby about twelve hours ago, was Harlow. In her arms was a little bundle wrapped in pink. I hugged Terror and congratulated him then went to Harlow while Devil greeted Terror. She smiled and held out her arms. I took Emerson in my arms. She felt so light after Jayce. I could see the red hair Devil had mentioned. I teased Harlow. "I see there's another redhead in the Warriors."

She groaned. "God help us all. Terror said she looks like and will most likely act like me, so I'm gonna apologize to everyone in advance. She'll be a hellion." We laughed and Devil came over and examined her again as I held her. He looked at Harlow.

"When will she get her first gun?"

Harlow winked and said "eight." Terror spoke up.

"Emerson doesn't need the gun. Daddy will. To kill all those horny guys who'll come around. If we home-school her, they would never know she exists." Harlow shot him a frown and shook her head no.

"I assume Bull has seen her?" Harlow chuckled and told me to unwrap Emerson. I did and she was in a onesie that said, *Grandpa's Little Princess.*

 She explained, "He brought it with him last night on the bike. Insisted she had to wear it today. He went to get some coffee and a bite to eat. He's in heaven. How did Hunter do last night? He stayed with you right?"

"He did great. He and Angel played, watched a few cartoons, and then he slept in her room. They're with Ms.

Marie right now." They both thanked me for watching him. "There's no need to thank me. I was glad to do it." As I got done telling them this, Bull and Demon walked in.

Bull greeted us but he had eyes only for Emerson. I handed her over to her smitten grandpa. We stayed for a little longer. Long enough to be entertained by Demon and Bull arguing with each other that the other one was hogging the baby. Devil and I left them to debate. We gave hugs and kisses before leaving.

Back outside Devil Dog said he thought we should go to the Fallen Angel for lunch. I realized I was hungry. We headed over there. Inside they were rather busy, but we were seated in the reserved booth. In no time I was eating the best burger I'd ever tasted. We were talking about anything and everything. It was really nice to get away with just Devil.

When we were done, he asked if it was okay to stop by the garage. I told him yes. I'd not seen the new one they had taken over in town. As we pulled in, out came Viper and Hawk. Both of them didn't look happy. We got off the bike and went over to speak to them. Devil Dog was the one to ask what was wrong. "What's wrong? You two look like you could kill someone."

Viper growled. "It's that damn, Cody. He was on close last night. He was supposed to finish that Camry, so he could start on the Explorer first thing this morning. And he was to be here and open at seven. Well, we rolled in around seven forty-five and no Cody. He finally came wandering in around eight thirty. That's when he in-formed us, he didn't finish the Camry. We're behind and have more coming. He doesn't stay on task. His work when he does it is good. But being on time or working on a schedule to be productive is not his forte. I don't think he's gonna survive past ninety days."

"Did he say why he didn't finish it or why he was late?" Devil asked with a frown. Hawk answered this time.

"No. Just said he didn't get it done and as for why he was late. He said he had shit to take care of. I wanted to take a pipe wrench to his head." He growled. I had to stifle my laugh. Devil was looking concerned. He wasn't supposed to be working today but by the sounds of it, they needed him. I tugged on his arm.

"Honey, call Tanner or Jordan to come get me and you stay and work." He shook his head.

"No babe. I promised I'd spend the day with you."

"Well then you can make it up to me another day. The garage needs you. It's fine. I'll work on finishing another website and look after the kids. Nothing strenuous. I insist." Hawk and Savage were calling me a godsend. Devil finally gave in and he called Tanner to come get me. I went inside to watch him while I waited. I could see the guy who must be Cody. He was prancing around. I'd gone to get a soda in the office and was coming back out to the bays when he cornered me.

"Hey baby, what's a hot piece of ass like you doing around here? I haven't seen you before. Are you a new bunny for the club? If so, I need to see about getting me some of your sweet ass. Damn you're sexy as hell." I was stunned. Then I remembered I'd put on my jacket over my property cut. I stared at him saying nothing while

I tugged off my jacket. When it was removed, I turned around so he could see the back. His eyes got huge and he backed away.

"Fuck, I'm sorry. I didn't know you were anyone's old lady let alone Devil Dog's," he sputtered. That was the moment when Devil's hand landed on his shoulder. Cody swung around.

"If I ever see or hear you talk to any woman like that again, I'll beat your ass into the pavement. Understand?" Cody nodded and then scurried off to work on a truck. I laughed.

"Honey, I think you made him piss his pants. What a little creep. I hope you guys find someone else. He doesn't strike me as Warrior approved." Ghost agreed. Soon after Tanner pulled into the parking lot. I gave Devil a kiss and headed to the car. He promised he'd be home by six for dinner. I waved at the other guys as we left.

Back at the compound, I stayed busy for the remainder of the afternoon. While the kids napped, I did some laundry and got dinner prepped. It was almost five when my phone rang. I checked it before answering. It was the prospect Tanner. I answered it.

"Hi Tanner. I'm surprised you're calling. What do you need?" He cleared his throat.

"There is a man at the gate insisting he has papers he has to give only to you. Can you come down to the front gate, please?" I told him to give me a couple minutes. When I hung up, I called Sherry.

"Sherry, can you come over and watch the kids for a couple minutes? Apparently, I have someone at the gate." She said she would send Tiny over. I thanked her.

Tiny was at the door in two minutes. I told him why I needed him and reassured him it would take only a couple of minutes. He told me to take my time. As I walked to the gate, I wondered who it was. Surely it wasn't Alex. Would he be that dumb to violate the restraining order again? Tanner was waiting. He walked with me to the small entrance side door. He went out with me and stood mostly in front of me. I knew he wanted to make sure he protected me. The guy standing there was in a suit and someone I didn't recognize. I nodded in greeting.

"Hello. How can I help you?" He just looked at me without any kind of expression.

"Are you Ashlee Andrews?" I nodded yes. "Here," he handed me an envelope. "You've been served. Have a good day." With this said, he turned and shot to his car. All I could do was look down at the envelope stunned.

Tanner took me gently by the arm and led me back inside, so he could shut and lock the door. "I don't want you out there Ashlee. It might not be safe. What did he give you?" I shrugged and tore it open. As I read my heart beat faster and faster. When I was done, I thought I was going to faint. Tanner led me to the "guard shack" as they called the little hut they had by the gate. He was texting and grabbing me some water. I sat there stunned.

I didn't know how long I sat there before I heard the roar of bikes. I looked at the clock on the wall and saw it was five thirty. In through the gate flew Devil, Savage, Hawk, and Torch. They stopped right inside the gate in front of the shack. Devil jumped off his bike and came over to me.

"Precious, what is it? Tanner texted some guy dropped off an envelope and when you read it, he thought you were going to faint. What is it?" I handed the envelope to him as I sat speechless. He read it. When he was done, he was swearing and looked ready to kill. The others asked him what was wrong. He answered.

"It was a summons to appear in court. Apparently, Alex is not withdrawing his request for divorce, but adding an accusation of adultery, which is considered fault-grounds for divorce. This isn't good news. I know it has to have some really bad implications. I need to get Dyson over here to look at it and tell us what we're now facing." He turned to me. "It's okay, babe. We'll get through this. Let me call Dyson and then we'll go to the house."

The next several minutes were a blur. I didn't really recall how I got to the house. Tiny was there and he spoke to Devil. I vaguely saw him take Jayce and Angel with him. I sat on the couch numb. Alex was doing this, and I knew it was because it was something terrible. I was pulled from my daze by Devil.

"Ash, babe, Dyson is here. Let's see what he has to say." I looked up to realize my living room was full of Warriors and the club lawyer. He was reading the paperwork. When he was done, he looked up. He was angry.

"This isn't good." Devil asked him

"Why. What does it mean for her case?" Dyson sighed.

"Essentially he is saying Ashlee was and is committing

adultery. He's basing his case for suing for divorce on it. This could lead a judge to rule in his favor not only when determining the amount of alimony but also distribution of assets." Devil shrugged.

"So, we don't need any of his money. She was only asking for it to prompt him to give her the divorce quickly."

Dyson nodded. "I know. But by accusing her of adultery, it could impact the custody of the children. The judge could see this as the children not being her number one priority. They'll likely want not only themselves, but a forensic child custody evaluator to examine and assess evidence of adultery and its potential impact on the well-being of the children when deciding who gets them."

Hearing his warning made me cry out. Devil turned to me, but I jumped up and raced to the bathroom. I barely made it before I threw up everything in my stomach. I kneeled on the cold tile floor, crying as I dry heaved after emptying my stomach. Devil was talking to me, but I couldn't understand what he was saying. All I could think of was Alex was going to get my kids. That piece of scum was going to try every trick in the book to get them. Not because he loved or wanted them. But to punish me and make me come back to him.

I vaguely remember hearing several raised voices, Devil handing me a cup to drink which tasted like mint and then being carried to our bed. I curled up in a ball and cried. I couldn't let him take my kids. If it came down to it, I'd have to either go back to him which would kill my soul or get rid of Alex. I couldn't stop sobbing and I think a couple of times I screamed. I felt a tiny sting on my hip and then I was getting drowsy. I opened my eyes to find Ms. Marie sitting on the bed. I closed my eyes. I didn't want to think. I wanted oblivion to take me. I sank under the waves into darkness.

Chapter 13: Devil Dog

I watched as Regan gave Ashlee a sedative. I didn't know what else to do but call her when Ash wouldn't stop crying and then she started screaming. It terrified me. She didn't seem to know where she was or what was happening around her. She'd vomited and dry heaved for ten minutes. As the drug took effect and she began to drift and get quiet, Ms. Marie showed up. "Go do what you need to do Devil. I'll stay with her." I thanked her and left as she sat down on the bed with Ashlee.

Back in the living room I paced. The guys were somber, and Dyson was watching me. I stopped to face him. "You do whatever you can to get this threat taken away. She can't take much more of him. He dares to accuse her of this, and some judge could give the kids to that raping, abusive prick over their nurturing, loving mother! Fuck that, Matt. You take care of it or I will." He held up his hand.

"I'll see what I can do. But she's staying here with a bunch of men. He can easily accuse her of being with any or all of you. It might be better if she lived somewhere else until this is over." I stepped into his face.

"That isn't fucking happening! You put her out where he can get her, and he'll have her, and those kids gone in a heartbeat. He might even be able to hide them forever. And what do you think he's gonna do to her, now that she's actually left him and was living with another man? He'll end up killing her, Matt!" He nodded.

"I know. It was a suggestion. But don't tell me anymore. I don't want to hear about the 'or I will' explanation. Let me go and see what I can do." He was led out by Jordan.

Savage grabbed my arm. "You need to sit and calm down, brother. Ashlee needs you. Come on sit." I sat down on one of the couches. The guys either took the other seats, pulled in dining chairs or sat on the floor. I looked around at them.

"You saw what this is doing to her. She's terrified. Fuck did you hear her screams?" I rubbed my face as they all nodded. "If she thinks he'll get those kids, she'll fucking go back to him to protect them. She'll go back to be beaten and raped and God knows what else if he gets custody of them. I can't let that happen. She's my fucking life! Those kids are my life. I'm not going to give them up." In the door came Bull. I thought he was at the hospital. He came over to me.

"The guys called Terror and told him what was up. I said I'd come. He wanted to but I insisted. How is Ashlee?" He asked with concern.

"She had to be sedated because she couldn't stop crying and screaming. Ms. Marie is with her in the bedroom. Bull, since you're here in Terror's place, I'll tell you right now. As soon as we find him, I'm going hunting. I can snipe his ass from a mile away and no one will ever know it was us. They may suspect, but they'll never be able to prove it. He's a dead man. He's threatening my fucking family. He will die and soon."

Bull patted my shoulder. "It's okay, Devil. I know. We'll do whatever it takes to keep her and those kids safe. I told you that. Don't worry. When the time comes, you can kill him, and we'll make sure he's never found. Right now, why don't you concentrate on taking care of her? Where's the kids?"

"They're over at Tiny and Sherry's house."

"Good. I'll see if they're okay to watch them tonight. If not, me and Marie will watch them at Terror's house. Hunter is with Alannah right now. We'll leave you two alone. Call me if you need anything through the night." I thanked him and the others. Bull went down the hall and came back with Ms. Marie. She gave me a hug and kiss. They all left leaving me to think. I went down the hall to Ashlee.

She was curled up in the fetal position in the middle of the bed. Her face was tear stained. She had a frown on her face even in her sleep. I got undressed and crawled in behind her. I tugged her into my arms. She didn't wake up, but she did snuggle into my chest. I kissed her hair and whispered to her as I stared out the window at the moonlit night.

"I swear to God, Precious, I won't allow him to take our kids or touch you again. He can threaten all he wants, but he won't win." It was a long time before I fell asleep.

I jerked awake sometime later. I didn't know how long I'd been out. Ashlee was thrashing around in the bed and whimpering. I was trying to gently get her to wake up when she screamed and yelled out.

"No please Alex don't do this. I don't want to have sex. No, stop! That hurts! Get off me! Get off!" I wanted to hit something. She was obviously reliving one of the times he raped her. Jesus Christ! She'd never done this before when I was around. I shook her harder and yelled her name louder. She came shooting up in the bed and she was fighting. She was like a wild animal. I finally got her pinned down and her eyes on me. It took a few seconds for recognition to show in those haunted eyes. When it did, she gradually relaxed. I cautiously rolled off her. She looked around the room in confusion.

"What happened, Jack?" I smoothed back her hair from her face.

"Do you remember earlier, Ash?" She frowned in concentration. I knew the moment she remembered, because her face went pale and she started to shake. I wrapped her in my arms. "Babe, it's okay. You're fine. Please don't get upset again. Alex is not going to get those kids or you. He can play all the damn games he wants, but in the end he'll lose." She looked at me half in hope and half in despair.

"Where are the kids," she asked?

"They're with Tiny and Sherry or, if not with them, then with Bull and Ms. Marie. They'll take good care of them. I didn't want them to get scared." She teared up.

"I'm the worst mother in the world," she sobbed. I looked at her stunned.

"How in the hell can you say that? What makes you even think that Ash?" She cried softly.

"First, I leave them for almost a week while I'm in the hospital. Now, I keep having to ask other people to take them because I'm upset, or I have to do something. What kind of mother does that?" I shook my head in bafflement.

"Baby, you're not failing the kids. You take wonder-ful care of them. You were in the damn hospital after almost being run over by a car, woman. And having someone take them here and there is nothing. You need care and I plan on you getting it. This whole damn com-pound is more than willing to help with the kids when it's needed, and no one will ever think you're being a bad mother or shirking your duties. Fuck! You're amazing with them, baby." I leaned down to capture her mouth. She gave in to my kiss and opened her mouth so I could enter it. When we broke apart, she wasn't crying any more. She was quiet. Then she looked at me.

"Was Regan here or did I dream that?" I sighed.

"She came. You were crying and then screaming and wouldn't stop. She came and gave you a sedative." She cringed and hid her face. I pulled it out of my chest so I could see her. "What?" She opened her eyes.

"What kind of wimp am I? I had to be sedated, Jack. Jesus, I thought I was strong, but I guess not. You should find yourself a woman who's worthy of you. Someone strong like you." Her words stabbed at me. I got angry.

"What the fuck is that supposed to mean? Now you think you're some kind of pansy who can't take it and I should walk away and find someone else? Is that what I'm hearing? Because if it is, you're more confused than

I thought! I fucking love you and I wouldn't leave you for anything! And you're one of the strongest women I know. Look at what you lived through for years. You never gave up. Right now, you're tired and that's understandable. But never say you're weak or that I deserve someone better. I don't know what I did to deserve you, Precious." As I finished my rant, she launched herself into my arms and attacked my mouth.

She was kissing me and tearing off her clothes at the same time. I eased her back. She looked at me. "Please Jack. Make love to me. Make me forget for a little while. I just want to feel you inside of me. Loving me." I couldn't resist her plea. I helped her out of her clothes and proceeded to tease her until she was begging for release. Then I made love to her slow and deep until we both collapsed in a heap of sated bliss. She fell asleep almost as soon as we were done. I held her in my arms and drifted to sleep hoping she had no more nightmares.

I woke up the next morning to the sound of the doorbell. I eased out from under Ashlee and grabbed my shorts before heading down the hall to the front door. I opened it, and there stood Terror. I invited him inside. I went to the kitchen to make some coffee. He took a seat at the table.

"Sorry, I didn't know you would still be in bed," he said. I looked at the kitchen clock and saw it was almost ten. Shit! We'd really overslept.

"It's alright. I didn't know it was this late." He glanced around.

"How is Ashlee this morning? Bull filled me in on everything. I'd have been here sooner, but they made us wait until this morning to discharge Harlow and Emerson." I stopped him.

"No need to apologize, Terror. You needed to be with your wife and new baby. Ashlee is still asleep. She woke up in the middle of the night having a nightmare about Alex. I think she was relieving one of the times he raped her. Shit, she's never done that around me before. It tore me up. She's feeling like she's weak and that she's not being a good mother and even told me I should find someone better! She's really messed up over this shit."

Terror's mouth was hanging open in astonishment. "She thinks what? How can she even think that? She's strong as hell. Like all our old ladies." I nodded.

"I know. I told her that too." We sat silently drinking coffee lost in our own thoughts. He was the one to break the silence.

"What do you need us to do?" I growled in frustration.

"I don't know what else to do. Smoke is trying several things to track him. Dyson is pursuing the legal end. I just wish we could find out something about him or some proof of what he's really like, so we could at least kill his chances of getting the kids. That's the main thing she's worried about. Because if he does Terror, she'll go back to him to try and protect them." He grimaced.

"Dyson was hiring a PI to look into him. So far, we haven't heard anything from him. How about we see if the Dark Patriots can find something on dear old Alex? They have resources we probably could never imagine. My gut tells me this isn't the first time he's been like this.

We need to find enough dirt on him to discredit him in front of a judge." I sat up excited. That was a good idea.

"Do it. Tell them I'll pay for their time. I want this bastard cut off at the knees. Then we'll bury his ass for real."

We'd just agreed to the new course of action, when Ashlee came wandering into the kitchen. She still looked pale and her eyes had dark circles under them. She greeted Terror and asked after Harlow and Emerson. He gave her an update. I put on the kettle for her tea. She rarely drank coffee. As it heated, I told her about the plan to get Sean, Gabe, Griffin and their guys on the case to find something on Alex. She seemed to perk up a little hearing this. I got up to fix her tea. I asked if she was hungry but she said no. Not long afterward, Terror excused himself to go home to Harlow and the kids.

I turned to her when he was gone. "Precious, you should eat. You had no dinner last night and now no breakfast." She shook her head.

"I can't, Jack. My stomach is rolling. I feel like I could vomit again. I'll be alright. Can we go get the kids? I need them. And what are you doing home? It's Friday. You should be at the garage." I looked at her in astonishment.

"You think I'd go to the garage when my woman is going through shit like this? I'd never leave you to do this alone." She looked startled.

"But honey, they're so busy and already behind because of Cody. I don't want to interfere with club business." I hugged her.

"Thanks for worrying babe, but Falcon volunteered to

go and work in the garage today. Him and Tiger are almost done with the bike they're building and are ahead of schedule. They both have experience working on cars and trucks as well as bikes. He told me last night he was going to go and cover for me today."

With this worry off her mind, we headed over to Tiny and Sherry's to get our two rug rats. Sherry greeted us at the door and told us to come on in. Angel was busy playing with Sam. Jayce was in the living room sleeping on Tiny's chest as he reclined in the chair. He grinned when we saw him.

"Works every time. Snuggle up to my manly chest and they're out like a light," he teased. Sherry laughed.

"You're so full of shit." He smacked her ass as she passed him. Ashlee was over with Sherry talking. He nodded over at her.

"How is she this morning?" I shook my hand from side to side.

"So, so. She had a hard night and it's still bothering her. Thanks for taking the kids and everything. You know if you ever need us to watch Sam, just let us know." He nodded.

"I know. And I appreciate it. He had fun playing with Angel. Jayce only got up twice which was a surprise. I swear Sam got up every two hours, I think. You let us know if you need anything else. Are you working at the garage tomorrow? If so, I can cover for you. She needs you at home with her for a few days. She looks pale."

"Thanks, Tiny. Falcon is covering for me today and I wasn't on for tomorrow. And she isn't eating yet.

She didn't have dinner and refused breakfast. Says her stomach is still too upset. I'll keep an eye on her and get some food in her soon. She really just wanted the kids. She thinks she's being a bad mother or some bullshit." He grunted in surprise.

We visited for a bit longer and then left after thanking them one more time. When we got them back to the house, we spent time with them. With Jayce it was mostly holding and cuddling him. With Angel it was playing dolls and watching her favorite television shows.

When lunch rolled around, Ash fixed Angel grilled cheese and a bowl of mixed fruit. I had the grilled cheese too and insisted Ashlee eat. She struggled to get down half a sandwich and a little bit of fruit. Not nearly enough. I decided to not say anything and see what happened at dinner.

After lunch the kids went down for a nap. I took Ash to the bedroom and made her lie down. I held her and thankfully she fell asleep. Two hours later when all of them were awake, we bundled the kids in their coats and went to check out the new house.

Guys were hard at work, so we stayed out of their way. The basement was done, and the concrete flooring poured. They were going to start the framing. This team did it smart. While some had been doing the masonry or pouring the concrete, others had pre-built the framing for walls. They'd be able to put them up in no time.

We finished by taking a walk in the woods. I carried Jayce in his chest carrier. Angel had fun looking at the stream, picking up pretty rocks and leaves. Ashlee told her to bring them home and she'd show her a magic way to color with them. When we got back, it was going on four. She fed Jayce again. She was still breastfeeding him but supplementing with formula. That almost week in the hospital had her milk decrease in production, even though she'd tried to pump to maintain it while in there. She'd dumped it until the drugs were no longer in her system. She said when he was six months old, she'd switch him over all the way to formula. That was about six weeks away.

I took Jayce to change his diaper and put him in his swing, so she could show Angel how to do the leaves. She had her use different colors and place the leaves under the paper and then rub across them, so the impressions showed on the paper. Angel thought it was magic.

She was happily coloring for over an hour. At five thirty Ash began to get things ready to cook dinner. I insisted on helping. We made a simple meal of wild rice, blackened salmon, and steamed carrots and broccoli. I was surprised to see Angel eat salmon and broccoli. Ashlee explained that Angel wasn't a picky eater and would try almost anything once.

Dinner clean up didn't take long, then it was more time with the kids, bath time, reading and they were both out by eight o'clock. The two of us settled down to watch a movie. Ashlee was out before it was even halfway over. I carried her to bed and got her undressed and under the covers. I hoped we ended up having many more relaxed days like it had been this afternoon and evening. Just regular family time.

The next week flew by without any word from Alex. Dyson had told us he was working still to get information to make him back off and take the adultery off the table. Ashlee tried to act normal, but I could tell it was still bothering her. She didn't sleep well at night and I had to watch her to make sure she ate. This morning we were having church. Ash had brought the kids to the clubhouse, so she could hang out with the old ladies. They were going to discuss more wedding ideas. She'd finished the website redesigns and the club loved them.

We'd run through most of the club business when Viper brought up the garage. "Business is booming. But Cody isn't working out. He's continually late, doesn't stay on task or keep productive. His work is good when he does it, but it's not enough. I want to suggest we start looking around for another mechanic now. As soon as we find one, we'll cut him loose. I'm hoping we can replace him before the ninety days are up." No one had any objections.

"I'll ask Tanner and Jordan if they might know someone."

Terror brought us back to task. "There's one more thing that came in just before this meeting. That's why Smoke and I were late." This got our attention. He looked at me. "The Dark Patriots called. They found out some shit on our little pain in the ass, Alex Andrews." This made me sit up rigid. "Smoke, why don't you tell Devil Dog what they found?" Smoke smiled. He tapped a few keys on his laptop.

"Alex Andrews has been a bad boy before he ever met Ashlee. Now, Alex is older than her by six years. When

Alex was seventeen, he had a girlfriend. From what they found out; he became abusive with her like he did Ashlee. There were trips to the ER to treat her for falls down the stairs and other bullshit. What finally ended the relationship was her allegation that he raped her. He never stood trial or was arrested, because her dad hushed it up to protect her and they moved far away. Alex ended up moving from Oklahoma to here soon afterward. The next few years were quiet. Nothing seems to have been reported on him being abusive to anyone. It was during this time; he became friends with the now police chief in Maryville." He paused.

"When he was twenty, he started to date another woman. They were together for over a year. In that time, she went to the ER five separate times with significant injuries, broken bones, concussions, severe bruising to some internal organs. The woman kept saying it was from falls, car accidents, and things like that. The ER doctors didn't believe her and documented their suspicions in the records. No police reports were supposedly filed against him. Then one day she just up and disappeared. He claimed she'd left to go live in California with an aunt and they'd broken up. Apparently, no one cared enough to follow up. According to the Patriots, they said there is no aunt and his girlfriend has never resurfaced anywhere in the U.S." I stood up to pace when he said this.

Smoke continued. "They are almost positive he killed her and got rid of the body. They also think his friend the chief helped him to do it. One of Sean's cyber people found evidence in the police system of a report filed by her, about Alex a week before she went missing. It said she came in beaten and claimed he did it and that he also raped her. The officer who took the report, reportedly left the force a week later and moved away to another state. The report was deleted from the police files, but not from the server, so it was recoverable. The system shows only two people ever accessed the record. The officer who wrote it and the police chief. The chief is the one who deleted it." All the guys were now muttering.

"Now for the last part. He met Ashlee when she was eighteen and he was twenty-four. Things had been quiet again after the girlfriend who allegedly went to California. There are six reports obtained from the hospital related to her having to come in to seek medical attention. Again, the doctors suspected abuse and recorded their suspicions. There was one attempt after what looked like the first beating, when she went to the police. The chief was the one to speak to her. He sent her home. One officer agreed to talk to the investigator off the record. He said they were told by the chief; she had a mental condition and was a pathological liar. So, if she ever came in, they were to refer her to him, since he knew her and could help talk her out of her fantasies. According to this officer, she never came back. However, the husband had been in more than once to talk to the chief in private. The Patriots were able to find old texts where Alex reached out to the chief telling him Ashlee was gone and he needed him to use his resources at the police station to find her."

I was now standing still and shaking in rage. "You mean he's done this at least twice before and one of those times we're almost sure he killed the woman? And with

Ashlee, he had help from the police to discredit her and also find her whenever she ran from him?" Smoke nodded. "How can we use this?"

Terror spoke up. "Gabe is going to have one of their operatives reach out to Alex. We know he's not at home, but we do know his phone number. He used it to call Ashlee. This operative will let him know what we know and that we have evidence to support it. If he does not drop his divorce filing and give Ashlee her divorce unattested with full custody of the kids, we'll give this over to the police and not the ones in Maryville. He'll be facing years if not life in prison. Sean said they have enough to convince a jury, especially with Ashlee's testimony."

"Good. Tell them to do it as soon as possible. She needs this off her shoulders. It's killing her. Get Dyson to work on pushing this divorce through fast. I want to marry her as soon as possible. Once he backs off and withdraws the claim, we find him, and he can meet with an unfortunate accident. That way, he will be permanently gone and unable to hurt another woman or child again." All the guys shook their heads in agreement. Terror said he'd talk to Sean, Gabe and Griffin to get things rolling. We were dismissed. I went to find Ashlee. I had to tell her about Alex.

I found her sitting with the other ladies. I asked them to excuse us and I took her outside. She gave me a curious look. "Babe, I need to tell you something. Just sit and listen then when I'm done, we can discuss it. Okay?" She nodded. I ran her through the highlights of the club finding out some shit on Alex and the plan to use it to blackmail him into dropping his bid for custody. At the end she sat there stunned. She looked at me hesitantly.

"You really think this will work?" I nodded. I took her in my arms as she sagged in relief. It took her several minutes to pull herself together, so we could go back to the clubhouse. I told her for now, we wanted to keep it from the other ladies. She agreed to not say a word.

The rest of the day was spent enjoying the unusually warm day. Since the pool was heated, we took the kids swimming. We cooked hamburgers and hot dogs on the grill. When the sun started to go down, we moved inside the clubhouse to watch movies, play pool, and cards. I was playing cards with Savage, Menace, Storm, and Capone. Ash was on my lap. I looked over once and saw Viper in deep conversation with Tanner. Viper was nodding his head. I briefly wondered what they were talking about and then I forgot about it.

We got the kids home and in bed late. It was after nine. I coaxed Ashlee to take a shower with me and then we got into bed. I started nibbling on her neck and ear. She laughed. "Just what do you think you're doing Jack Cannon?" I growled.

"I'm getting ready to devour my woman and then I'm going to make love to her until she's weak and speechless. Are there any objections to this plan," I asked with a wicked grin on my face? She laughed.

"Well don't let me stop you. Devour and make love away."

I licked her neck and nibbled on her ear. She sighed. I worked my way to her pouty mouth, where I sucked and nibbled on her lips and plundered her mouth with my tongue. Hers dueled back with mine. I moaned when she gently bit my bottom lip. Fuck, she could turn me on with a look let alone a touch. She ran her hands all over my chest scrapping with her nails causing goosebumps of pleasure to rise on my skin.

I worked my way down to her chest. Her breasts were hard peaks and so round. Even with her not feeding Jayce as much, her breasts remained lush. I could get lost in playing with them and giving her pleasure. We'd discovered she was extremely sensitive to breast play.

I sucked her left nipple into my mouth. My tongue lashed her nipple to an even harder peak. She moaned and ran her fingers to the back of my head where she sunk her fingers. I laughed and switched to the other side. Her moaning was getting louder and more con-stant.

"Jack, you're killing me. I need you, honey. Please." She was flushed and had a pleading look in her eye. I shook my head.

"No, not yet. You're not speechless or weak yet, Precious. Just relax and let me make love to you." She whim-pered but did relax into the mattress. I went back to her breasts and worked them until she came panting just from my play. Once she came down from her orgasm, I licked down her stomach to her beautiful pussy.

She was so wet, and I could smell her scent in the air. I took a deep breath. "Umm, babe, I love to smell your sweet scent almost as much as I love to taste your sweetness," I growled before sliding my tongue down her folds and back up to her clit.

I paid particular attention to that hard-little nub sucking and nibbling on it. She was again climbing toward another orgasm. I could tell by the way she was breathing and because she was thrusting her hips off the bed more and more. I slid two fingers into her tight entrance. She cried out and thrust back on them. I kept thrusting in and out as I licked and sucked on her sweet juices. I could eat her for hours. Suddenly, she clamped down hard on my fingers and yelled as she came for the second time. This one was more intense than the last one. But it wasn't going to be her last. I meant what I said. I wanted her weak and speechless.

"Oh God, Jack!" she yelled as she kept coming. I eased her down and then crept up her body to kiss her. I wanted her to taste how sweet she was. She didn't pull away or act grossed out at tasting herself. She kissed me like she was starving. When we broke apart, I sat up with my back to the headboard.

"Babe, I want you to straddle me, but face away from me. This is called reverse cowgirl. I think you'll like this position a lot." She was quick to get into position. As she held herself hovering over my cock, I lined it up with her entrance and she sank down so slowly it made me groan. She laughed and then went even slower and circled her hips over and over as she sank. When she had taken all of me inside, I had to hold her hips so she couldn't move.

"Ash, don't move yet. I don't want to come too soon and if you move, I will." She nodded and stayed still. When I had myself back under control, I lifted her by her hips. She took over riding my raging hard cock.

She started moaning and panting again and riding me faster and harder. I slipped my hand under my pillow. Before we'd gotten in bed, I'd hidden a bottle of lube under it. I lubed up a finger. As she raised back up, I circled her puckered hole. She stopped and glanced back at me.

"Can I?" I asked her. She nodded. As she came back down, I let gravity push my finger into her ass. She whimpered long and hard as she did. I knew it had to burn but she never stopped. Then she rose back up. From there things got faster, harder, and deeper.

I was thrusting up with my hips now, to bury my cock deeper in her pussy, as I fucked her super tight ass with my finger. She kept crying out.

"More, Jack, More. Oh God!" I felt the sweat running down my chest. I was panting and could feel my release rising up into my balls. I pulled her down harder as I thrust up and I rubbed inside her ass on what many called the "A" spot. It was just what she needed. She came screaming my name and I released my load, grunting, and groaning in ecstasy. Her pussy and ass were so damn tight and were milking both my cock and finger. She finally collapsed back on my chest. I held her back to my front with my softening cock still buried inside of her.

"Are you okay, Precious?" She merely nodded. I laughed. "See I told you I planned to make you weak and speechless. Looks like I did." She smiled at me. After we rested, I helped her up and into the bathroom to clean up. As we crawled back in bed, she looked at me a little apprehensive. "What is it, babe? Is something wrong?" She squirmed a little before she spoke.

"No, nothing is wrong. I want to ask you something and I'm sort of embarrassed to ask it."

"Ashlee, you can ask me anything and there is no need to ever be embarrassed. What do you want to ask me?" She took a deep breath.

"I want to ask you if you'd want to put your cock in my ass rather than just your finger. Would you like that?" I blinked. That wasn't what I expected her to ask.

"Babe, I want only what you want. Would I like it, of course. But it's your pleasure not the lack of it, I want. Do you want us to have anal sex? I know your experience with it was horrible and painful. I'm surprised you let me play with my fingers to be honest. Tell me, do you like the sensations when I do?" She nodded shyly.

"Yes, I do. Very much. Once I'm past the burning and discomfort, it feels really good. I'm wondering if you did it, would I feel the same with your cock. You take care to ensure my comfort every time. I think that would make a difference. So yes, I do think about trying it, but only with you would I ever consider it."

I pulled her closer. "Then we'll try it. But I want to be sure you're really prepared. Going from a finger to my cock is a big difference. I need to work you up to it. Which means I need to use toys. Will you be okay with that? I know it could bring up bad memories." I wanted to do nothing that would cause her to flashback to the times Alex raped her with toys anally. She kissed me softly on the mouth.

"As long as I know it's you, I think I'll be fine."

"Okay, then we'll work at it. But for now, we both need to get some sleep. Good night, Ash. I love you, Precious." I gave her a kiss. She moaned and then kissed me.

"I love you too, Jack. So very much. Good night, honey." She fell asleep before I did. I laid there thinking about what I wanted to do to prepare her. I admit I was excited she wanted to try it. Hopefully, she found it pleasurable and not a trigger for unpleasant memories.

Chapter 14: Ashlee

It had been a few days since the man had served me with those papers from Alex and the subsequent worry. With the information the club had found out on Alex, we were all hopeful it would be enough to get Alex to get him to drop his suit. And just grant me the divorce and full custody of the kids. I lived in hope it was enough to get him out of our lives once and for all.

I shook off my thoughts. I needed to focus on work. I was at the spa today. I'd launched all the new websites for the club. I'd also contacted the college again at Devil's urging. I planned to start my online classes in January. I would have to stop working, but Harlow assured me they could hire someone to replace me. Everyone seemed very psyched I was going back. Most of the old ladies had college degrees. Even those who didn't, were very business savvy women that the club trusted to help run the various businesses.

One of our regular customers came through the door. She came for a facial once a month religiously. She had great skin and I'd asked her to tell me her routine. It was never too late to take care of your skin. I'd avoided the sun most of my life so that was a plus. I got her checked in and then in the steam room to wait for her appointment. The steam room had been one of the renovations the club had added when they bought the spa. I had to say, they were busy and if the new website attracted more business, they'd need to hire and expand. I stepped outside to get some air.

Today, Storm and Razor were on guard duty. Storm was out front. He came over when he saw me step outside. "Everything okay, Ash?" I nodded.

"Yeah, I just needed some fresh air. You must be bored to death." He laughed.

"Actually no. I get to see some hot women coming and going at this place. It makes it bearable." I had to laugh when he said that. Like all the Warriors, Storm was hot. I knew he had no trouble getting women. As we were joking and talking, I glanced around.

My breath caught. Standing down the street watching us was Alex. I knew it was him by the jacket and hat he was wearing. Storm noticed the change in me. "What's wrong, Ash?" I swallowed.

"Storm, please act casual and keep talking. Don't turn around. Off to your left, down the street is a man in a navy-blue jacket and a black hat. I swear, it's Alex. He's watching us. I know those clothes. He wears them as casual clothes."

Storm kept his cool. "Don't look his way again. I want you to talk to me and laugh for another minute and then go back inside to work. When you get inside, go tell Razor in back what's happening. I'm gonna play on my cell and text the guys. Whatever you do, don't look that way again. We don't want him to know we've seen him." I nodded and fought to keep the smile on my face. We talked for another minute while I laughed and then headed inside.

As soon as I was clear of the windows, I headed through the back rooms and out the back door. Razor looked up when I came out. "What is it, Ashlee?" I told him what I saw and what Storm had said to do.

"Okay, go back inside and make sure this door stays locked and closed. Find some reason to be in the back away from the windows as much as you can. Let us take care of this." I told him I would and went back inside the spa. I spent my time washing more linens and towels, folding them, putting them away, filling empty cabinets with more supplies. The front bell would alert me to anyone I had to go to the front to help.

Ten minutes later I heard a commotion and bikes coming. I couldn't stay in the back. I had to see what was happening out front with Alex. I peeked out. Alex wasn't in his place. Storm was still out front, and I could see some of the guys combing the area on their bikes. Devil was one of them. About fifteen minutes later, the chime rang, and I came back to the front reception area. Devil was there. I ran into his arms. "I know it was him, Jack. I know it. He got away, didn't he?" He nodded.

"I believe you, Ash. He must have gotten spooked. Razor left Storm out front and worked his way over, but he ran. There was a chase. He lost him in the maze of alleys back there. We searched but there's no sign of him. What we did find is this." He held up a note. I took it from him. Typed on it was a message. Y*ou think you've won. Think again. You won't get to enjoy your freedom with that biker*. I felt the panic rise.

"Jack, what does he mean? I've won?" He took me over to sit in one of the chairs.

"Dyson called and said Alex had rescinded his divorce filing. He had his lawyer drop it. He told the judge he won't fight it. He also agreed to give you full custody of the kids. But we know he's only doing this, because of the information we found and threatened him with. He has something else planned." I rocked in the chair.

"Jack, tell me what you guys found out. I need to know" I could see he didn't want to tell me. I also saw the moment he decided to tell me all of it. Devil gave me a rundown of everything they'd found out and suspected. I felt the bile rising. I stood up and paced.

"So, what you're telling me is I married a rapist and murderer and that is the father of my children. I'm going to be sick." Devil jumped up and grabbed my shoulders.

"No, I'm the father of those kids. He's the sperm donor. You had no idea what he was, Ashlee. He abused and raped you, too. Thankfully you got away before he murdered you. We'll figure out what he plans to do next. We'll just have to be careful." I leaned my forehead on his chest. "I just want this to be over so badly, Jack. I want us to be able to move on with our lives."

He kissed me. "I know. Me too babe." The spa was closing early due to tomorrow being Thanksgiving. Devil stayed and took me home at three. I planned to help the others prep things for dinner tomorrow. When we got home, I changed, fed Jayce and then headed to the club-house. I needed to do something to get my mind off of what was happening with Alex.

The other old ladies were there, and the kitchen was a hive of activity. The kids were being watched by the guys in the common room. By seven we'd gotten every-thing we could do in advance all done. The guys ordered pizza for dinner, so we didn't have to cook.

After everyone ate, Devil and I took the kids back to the house. They were bathed and in bed by eight thirty and both had fallen asleep without a protest. I stood looking down at Jayce. He was now five months old. It was hard to believe I'd only known Devil and the Warriors for such a short period of time. Devil came up behind me.

"What are you thinking about, babe," he whispered. I led him out of the room and to our bedroom.

"I was thinking how it seems much longer than five months, since I met you and the rest of the MC. I feel like I've always been here in some ways. I can't tell you how thankful I am, that Harlow and the gang spoke to me that day in the store and gave me their phone numbers. I love you, Jack. I don't know what I'd do without you."

"Ashlee, I love you too. And you won't need to find out what you'd do without me. I plan to be here and for us to be together until I'm at least a hundred. Now, I have an idea. You need to relax. The pool is heated. Let's go for a night time swim. Before you say we can't, I asked Tanner to come over and stay in the house in case the kids wake up. He should be here any minute. Slip into a bikini and I'll be right back." He gave me a quick kiss and then left the bedroom. His idea surprised me, but it also sounded perfect.

I slipped on a bathing suit. It was one I hadn't worn that Regan had insisted I buy. It was a skimpy two piece that was halter style on top and the tiny panties were cut high on my legs and had rhinestones holding it together on each hip. The halter supported my less than tiny breasts and made my cleavage look huge and my breasts even bigger. I grabbed us a couple of towels. Devil came back in when I was in the bathroom getting them. I could hear him getting in the dresser.

"Babe, Tanner is here in the living room. I'm just changing, and we can go. Did you get everything you need?" I walked out as he was pulling on his swimming trunks. He looked up and froze.

"Jesus! Precious, where did you get that bathing suit," he rasped? I could see he liked it because his cock was starting to tent his trunks. I sashayed over to him.

"Do you like it? Regan talked me into it." As I asked him this, I gently squeezed his cock through his trunks. He groaned.

"Do that again and I'll throw you down right now and fuck you into the mattress. Fuck, do I like it? I love it! Never wear it where anyone else can see you. You're too much for them to resist." I laughed.

"Let's go swimming."

Instead of going out the front door, he took us out the glass doors in the bedroom. They led us onto the back patio. We made it to the pool area. He flipped a switch and muted colored lights lit up the pool and spa. I slid into the warm water. The night air had a bite, but the water made it bearable. Devil got in with me. I floated for a little bit then he took me into his arms. He was kissing me and caressing me all over. I could feel the slickness growing between my legs. He suddenly stopped when I was almost ready to explode. "Let's get in the spa. It's warmer." I let him take me to it and he threw our towels down on the nearby chaise.

The heat felt even better than the warm water in the pool. Devil sat back on one of the ledges and pulled me onto his lap, so I was facing him. I gave him a kiss. He growled. I knew he was still excited, because his hard cock was pressed between us. I ran my hand down to caress him.

"Looks like you have a problem, Jack," I teased. He grinned.

"I do. And I plan to have it taken care of." I smiled.

"Really, how are you going to do that?" He ran his hands up my back. Then I felt the ties on my top giving. I gasped and tried to grab it, but he whisked it out of reach.

"Jack! Someone might see us. Give it back." He shook his head no.

"It's unlikely anyone will. If they do come around, they'll leave when they see us. And babe, I don't care if anyone sees me making love with my woman. Besides, the bubbles in the water keep most things covered. Relax. I need to fuck my woman and I need to do it now. I bet you've never had sex in the water, have you?" I shook my head no. The idea did excite me. He ran his hands down to my hips and unclipped the sides. My bikini bottom joined my halter. I was now totally naked outside in a spa with my man.

He took my mouth in a searing kiss and his hands engulfed my breasts to massage and play with them. He had me panting and ready to explode in a matter of a couple of minutes. I broke away.

"Take off your trunks," I demanded. I needed him buried inside of me right now. He grinned and then lifted his hips to push them down. I helped him to drag them off. His big, hard cock was bobbing in the water. I grasped him and sat down on him sinking down fast and hard. He groaned and his hands tightened on my hips.

I leaned forward to kiss my way up to his ear. "Jack, fuck me. Fuck me hard and deep. I want to still feel you tomorrow." My words seemed to do something to him. His expression became almost feral. He growled and then he was lifting my hips and then slamming them down as he thrust up. He was so deep. I whimpered as the hard veins on his cock scraped the swollen tissues inside my pussy. He watched as I rode his cock with his help.

My breasts were bouncing in the water. His eyes never left them as he sped up. He growled out, "I need to be deeper." He stood with me still filled with his cock. He got out of the spa and walked us over to the chaise he'd thrown our towels on. He lowered me to it. As he did, he pulled out. I whimpered in protest.

"Get on your hands and knees. Now," he ordered. I scrambled to do so. I was too excited to feel the cool air. He grabbed my hips and slammed me back on his cock. I cried out. The pleasure was almost painful. Then he went wild. He pounded in and out of me, burying himself to the hilt over and over again. His cock was nudging my cervix. I could hear our skin slapping together. He was grunting with every thrust and moving inside of me like a piston. I knew I was about to come, and it would be remarkable.

As he kept thrusting, he began to groan. "So fucking beautiful. God, I love you. You're so tight and wet, baby. You're scorching hot. Come for me. Let me fill that sweet pussy." His words did something to me. I was thrusting back to meet his thrusts and whimpering out.

"Harder, harder, please honey, I need to come." His movement got even more crazed and I felt the orgasm start in my toes and rush up my legs, through my core and into my chest. I screamed and cried as I clamped down on his cock. He came roaring out his own release. I could feel his seed splashing on the tender walls of my pussy as I milked him dry. My vision got dark around the edges and I barely remained on my knees. He collapsed to lie over my back. He was still gliding in and out slowly as he kissed the back of my neck and shoulders. He was praising me.

"You're amazing. I've never had anything like what I have with you, Ash. You're made for me." He finally stopped once he went totally soft and wrapped me in his arms.

We sat on the chaise with me wrapped in towels and on his lap for a little while just recovering and enjoying the quiet. He insisted we should go inside before I got too cold. He grabbed our swimming clothes and wrapped me tighter in the towels. He walked me back to the house, in the cold without a stitch on. When we got inside, he pulled on a pair of shorts and went to dismiss Tanner.

When he came back to our room, I was sprawled out on my stomach boneless. His eyes got a gleam in them. I moaned. "You can't be serious. There's no way you can go again." Even as I said it, his cock began to lengthen and grow. He got a wicked smile on his face.

Devil casually reached down and stroked his cock. I was now getting wet again just looking at him. He went into the bathroom and turned on the water. When he came back out, he pulled me up off the bed and into his arms. "Wrap your arms and legs around me. You need to shower and warm up, Precious. Let me help you with that."

He put me in the shower under the hot water. As it chased the chill away, he kissed me and caressed my body as I did the same to him. Next thing I knew he had my back pressed to the cool tiles and had thrust into me. He took me against the wall like he'd done by the pool. When I came this time, I knew I lost consciousness for a little bit. I remember him shouting out his release and then nothing. When I came back to awareness, he was calling my name with worry in his voice.

"Precious, talk to me! Are you okay? Babe, say something!" I opened my eyes.

"Wow. That was amazing, Jack. You actually made me so excited that I fainted when I came." He stared at me in shock and then laughed.

"Fuck, you scared me when you wouldn't open your

eyes or say anything. I guess I should take it as a compliment you fainted. I also think you'll still be feeling me tomorrow like you wanted." He teased wiggling his eyebrows. I laughed and slapped his ass.

"I guess I will." He eased out and sat me down on my feet making sure I was steady before letting me go. We finished up by washing each other and then fell into bed. I drifted off dreaming about how he'd taken me tonight. It was amazing.

Thanksgiving at the clubhouse had been wonderful. It was the first for me and the kids. Alex had never let us celebrate it or have people over. It was one big, loud, fun and perfect celebration. All the food turned out great. I ate way too much but nothing compared to the guys. When we had been making it, I thought the others were crazy for how much they were cooking. Now that I saw them eat, I was thankful we ended up with enough!

Emerson was passed around like a living doll. We had to fight Terror to get our hands on her. He was totally enamored with his little girl. I was holding her when Devil came up. He wrapped his arms around both of us and looked at her over my shoulder. His words stunned me.

"Let's have one. I want one who'll be a part of you and me. I love Angel and Jayce. I want more." I looked up at him to see if he was joking. His expression was completely serious.

"Jack, do you know what you're saying? Do you really want to have a baby with me? Right now? I'm not even divorced, and we're not married." He shrugged.

"The divorce will be granted soon. We're getting married. I want a baby. But I'll wait until you want one too. I just hope it's soon. You look so beautiful and natural when you hold Emerson or any of the babies. The thought of keeping you pregnant makes me hard," he whispered. I elbowed him in the stomach and whispered back.

"Everything makes you hard. I think you're a sex fiend," I hissed.

Devil just laughed. "Yeah, I'm a sex fiend but only for you. I can't get enough. I want to be buried in you morning, noon and night." I shook my head.

"Like I said, you're crazy." He nodded in agreement.

"Crazy for you. Think about it and let me know when you're ready. Just know, I'm ready when you are. I'll plant a baby and we'll watch it grow." He took my mouth before he walked off to talk to Menace. Harlow came over to me.

"Looked like the two of you were in an intense conversation. Is everything alright?" I nodded.

"Everything is fine. He just decided to drop the bomb that he wants to have a baby, like right now. But he's willing to wait until I'm ready. He just wanted to let me know he wants one." Harlow's mouth dropped open. She glanced at him.

"Well damn, he's like the rest. They all get to be cavemen and want to mark their women. Every one of them got their women knocked up almost right away except Viking and Tiny. They took their time. What do you think? Do you want any more kids and if so, when?"

I thought about her questions. "Yes, I want at least a couple more. I love kids and I want Devil to have some of his own. As for when, a part of me thinks I'm crazy to want another one when Jayce is only five months old. But another part says don't wait. Take my happiness now, since we never have any guarantees on how long it lasts." She smiled.

"Then I think you know the answer. Hopefully we'll see a little Devil running around within the year." She took Emerson and walked off to give her to her father. I went to the kitchen for a drink. I turned around to find Devil standing there.

"You look pensive, babe. Did my confession upset you that much? I'm sorry, Ash. I don't want to put pressure on you. Please, just forget about it. When the time is right, you tell me and then we'll try for a baby. Okay? Now, let's go mingle some more." He took my hand and turned to leave the kitchen. I tugged on my arm, so he'd stop. He looked back at me with a question in his eyes.

"You didn't let me tell you what I was thinking. I want to have children with you, Jack. And a part of me thinks it's crazy to get pregnant when Jayce is only five months old." He nodded and tried to lead me out again. I stood still. "But, the other part of me says to take my happiness now. We're never guaranteed how long it will last. And that part is louder than the other. So, if you want to have a baby even though I'm still technically married and we're not, then I say, let's have a baby, Jack." His eyes got huge and then he grabbed me and swung me around and then danced me around the island in the kitchen. When we came to a stop, he whispered.

"I can't believe you said yes. God, I love you, Ashlee. I can't wait to have a baby with you." I kissed him. Someone clearing their throat brought us back to the present. I looked at the doorway. There stood Savage, Terror, and Ranger. They all had grins on their faces. Terror was the one to say something.

"Did we interrupt something?" I looked at Devil. He had a questioning look in his eyes. I nodded yes. He looked at them and smiled.

"Yeah, you did. Ashlee just agreed to have my baby." They all were nodding like they didn't understand what the big deal was. He enlightened them. "As in we want to start right now and have one as soon as possible." This got their attention and all of them looked stunned and then started to congratulate us. Before the hour was up, everyone had heard we planned to get pregnant immediately. Some teased us we should go now and start. Many volunteered to watch Angel and Jayce. They teased me so much I was blushing, but I was happy. I'd be throwing away my birth control pills tonight.

We spent the evening with everyone at the clubhouse. Bedtime was pushed back for all the kids and there were games of cards, pool, and darts. The kids played with their toys and ran around the room then sat down to watch a Disney movie. Most of the adults joined them. It was going on ten when we finally took our two home to bed. I didn't bother washing them. We slipped them out of their shoes and clothes and into pajamas. Neither of them even woke up. Then Devil took me to bed to practice getting pregnant. At least that is what he said we were doing. Whatever it was, it was wonderful. He rocked my world.

Chapter 15: Devil Dog

It had been just over two weeks since Thanksgiving. No one had seen or heard from Alex, which made me nervous. Dyson had called to tell us it looked like the judge was going to sign off on granting her the divorce and giving her full custody of the kids. He anticipated it would be done by the end of the month. That meant by January, Ashlee would be a free woman. Dyson cautioned us to wait thirty days after the decree was granted just in case Alex decided to appeal it. If he did, the divorce would become void. I promised him we would, but it was only to grant her time to finish planning a wedding. Alex wouldn't be appealing anything.

Today after church, we were all going on a ride and then having lunch at the Fallen Angel. The kids would be watched by Cindy, Paige, Monica, Tanner, and Jordan. Ms. Marie had been convinced to come along. Bull and a couple of his guys had showed up to spend a few days since he didn't make it over for Thanksgiving. We all knew it was because he couldn't resist seeing his granddaughter, Emerson or Hunter. He told everyone she was an exact duplicate of Harlow when she was that age.

As we were getting situated to ride, I saw Ms. Marie. She was dressed in boots, jeans, and a long-sleeved shirt with a jacket on. Her hair was wrapped in a do-rag. She looked like a biker chic. For a woman in her sixties, she was still very attractive and didn't look her age. Most would think she was in her early to mid-fifties. Or act it for that matter. What she did next stunned most of us. We expected her to get in the SUV to ride with Harper, since she was pregnant and couldn't be on the bike. Bull yelled over to her.

"You ready, Marie?"

She nodded and said, "I sure am, Nicholas." Then she walked up to him and swung onto the back of his bike. We all stood there frozen. She was fastening her helmet. Bull noticed us looking.

"What, never seen a woman on the back of a bike before? Marie said she hasn't ridden in years and misses it. So, she's riding with me."

All of us got ourselves together and on the bikes. We roared out of the compound like a giant wave. We rode for a couple of hours in the Sevierville area and then back to Dublin Falls. It was a nice day for the ride. Even though it was early December, the temp got up to the mid-fifties. It was after two o'clock when we rolled into the Fallen Angel. We were all starved.

Our waitress ended up being Julie. Her husband, Sam, helped to manage the place and acted as the main bartender. She seated us in our usual booths. Everyone gave their orders for drinks. Riding made you dehydrated. We were all sitting and chatting. Ashlee was quiet.

"Precious, are you alright?" She gave me a small smile.

"Yeah. Just tired. The ride took more out of me than I

thought. I could almost lay down here and take a nap on the table," she joked. She did look tired.

"When we get back, you're going to take a nap and no arguments. I can keep an eye on the kids. You need sleep." She said we'd see. I didn't say anymore, but she'd be taking a nap even if I had to tie her to the bed.

After our drinks came, we gave Julie our orders. Everyone was having a good time talking and horsing around with each other. We tried not to be too loud, but with well over thirty of us, we were going to be loud. Ms. Marie was telling us about the last time she rode on a bike. Apparently, her husband had rode and they went riding all the time. While she was talking, Ashlee said she had to go to the bathroom. I rose to go with her. Terror was looking at his phone and at that moment looked up and shouted for me to come over. I could tell it was really important from his tone. I asked Ashlee to wait a minute.

"What's up Terror?" I asked. He showed me his phone. Sean's group had just sent him a file and it showed a couple of places they thought Alex had been staying since he still hadn't returned to his house or the business. I got excited. Maybe we could end this once and for all with him. I clapped him on the shoulder and gave him a smile. I looked up to tell Ashlee the good news, but she wasn't standing there. I dashed over to our seats. Alannah saw me looking.

"She went to the bathroom with Harper. She said she couldn't wait. They should be back any minute." I thanked her. I hated that she didn't wait but she didn't go alone. We were in a full restaurant. I waited a couple of minutes and neither of them were back. I stood up. Viper looked up. I explained where I was going.

"Harper and Ashlee should be back by now. I'm gonna go check on them." He got up as well.

"I'll go with you." We headed down the hall where the bathrooms and back office were. I knocked on the bathroom door. No answer. I knocked again and called out,

"Ash, Harper are you two alright?" Still no answer. The hairs on the back of my neck stood up. I pulled out my gun at the same time Viper pulled out his. I tried the knob and found it locked. I moved back and kicked it in. As the lock gave, the door swung inward. Sitting on the floor gagged and tied was a pregnant Harper. Her eyes were spitting rage. Viper rushed over to her. I looked around and saw no sign of Ashlee. Viper removed her gag and started to cut her bindings. Harper looked at me.

"It was Alex. He must have been watching and he caught us from behind when we came in here. He held a gun on her and threatened to shoot her if I didn't cooperate and stay quiet. He made her gag and tie me up, while he stood over us with the gun. He told her if she screamed or fought him, he'd shot me in the stomach. He took her out of here, Devil. It's been about five minutes. He got us as soon as we got back here." Her words cut me like a knife.

He had her. We knew he most likely had killed at least once before, and he had my Ashlee. I tried to concentrate. By now the hall was filled up with Warriors. Viper must have sent them a text while I was talking to Harper. Regan, Ghost, and Janessa pushed into the bathroom to check on her. I prayed he hadn't hurt her. She was telling them she was fine that he never laid a hand on her. I swung around to Terror.

"Show me those places again. He took her and he'll need a place to take her." Terror grabbed my arm and we went into the office. It was crowded when almost all the guys came in. The rest were guarding the hall and the women.

Smoke sat down at the computer and pulled up the map Terror had on his phone. There were three locations. All of them within an hour or less of Dublin Falls. And all were remote. Smoke pointed out one of them.

"Sean and his team said they think he's primarily been here. It has the remotest position. He could hole up for months and he has terrain he can use to hide. I can find out for sure. She has the tracker. I just need to access the system. Give me a few minutes to get it up and running on this computer." While he was working on it, I studied the map. I wanted to race after her, but I knew we needed a plan. If nothing else the military taught me to plan and not run haphazard into the situation. I fought to remain calm.

Smoke cursed and then pulled out his phone. He dialed a number. Whoever answered on the other end, got an ear full. Smoke snapped at them. "The system isn't working. I can't bring anyone up using their trackers. What in the hell is going on?" He paused and listened. I couldn't hear whatever was said but our usually cool Smoke, went ballistic. "Whose dumb fucking idea was it to take it offline to work on an upgrade? And even if you were, I was supposed to be notified in advance of anything like this or if the system ran into problems. You assured me that my family would be safe testing this out. I have one of my brother's old lady taken by a goddamn mad man. You get that system back the fuck up, now." He shouted before clicking off his phone. He looked at all of us.

"The agency took it offline without telling me to do some kind of upgrade. Until they bring it back online, which will probably take them time, since they have to ask so many damn people's permission, we need to do this the old-fashioned way. I'm so damn sorry. Shit!" I could see he was pissed and worried. I squeezed his shoulder.

"It's not your fault. Let's look at those locations and form a plan." He nodded. We studied it some more and then I laid out to the guys my plan. "I want to take a team and we'll go to the location Sean said was most likely the one he's been using. But on the off chance we're wrong, I want the other two checked out. So, three teams in the field and one back at the compound as our operations center. Smoke, you can lead that team." He nodded. I looked at Terror.

"I'd like to take Ghost, Ranger, Capone, and Menace with me. For the other teams Sniper, Blaze, Tiny, Torch, and Hawk. The third one will be Steel, Hammer, Viking, Falcon, and Gunner. The rest along with Bull's guys can stay at the compound to cover the other women and kids as well as support you and Smoke. Does that meet with your approval, Pres?" I knew he should be calling the shots, but this was my old lady. I needed to be the one to lay out the plans. Terror nodded.

"We're with you, Devil. Let's go." Lunch was forgotten as we all headed back to the compound. We had gear to get. Harper refused to go to the hospital since she said Alex hadn't touched her. My mind was whirling with the thought, *what if he'd already killed her*? Harper put her hand on my arm.

"Devil she's still alive. While he was having her tie me up, he kept ranting about how she would now come back home where she belonged, and she'd never leave him again. He said something about after she proved she could behave; he'd let her get the kids back. He's a lunatic but I don't think he intended to kill her. Otherwise, why not just kill her here?" Her words did give me a little hope. I gave her a kiss on the cheek.

"Thanks Harper." Back at the compound we got down to gearing up and heading out. Since we had no idea what we might find, each of us had one of the team member's driving a vehicle. In under a half hour, we were on the road. Smoke and Terror said they would contact the Dark Patriots in case they had more intel for us. The drive left me with too much time for thoughts and fears to crowd my head. I worked to clear them. I had to treat this like a regular mission. No emotions, just get the job done.

When we were just under a mile out from the location we were given, we stopped. I rallied the guys with a final run through then we headed out. Though I had been a sniper, I wanted to be with the ones who went in. I couldn't wait outside on overwatch to see if they found her or not. Ranger would take over as the overwatch on this mission. He headed to a nearby hill. Before we all dispersed, I told them, "I want him alive. So, whatever you do, try if you can not to kill him. He deserves to suffer." They all nodded.

We jogged the rest of the way to the location. It was an old dilapidated cabin. No one was visible, and I didn't see a vehicle, though there was a small barn with the doors closed. Capone snuck up to look in the window of the barn. He nodded and held up one finger. We knew he'd spotted one vehicle. He came back. Before we split up to check out the place, Smoke came over our comm links we were wearing.

"They got it back up. She's at your location, Devil. I have her tracker pinging my system hard. She's about three hundred yards north of you. Good luck." His directions placed her in the house. We signaled each other and split up. Capone and Ghost were going in the front door and Menace and I were each making our entrance through a back window. I jimmied the window on the east side of the house and slid inside. It was a tight fit. I found myself in a dark bedroom. I looked around, but it was empty. I crept to the door and cracked it open. From what I could see, it was clear. I opened the door a little more.

I caught sight of Menace. He was coming out of a room opposite of me. We both went down the hall quietly opening doors on opposite sides. I came to the third door on the right and when I cracked it open, I discovered a set of stairs. It must lead to a basement. I whispered the information to Menace. He nodded and indicated he'd follow me. We crept down those steps as quietly as possible. As we descended, I started to hear a voice.

"You damn slut! You left me to go to a fucking dirty biker, Ashlee! A biker! After all the things I gave you, you ran away. Why do you keep doing that? Don't I give you everything? Don't I take care of you? I love you and just want you to love me. But you won't do it. You said you love him, that biker. What's his name, oh yeah, Devil Dog? Well, I have news for you, Ashlee. I don't care what any judge says, you're my wife and you're gonna stay my wife. No one can have you. We said vows, and it was until death did us part. We're gonna be together forever. This Devil Dog better stay away." He was insane.

Then we heard Ashlee. "Alex, it's over. I'm not your wife. I don't love you. As for you giving me everything, how can you even say that? You've basically made me a prisoner in the house. You beat and raped me repeatedly and then you expected me to love you and stay! You're crazy. Devil Dog will find me and when he does, you'll be sorry. You should've walked away, Alex. The judge is going to grant the divorce any day and when he does, I'm marrying Devil Dog and he's going to help me raise the kids and we're going to have more kids." While I was proud to hear her standing up to him, another part of me was praying she'd stop because he was unstable.

He shouted back at her, "Marrying him? Having more kids? Never! The only man who should ever be in your body is me. As for beating you, I only did that when you needed it. You're my wife, and you can't rape your own wife. It's your duty to make love with me when and how I want it. It'll take time for me to fuck away your memories of him. I think your punishment should be to be used, repeatedly." I knew he was referring to the dildos he used to anally rape her before. I'd heard enough. I signaled to Menace. He took up a position on the stairs in case Alex ran. I eased down the rest of the steps.

His back was to me, but Ashlee saw me. Her eyes got big and he must have noticed because he swung around. He scrambled to grab the gun on the table, but I pointed mine at him, and he stopped.

"I wouldn't do that if I were you. Menace, come on down and keep an eye on him while I untie Ashlee." Menace joined us. Alex was eyeing him with a wild look in his eyes. I hurried to get Ash loose. He had her tied to a chair securing both her ankles and wrists. After I got her loose, I pulled her in my arms and ran my hands down her body. "Are you okay, Precious? Did he hurt you? Did he do anything to you?" I was hoping he hadn't had enough time to rape her. Her clothes were ripped in places but that could have been from a struggle. She had a bruise on her right cheek and a graze down her left arm. She shook her head.

"No, he didn't get a chance to do much. Please, Jack, get me out of here. Take me home with you and the kids."

Her words made Alex even more unstable, and he started to scream. "You can't go with him. You're my wife, *my* wife! He can't have you, Ashlee. Only I can. My beautiful little Ashlee, so soft and sweet. You're my reward. I thought you were different from the other women but you're just like them. You want to leave me. I have to keep you hidden so no one takes you away. He's trying to take you away from me. I can't let that happen," he ranted. Suddenly he lashed out at Menace hitting him in the side of the head with a piece of metal he had hidden along his side. Menace hit the ground and was out cold.

I was busy helping Ashlee to the stairs when it happened. I pushed her away and aimed my gun, but he'd grabbed the one on the table and pointed it at me. We were in a standoff. I made sure to edge away from Ashlee. I could take a shot, but there was always the chance he could get one off and accidentally shoot her.

"If you're dead, she'll have to come home. There'll be no more being in love with someone else," he yelled with glee. I could see it in his eyes. He was going to pull the trigger. I prepared to shift to the right so he would miss me, and I would be between him and Ashlee. As I went to move, everything seemed to slow down into slow motion. I was moving but slowly. I saw him start to pull the trigger and then out of the corner of my eye on the right, movement flashed in front of me and then it was gone. I prepared myself to feel the pain of the bullet. I felt myself pull the trigger on my gun. In the distance it sounded like I heard a scream.

As everything came back to real time, I noted I wasn't feeling any pain. Alex was lying on the floor bleeding, but alive because he was screaming. And then it registered, the movement I had seen was Ashlee. She was on the floor curled up in front of me. I dropped to my knees.

"Babe, are you okay?" She moaned and rolled over onto her back. That's when I saw the blood and the bullet hole in her upper chest. She was pale, and she was gasping for breath. I screamed for help. Ghost appeared out of nowhere. She reached up to touch my face. I knew I was crying. "Precious, why? Why did you get in front of me? You had to know he was going to shoot. Why?" She tried to smile.

"Because I love you. I couldn't let him kill you, Jack. I couldn't live without you. Please take care of Angel and Jayce for me. Tell them I love them." As she gasped out the last word, she slumped back with her eyes closed.

I screamed, "No! Fuck, no, open your eyes, Ash. Please baby, you can't leave me." I felt hands on my shoulders, and I struggled to get away but more joined them and I was pulled back. I could hear voices talking, but what they were saying was just garbled. Ghost and Ranger were working on Ashlee. Capone had tied up Alex, who was bleeding from the shot I'd placed in his shoulder. I looked around to see Terror and Tiger there. I had no idea how or why. They were helping Menace hold me back. I saw Ghost say something and then they were lifting her and racing up the stairs. Terror was on his phone. They ran out to the SUV they'd apparently arrived in. They put her in the back and Ghost climbed in with her. I got in the backseat. Things were now beginning to make sense when people spoke.

Terror jumped in with me and Ranger got behind the wheel. He raced the car out of the driveway. Ghost was looking at me. "Terror had called Sean and his guys to be on standby at this location since it was the most likely one. Sean sent a helicopter with his team here. I won't lie, she's bad, Devil. Really bad. She needs to be in the hospital ASAP, and we don't have time to wait for an ambulance or to drive her ourselves. She'll be dead before we can make it. It's almost an hour driving, but only ten minutes flying. The helicopter is waiting for us a mile out. We're going to have to fly her to Dublin Falls General. You need to stay out of the way and let us work.

You won't be able to fly with her. I swear I'll go with her. There just won't be enough room. Do you understand?" I was numb. I simply nodded.

The whole time he spoke to me, he was working on her. I saw he had an IV in her arm and was pressing on her wound. Blood continued to soak the dressing. She was still unconscious, and her breathing was faint and labored. The car skidded to a stop. In front of us was a helicopter with its rotors spinning. Sean was outside of it. I could see a pilot and another person inside. They raced over and helped get her out and into the helicopter. Ghost jumped in to go with her. I almost broke and insisted I go too, but I knew there wasn't room. They had her in and they were taking off in less than two minutes. I watched them take off with my life. As they raced away, I sank to my knees on the ground.

Terror crouched down beside me. "She needs you to be strong for her, Devil. You have to believe she's going to be alright. She's a fighter. Look at what she's survived. Ghost and Sean will do everything they can to make sure of that. Let's get in the car so we can get to the hospital. The others will take care of Alex. We'll deal with him later. Come on." He helped me to my feet.

I followed him like a robot. As we raced on the curvy roads to get to Dublin Falls General, I prayed over and over for God to let her live. It felt like it took forever to get there even though a part of me knew Ranger had broken every speed limit to get us there as quickly as possible.

We stopped outside the doors to the ER. I jumped out of the car and raced inside. Terror was hot on my heels with Ranger not far behind. When I got inside, I saw Ghost. He was sitting in a chair with his head hanging. Sean was pacing the lobby. I ran to Ghost.

"Is she okay? Are they working on her?" He looked up. I could see her blood on his shirt and hands. He looked wiped.

"Devil, they took her straight into surgery. Sean called it in mid-flight, so they knew to have a surgical team waiting at the door." He stopped.

"What aren't you telling me, Ghost?"

He sighed. "They said they don't think her chances are good, brother. She's lost a lot of blood and the bullet likely tore up a lot internally. We almost lost her in the air. They told us we need to pray." His words went through me like a knife. I yelled and kicked a chair. Ranger, Terror, Sean, and Ghost all grabbed me and dragged me outside.

I stood there screaming out my rage. I'd waited what felt like forever to find my soulmate, then Ashlee came along. We were just starting our lives together. We wanted to get married and have a baby. The thought of not getting to do that, of trying to live without her, was unthinkable. I just screamed until I went hoarse then sunk to my knees. They stood protectively around me. I heard more bikes roar into the parking lot, but I didn't pay attention to them. I heard numerous voices and still I sat there on my knees with my head bowed.

Suddenly, I felt a soft hand on my face. I looked up to see Harlow. She had tears in her eyes. She kneeled down beside me and I wrapped my arms around her. I knew I was sobbing like a baby and I didn't care. "Harley, what will I do if she dies? I can't live without her. She's my soul, my life. She was supposed to be with me for the rest of our lives. We were going to have more kids and raise them to be Warrior Hellions. Tell me how can I go on if she dies? They say her chances are poor and we should pray. Jesus Christ!"

She held me as I sobbed. Then she started to whisper, "You listen to me, Marine, she isn't going to die. She's too tough, and she has this whole club and more behind her. She's going to pull through. You can't think any other way than she's going to make it. Now, you need to calm down so we can go inside and wait for news. They'll kick us out if you tear the place up. Come with me." I blindly took her hand and stood.

She led me to the surgical waiting room. The rest of the club followed. It looked like all the guys who went to the other two sites had returned and come to the hospital. Most of the old ladies were here. They all looked teary-eyed. As the hours passed, I felt like I was losing my mind. Not a word. Janessa even tried and got nowhere.

Several times Harley made me drink something or even once eat a sandwich. I did it on autopilot. Sean came over. "Man, I'm sorry, Devil. We just found out the information on those locations about an hour before he took her. I'm so fucking sorry we couldn't find him sooner. Shit!"

I shook my head.

"Sean it's not your fault. If it wasn't for your intel, we might not have even found her at all. And your helicopter may have saved her life. Thank you." He shook my hand.

It was going on six hours when what looked like a doctor came out wearily pulling off his mask. He asked for the family of Ashlee Andrews. I raced over to him. His eyes took in me and my club. He swallowed nervously. "The good news is she made it through surgery. It was very touch and go. The bullet clipped an artery and did other internal damage we had to repair. There were problems and we almost lost her. She coded on the table." His words made everything go fuzzy. She'd died on the table! "However, we got her back. She's one strong young lady. The next forty-eight hours are critical. It will determine if she will make a recovery or not. I would advise you to all continue to pray. She's not out of the woods by any means. She'll remain in ICU under sedation for at least the next forty-eight hours."

I found my voice enough to ask him if we could see her.

"You can see her but only immediate family and one at a time. We'll keep monitoring her very closely. I forgot to ask when I introduced myself, what is your relationship to her?" he asked me.

I briefly wondered why it mattered.

"I'm her fiancé."

He gave me a grave look.

"We don't know yet and might not know for a while, if she'll maintain the pregnancy or not. She's not very far along but luckily, we check for pregnancy as a routine test before surgery. Her HCG count was high, so we adjusted what medications we gave her during the surgery and what we'll give her after. I hate to add to your worry and burden, but you need to be prepared that she's still at high risk to miscarry, even if she pulls through. I thought you would want to know. I need to get back, but a nurse will be out soon to let you know when she's been moved to the ICU." He shook my hand and left.

I stood there frozen. All I could think about was him saying she might not make it and that she was pregnant! Hell, we'd only stopped the birth control pills just over two weeks ago! How in the hell could she be pregnant that quickly? I looked at the others. I had to have heard him wrong. I caught Harlow's eye.

"Did he just say she's—"

She interrupted, "Pregnant? Yeah, he did."

I sank down in a chair.

"How? We barely stopped the pills two weeks ago. She can't be." I kept questioning it because in the back of my mind, if I accepted that she was pregnant and she died, I'd be losing two people not one. I couldn't face that.

The vigil continued as we all sat there quietly thinking about what the doctor had told us. An hour later, a nurse came out to say she was out of recovery and in the ICU. We headed up there. It was unfortunately a very familiar place for us. Regan and Janessa went to the nurses' station to speak to them. When they came back, they were smiling.

"You're in luck. The charge nurse tonight is Vicki. She's taken care of some of us before. She knows the Warriors' protocol for guards and staying, so she won't give you any trouble. You can go on back. She's in room 315." I stood frozen for a minute. I was afraid to see her. Harlow took my hand. "Let's go. I'll come with you." She led me down the hall and into room 315. When we entered and I saw her, I couldn't breathe.

She was hooked up to so many wires and machines all making noise I could barely see her. She looked as white as the sheets. Her chest looked like it was barely moving. She was swallowed up by the bed and dark shadows were under her eyes. I moaned as I crept to the side of the bed and touched her hand.

"Oh, babe, what did they do to you? Precious, I hope you can hear me. It's Jack. Baby, you need to stay strong and pull through this. Do you hear me? Angel, Jayce and I need you. We can't live without you. And the doctor said there's a new baby on the way. Did you know that? You're carrying our baby already. I need for both of you to pull through this. Please, Precious. Do it for me. I love you so fucking much it hurts." At this point I broke down in tears again. Harlow helped me to sit. I looked at her. "Harley, pray for her please. Pray for both of them. But if I have to make a choice, then please let God save Ashlee." She stayed with me for a while and then left me so I could have time alone with her.

Throughout the night and the next day there was always one person with me in her room. The club was supporting both of us. I called and talked to Angel at one point since she was missing us. Her little voice stabbed me in the heart. There wasn't really any improvement by morning but also no decline. We were still in a wait and see mode. By the time twenty-four hours had lapsed, I wanted to scream. It was ten at night and Regan was with me this time.

We were talking when an alarm went off. I jumped up and so did Regan. A nurse came running in the room. There was a flurry of activity. No one would tell us what was going on. They just ordered us out. I paced the hall. I turned to Regan. She saw the look on my face.

"From the little I saw before they kicked us out, her blood pressure dropped, and her pulse spiked. We'll have to see." I grunted and continued to pace. Forty-five minutes later the doctor came out. He came over to us.

"She seems to have stabilized. We think she threw a clot, and it made her have a cardiac incident. We've administered some blood thinners and will be monitoring her for more issues like this." We both gave a sigh of relief. He gave us a small smile. "There is more that I consider good news, at least for the moment. Even with this new shock to her body, her body continues to fight to maintain the pregnancy. Hang onto that hope." He left us there with me feeling lost. We were allowed back in the room.

Over the rest of the night, I spent hours just talking to her. Regan was replaced by Ghost. He gave calm, silent support like Regan or even Janessa. Maybe it was because they had medical training. Around six the next morning, they started running more tests, taking more blood. Her doctor came in around eight.

"Well, her tests show she's not having any new active bleeding. Her blood counts are going up. Her vitals are stable. No more incidents like last night. I'd say as long as she makes it to the forty-eight-hour mark without issues, she has a fair to good chance of making a full recovery. That's an improvement from last night." I thanked him.

By this time, I'd been here almost thirty-six hours. The nurses showed me where I could shower. The guys had brought me clothes and hygiene stuff. Janessa and Wren sat with her while I showered. I did feel almost human when I was done. Harlow had brought me breakfast and coffee which helped to revive me more. They told me that Angel was acting out because she wanted us. I took time to call and talk to her. She was only three. She didn't understand why she couldn't come see us or why we weren't at home with her and her brother.

The day passed slowly and in a haze for me. No one mentioned Alex and right now, he wasn't my focus. But when things were resolved with Ashlee, he would be, and God help him. At ten that night, her doctor came to see us again.

"I understand she's been stable all day. We're going to start weaning her from the sedation and off the vent. She may wake up confused and fighting. So, for her safety, we're going to restrain her hands. We can't have her pull that tube before we know she's able to breathe okay on her own. I'd usually suggest you leave when we do this, but I don't imagine you will. She's going to take a while to recover, two maybe three months. If she continues to improve like she is, she might be out of here in time for Christmas. But that's a big might." He left us to do the rest of his rounds.

I looked at Harlow and Wren. They both had smiles on their faces. I tried to, but I was scared to get my hopes up. They seemed to understand without me telling them this. It was close to an hour later, when a team came in to start the weaning process. By then Regan and Janessa were with me. As expected, they asked us to leave, but I refused. The ladies explained they were nurses and worked there. The staff stopped trying to get us out of the room. The weaning process consisted of them changing settings on her breathing machine. Then they were monitoring how she responded to it. Regan explained they'd likely wean her for the next two to three days.

By the third day, the club brought Angel and Jayce to the hospital to see me. We still couldn't let Angel see her mom, but at least I got to spend time with them. They'd said she hadn't been sleeping or eating well with us gone. I held the two of them hugging them tight. They were my connection to Ashlee. After a few hours, Trish took them home. Ashlee had been here seventy-two hours and been in the weaning process for over twenty-four, which she seemed to be tolerating.

It was around noon on the fifth day, when they said they were shutting the ventilator off and bringing her out of the sedation. They'd warned us some patients had a hard time come out from under prolonged sedation and ventilation. I stood praying she'd be one of the lucky ones. What I'd apparently underestimated was how confused and scared she'd be when she did wake up. She came out of it trying to scream and she couldn't with the tube down her throat which caused her to look terrified. She thrashed around and if her hands hadn't been restrained, I could see she would have yanked the tube out causing more damage. Once she calmed down and they saw she was breathing fine on her own, they went to remove the tube. That was horrible to watch too, as she gagged and thrashed.

I finally stepped forward. "Precious, stop, you're fine. Calm down and they'll get that tube out of your throat. Please. You're gonna hurt yourself if you don't stop it." She looked at me and began to relax. I kept eye contact with her, so she'd concentrate on me as they finished removing her breathing tube. Once it was out, they gave her a sip or two of water. They left after doing a quick assessment. I sat down on the bed and kissed her. She was looking at me with a confused look on her face.

"Do you remember what happened?" She shook her head no. I gave her a quick rundown. When I got to the part of her stepping in front of me, she nodded.

"I remember now," she rasped. "I couldn't let him kill you. How long have I been here, what—"? I stopped her.

"Sean had a helicopter, and he came with some of his men. They were able to get you here, and that saved your life. The bullet did a lot of damage and they said you coded on the operating table and they brought you back. You've been in here for five days and they've been working you off the vent for most of the last three days. Jesus Christ, Ashlee! Don't ever do anything like that again. You keep yourself safe and let me handle shit. Do you think I would have been able to live if you'd died? What would I tell Angel and Jayce?" I could see her getting tears in her eyes.

"Babe, I don't mean to make you cry. I just don't want you to ever do something like that again. I couldn't go on if it did." She sniffed as the tears ran down her face.

"Jack, what would you have done if the roles were reversed? If I was about to be shot." I looked at her speechless because the automatic response I wanted to make was to tell her I'd have stepped in front of the gun too.

Instead, I said, "That's different, Ash." She shook her head.

"No, it isn't. Why would it be? Because you're a man? Because you were a Marine? Tell me why it was different, Jack. It was an automatic response for me to protect someone I love. Now, if you don't mind, I think I want to be alone. I'm tired and I'm too tired to get yelled at right now." She slowly and painfully turned away from me.

I came around the bed. "No, I'm not done. I won't argue anymore but I'm not leaving. You need to push this button if you're in pain. It will dispense pain meds every hour into your IV. If you push it early, it doesn't dispense. We need to talk about something else." She sighed and opened her eyes.

"What? I don't feel in the mood. I woke up after days and I thought I'd get to see my fiancé's loving face, only I got a pissed face. I'm not up to anymore, Jack. This can wait. Please leave. I just want to rest." I could see the pain in her eyes and not all of it was physical. I hadn't meant to jump on her as soon as she woke up. I gave her a kiss.

"I'll be back later. Rest up. Love you." She merely nodded. She didn't say the words back which had me worried. I left her room but not the hospital. Instead, I went to the waiting room. I was surprised to find Harlow and Terror there. They came straight to me.

"How is she? Did she come off the machine yet," Harlow asked? I nodded.

"Yeah, she's off and breathing on her own. She told me she wanted me to leave." I saw them exchange confused looks. "I kind of yelled at her about stepping in front of the gun and she got pissed at me when she asked me what I'd have done if the roles were reversed and hell, I don't know. But now she wants to rest without me around and when I told her I loved her. She didn't say it back. Fuck, did I just ruin everything?" I paced the room. Harlow grabbed my arm.

"I assume you indicated you would've done the same thing?" I nodded yes. "So, what makes it different? I mean, I know you're all a bunch of macho Neanderthals, but our instincts to protect those we love are just as strong as yours is."

Both Terror and I tried to protest, but she shushed us. "No, don't say anything. You just belittled her, Devil. You reduced what she did to an inconvenience or a problem. And made sound like if it had been a man, it was heroic but because it was a woman, it was stupid. Shit, I'd want you out of my sight too. Men are knuckleheads." She growled before going down the hall to Ashlee's room. I looked at Terror.

"What the hell just happened?" I asked him. He sighed.

"She showed us we're dumbasses who are still acting and thinking like cavemen, I guess. Man, I can't disagree with you being upset, but I can sort of see what Harlow meant too. Probably wasn't one of the first things you should have led with as soon as she came out of her coma. Did you tell her about the baby?"

"No, I didn't get a chance after I stuck my foot in it. Shit, all I can think about is losing her and what that would do to me. I never looked at it from her perspective of what she would have felt or done if he'd killed me. I just want to keep her and the kids safe. Fuck, I did mess up. I'll let her rest a little and then talk to her again." He nodded and we stepped out in the hall. I was going to suggest we get a cup of coffee when I heard alarms go off and saw people running. They were running into Ashlee's room. I froze then took off running toward it.

As I got to the door, Harlow was coming out. She had a scared look on her face. People were shouting and they had a cart in her room and were huddled around the bed. A nurse shoved both of us out and shut the door in our faces. I stood trying to watch through the window in the door. They were working all around her. I could see them pulling out needles and shit. Then I saw one of the nurse's pull stuff out of the crash cart. I hit the floor. Terror grabbed me.

"What's wrong, Devil?" I pointed to the window. He must have looked because I heard him swear. I could hear him and Harlow talking but their words were making no sense. I sat there waiting for them to come out and tell me she was dead. And the last fucking thing I'd done was give her hell!

I don't know how long I sat on the floor before several brothers showed up and practically carried me to the waiting room. I tried to fight them, but they wouldn't let go. Once there, I sank into a chair and closed my eyes. I sat there living in terror and dread of them coming to tell me she was gone. I'd fucking lose it. I could feel the panic rising. I was about to jump up when Regan came into the room. She headed straight to me. I swallowed the bile in my throat. She sat down and took my hand.

"Devil, she's okay so wipe that look off your face." At first the words didn't register. When they finally sank in, I looked at her afraid I'd heard her wrong. She shook her head. "You didn't hear me wrong. She's going to be okay. The alarms tripped because they detected a rapid drop in her vitals. Terror told me what you saw through the window in the door. It's standard to take a crash cart into the room. They worked on her because she ended up seizing on them. Apparently, the doctor had ordered a new medication for her pain control this morning. She hadn't had any yet. She pushed the patient-controlled analgesia machine while Harlow was with her. It caused her to have an allergic reaction and that caused her vitals to drop and then the seizure. As soon as they administered the meds to counteract it, everything settled down. She'll continue to be monitored, but she's going to be okay. They'll be marking it down to never give her that medication again and will put her back on the old medication."

I wrapped her in my arms thanking her over and over. She hugged me. "You're welcome. They want her to sleep for a bit. This is hard on her body." I nodded then a thought struck me.

"Is this going to cause her to lose the baby?" Regan shrugged.

"Only time will tell. There were no immediate signs of a miscarriage but again, she'll have to rest and recover. But I think if the shooting and this doesn't do it, then nothing is going to shake that baby loose. Why don't you go get some food and then come back? They won't let anyone in just yet. We'll stay here." I agreed and left to go try and eat.

Chapter 16: Devil Dog

It had been a day since Ashlee had come off the vent only to have a seizure due to an allergic reaction to a pain med. She'd mainly slept the remainder of the afternoon and night. I'd stayed by her bedside. She hadn't really awakened, so I could apologize for giving her hell about the shooting. It was dawn and I'd just woke up from my fitful sleep. I stretched and then looked over at the bed. She was lying there watching me. I jumped up and rushed over to her.

"Shit, babe, it's so good to see your eyes open again! Are you okay?" She nodded. She went to roll over and flinched. I slid my arms under her and helped her into position. She sighed. I kissed her. When I broke it, she went to speak, and I stopped her. "Say nothing. I need to speak first. I am sorry I jumped on you for stepping in front of the gun. I didn't mean to imply since you did it, it was stupid. Harley made me see how we're all a bunch of men who think like macho asses. I'm never going to like for you to put yourself in harm's way, but I can understand why you did it. I would have done the same. I just can't imagine losing you. Please tell me you don't hate me."

She gave me a surprised look. "Jack, I don't hate you.

Yes, you pissed me off and I couldn't deal with it at that time. That's why I told you to leave the room. I needed to think and get my bearings. I love you, Jack." I hugged her.

"I'm so glad to hear that. When I told you, I loved you and left the room, you never said it back. I thought you hated me." She laughed.

"No, I was just pissed and truly not paying attention to what you said. Now, tell me why I feel worse. I remember alarms and then a bunch of nurses and people coming into the room. Why?" I explained to her about the allergic reaction.

She shook her head in amazement. "Really? Wow. I've never had a reaction to medication before. Definitely want to know the name of that one. Now, you wanted to talk to me about something else. What was it?" Before I could say anything, her doctor entered. He greeted us and introduced himself to her. He ran through her status and assessed her a little bit. When he was done, he looked at her in amazement.

"Ms. Andrews, it's amazing to know what you've been through over the last six days to see you doing so well. All your tests are looking good, your wound is looking good. I'm amazed and if you keep this up, you can go to a regular floor tomorrow and home for Christmas, maybe. Just no more allergic reactions." She laughed. Then he continued, "and even more amazing is none of this has seemed to phase the baby. Your pregnancy is showing no signs of terminating itself."

She shot me a stunned look. The doctor caught it. "Oh, you didn't tell her?" he said to me, surprised. I shook my head.

"I didn't get a chance with all this other stuff happening. Will you excuse us so we can talk?" He nodded and left. I turned back to her.

"Jack, did he say a baby? What is he talking about?" I explained what they'd told us when she came out of surgery. She laid there stunned.

"How is that possible? It's only been what three weeks since I stopped the birth control pills? I couldn't have gotten pregnant that quick," she mused. I shrugged.

"Precious, they were very sure that you are. The blood work showed your levels were up and that only happens when you're pregnant. They've been monitoring you the whole time to be sure you weren't miscarrying. We can ask the doctor to either redo the blood or maybe they can do something else. Let's ask Regan and she'll know." She gave me a distracted nod. "Babe, aren't you happy about the baby?" I asked her with trepidation. I knew we'd agreed to try, but maybe she'd changed her mind or thought it would take longer for her to get pregnant.

"Oh no, I'm really happy, just stunned. How can it be that soon? I had to have gotten pregnant as soon as I stopped the pills. I want us to find out, please. I need to know for sure. And what about all the meds they've been giving me?" She asked in a panic. I reassured her on that front. Then I pulled out my phone and called Regan. She said to let her check something and she'd get back to me. We waited in anxiety. About a half hour later, Regan walked in and she wasn't alone. There was a man with her. She introduced him as Dr. Hunter. I knew his name. He was the OB for all the club's old ladies when they were pregnant. He shook our hands.

"Ah, another Warrior baby is suspected is what Regan has told me. I need a little info then we'll see what we want to do. First, what was the first day of your last period my dear?" Ashlee told him November 12th. "And were you on birth control pills or using something else for birth control?" We explained stopping the pill on November 28th. He nodded. "Okay assuming you got pregnant immediately and the way we calculate due dates and weeks started from the date of the last period not the actual day of conception, you'd be in your sixth week. Now, a blood test can be done to see if it is still positive, but I expect you want to see if the baby was conceived sooner even if you were on the pills. Let me get a tech up here so we can look. With your injuries and issues, we can definitely get the insurance to pay for an early ultrasound." I told him we'd pay even if the insurance didn't.

About twenty minutes later a tech came in with a machine. I watched as they did what they called a vaginal ultrasound. Which to be honest, made me wince to see him insert that thing up my woman's vagina. She seemed to take it all in stride. Dr. Hunter did the test himself. He was jotting down things and then moving around here and there, muttering to himself. I was about to yell at him when he looked up.

"Well, it seems from what I can tell, you did conceive as soon as you stopped the pills. In fact, it looks like you conceived within a day or two which could mean the pills were not working effectively or you could have missed doses. It is hard to tell. However, I can say this puts you at six weeks and your due date will be August 20th of next year. Now, for the other thing I've found." I felt my heart drop. She had a scared look on her face.

He continued, "I can see from your stomach you had a c-section. Looking at this, I see no reason why you can't have a normal vaginal birth with this one. Your chart mentioned you had one for your son due to a partial placental abruption. So that's good news. We'll keep an eye on both of you, but things should go well. I'll go ahead and prescribe your vitamins and folic acid. Make an appointment to see me in a month in my office. Congratulations! I always love to see more Warriors in my office." We thanked him profusely before he headed out.

Regan hugged and congratulated both of us before she left us alone. I leaned over the bed and took her face in my hands. "I love you Ashlee and you've made me so fucking happy. Now I have even more to love than just you, Angel, and Jayce." I kissed her deeply. When we came up for air, she laughed.

"Jack, I bet you never imagined this a year ago, did you?" I had to laugh and agree. We spent the rest of the day making plans about the baby and the wedding. She didn't ask about Alex and I didn't bring him up.

It had been three days since Ashlee had recovered from the seizure. She'd finally convinced me to take a break away from the hospital. Christmas was four days away and the doctors were planning to let her come home on the twenty-third. Before she came home, there was something I needed to take care of first. I headed to the compound.

A couple of the old ladies were keeping her company

at the hospital. My brothers were all at the compound when I got there. We headed out to the Hole. The Hole was our name for the building we had way back on the property in the woods. It's where we kept anyone we needed to question, torture, or kill. Alex had been left there to wait for me for the past week. They'd given him enough food and water to barely keep him alive.

When I walked inside the Hole, he was lying down on the floor of one of the cells. He looked up at us. He saw me and he sneered. "So, you finally came to see me, did you? Did the whore die yet?" The guys all growled. I smiled. My response took him by surprise. I nodded to Hawk.

"Get him out and in the outer room. I want him on his tiptoes and naked." He nodded and opened the door. Alex tried to struggle but Hawk just punched him in the gut. As he dragged him out to hang on a hook we had suspended from the ceiling, I looked Alex over. It was obvious some of my brothers had been paying him visits. He was bruised and cut in numerous places all over his body. Once they had him suspended, I walked around him. He tried to swivel to keep me in sight, but it wasn't possible. I came to a stop in front of him after doing two complete circles.

"No, Ashlee isn't dead. In fact, she's recovering nicely and going to be home in a few days to spend Christmas with us, you know, her real family. And Alex, we have great news. I know she told you we were going to get married, well that'll be soon. But the best news is the other thing she told you. Remember, she said we were going to have more kids, so Angel and Jayce would have siblings. I'm happy to say the first one of those is on its way. He or she will join our little happy family in August," I said with a big smirk on my face. He screamed in rage and tried to kick at me. I laughed.

"Sadly, for you, Alex, you won't be around to see either happy occasion. See you tried to take away my happiness. You shot the woman I love more than life itself. For that alone, I plan to kill you, but you tortured her for years. You held her hostage, beat her, raped her, and just plain terrorized her. That'll earn you more torture before you draw your last breath." He glared at me. "So, over the next couple of days, me and my brothers will be paying you visits. I'd do it all myself, but I need to be at the hospital with my fiancé. And we're going to share so much love with you, you won't know what to do. And Alex, let me tell you something, some of that love is going to really hurt. We have this thing about rapists in particular. We hate them and like to share with them what it feels like to be the victim. Just a little something for you to look forward to." His eyes got big around and he was sweating. I could see his false bravado and anger was fading into fear.

"I'd love to stretch this out longer. See several of my brothers were in special forces and they know ways to stretch out torture for days even weeks. I know some myself being a former Marine. But I want you gone before she comes home from the hospital, so that shortens the timeline. But don't worry, we'll be sure to get in all the quality torture we'd have done over weeks in those couple of days. We wouldn't want you to miss out on any of it. However, know this Alex, I will be the one who takes your life. That ultimate satisfaction belongs to me. Now, let me think about what I want to do first."

I walked over to a table where all our "tools" were laid out. I picked up a wooden rod.

I walked back to him. I nodded to Storm. "Tie his legs so his knees are bent, and I can see the soles of his feet." He went to get rope. I stood in front of Alex, smacking the palm of my hand with the caning rod. He watched every slap. He tried to struggle but Storm had him tied with his legs bent and tied with the soles of his feet at a ninety-degree angle to his thighs. I stepped back and let the rod sail through the air. He could hear it coming before it struck the soles of his feet. He yelled out in pain. I beat both of them over and over again with him screaming and sobbing more and more. Caning rarely left permanent injury or visible injury. However, it was very painful and ensured that even if by some miracle he got loose, he wouldn't be able to walk let alone run anywhere. This was done a lot in the Middle East.

After about a half hour of this, I got bored. He was hanging there with his head down, sobbing. The bottoms of his feet were blue and purple from the blood rising up under the skin. I went back to the table and picked up an iron comb. It was something used in the textile industry to comb wool and to prepare it for spinning into things like rugs. It was also a very painful torture tool.

I stood back in front of him and drew it down his chest. Alex screamed out in pain as the flesh was literally torn open. I proceeded to spend the next hour randomly running it over various parts of his body. I pushed hard, so it would remove more than skin, it tore away his flesh. He passed out halfway through, so we had to wake him up before I could continue.

After I'd torn up his chest, back, legs, and arms, I whispered to Torch. He went over to get a container which he brought back to me. Inside of the container was salt. I rubbed it into each and every one of the combing marks. He was sobbing and begging for me to stop. I shook my head.

"Sorry Alex, this doesn't stop. You didn't stop when Ashlee begged you to, so why would I stop when you beg? Now, we're going to leave you alone for a while. But we don't want you to get lonely so we're going to leave on some music." We left him hanging in there, but with his now sore feet touching the ground and the music blaring. Sound torture could drive a person mad. And I didn't want him to be able to sleep to escape the pain.

Outside I stopped to talk to my brothers. "I'm gonna go see the kids and then take them to the hospital. Ashlee is going crazy and she can see them now that she's in a regular room. Someone be sure to come out and work him over every hour or so. I'll be back as soon as I can. Just be sure he doesn't die before I kill him."

They all told me not to worry. They'd keep him company. Back at the clubhouse, Angel threw herself in my arms crying out her eyes. Once I got her calmed down, I took Jayce from Ms. Marie. He looked so big even after not seeing him for a few days. I got them ready and headed back to the hospital with them.

Ashlee burst out crying when she saw them. Over the next hour or so, she held them though she had to be careful of her wound. Angel asked her a million questions. Jayce just stared at his mommy. She fed him a bottle. Ashlee was sad that with her being in the hospital for a week, he now had no choice but to go on formula a hundred percent, because her milk had dried up this time. Or more specifically, they'd given her something to make it happen. When it was time for them to leave, Janessa and Alannah had come to get them. Angel didn't want to leave, but I told her that her mommy would be home in two days. She left without too much protest after that.

I sat back down on the side of the bed after they left. She searched my face but said nothing. "What is it, Precious? You look like you want to ask something." She looked away and then back.

"What happened to Alex? You nor anyone else has mentioned him. Where is he, Jack? Is he in jail or did he get away? Tell me." I stood up to pace.

"Babe, why don't we talk about this later?" She shook her head no. "Fine. He isn't in jail nor did he get away. He's somewhere safe at the moment. He'll soon no longer be a threat to you or the kids." She stared at me hard.

"Are you going to kill him?" I remained silent. I didn't want her to know anything else. She took my silence as a yes. I waited for her to tell me we couldn't kill him. Instead, she surprised me. "Don't let him get away. He needs to disappear and never have a chance to come back into our lives. That's all I want." I gave her a nod in agreement. She dropped the topic.

Around dinner time, Dyson came knocking on the door. We waved him inside. He greeted us. "I don't want to disturb you, but I thought you'd want to know this. The judge contacted me today. He knew you were in the hospital, so he called me. This morning he signed off on your divorce and filed the papers. You are now officially divorced from Alex. The judge granted you sole custody with child support and alimony as well as half the assets. I thought you'd both like to know this. Merry Christmas." We both thanked him profusely. This was the best early Christmas present ever. He accepted our thanks and wishes for a Merry Christmas then left.

"Jack, I forgot to ask. How do the doctors and police think I was shot? Do they know about Alex?" I shook my head no.

"We told them we were at the compound having a meeting with a friend who'd flown in to see us. You went out to head into town and someone ran you off the road and shot at you. You called us and we found you shot and bleeding. There was no time to call an ambulance, so our friend had you brought to the hospital in his helicopter."

"What about the car? I didn't do that so how did you back it up?" I grinned.

"Well, some of us did a little staging and we have your blood on dressings from the helicopter, so we made sure it got smeared around and there were enough casings from Alex's gun and holes in the car to make it believable. They bought it." She shook her head in amazement. The cops so far had stayed away from questioning her. But we'd also been telling them, she was still too sick to be questioned. I expected them today or tomorrow.

I was lucky we'd talked about the story we fed the cops, because two hours later Officer Cane and his partner Kennedy showed up. They questioned her and she made sure to tell them what we'd told them. They asked if she recognized the shooter and she claimed she didn't, because it happened so fast and the car wasn't familiar. I knew Officer Cane was thinking it could have been Alex. But he didn't push her after she told him she had only a few memories of the shooting. They left after we promised to let them know if she remembered anything.

That evening I went back to the clubhouse to sleep at her insistence. I made sure to pay Alex a visit with some of the guys. I could see he'd been beaten again. This time I tortured him with Palestinian hanging. It was a method where the person was strung with his hands tied behind his back and then hung. It was painful because it dislocated the shoulders. I'd have loved to leave him like that all night, but you couldn't do it for more than an hour without running the risk it would kill him. I worked some more of my frustration out on him by beating him with brass knuckles. My final torture before going to bed was to rip off his fingernails and toenails.

The next day I got up early to visit Alex before heading to the hospital to see Ashlee. When I entered the Hole, he was hanging from the hook almost unconscious. I turned off the loud music. He barely moved. I went over and jerked his head back by his hair. He groaned and cracked his eyes open.

"Good morning, Alex. Hope you had a good night. I wanted to drop in before I headed out. On the menu this morning, is to leave you with a reminder, so you don't forget me. I was thinking what I should do, and I realized you need to know what it feels like to be shot again. Ashlee is having to feel that every day as she recovers. Now, I could shoot you and then let you die, but there's no fun in that. So, see my brother Ghost over there, is going to patch you up. Not enough to alleviate the pain, but enough so you don't die from it. I wondered where I should shoot, and we decided why not kneecap you."

He shook his head. "Just fucking kill me. Why keep this up? I'm not gonna last much longer," he pleaded. I laughed.

"Oh, you still have suffering to go through and the guys will keep you company today. They can be some inventive and vindictive bastards." He hung there as I pulled my Glock and I put a .45 round in each knee. He screamed so high, I thought he'd hit a new note. Ghost quickly patched him up and I left for the day.

At the hospital I spent time with Ash talking about the wedding. The doctor said it would take her a couple of months to recover. We discussed wedding dates and I knew she had ideas for the dress, venue, and decorations she'd already talked about with the old ladies. We decided on March 17th on St. Patrick's Day.

That gave us just under three months and was still five months before the baby was due. She was up walking every day and was getting around better. I took her for walks around the hospital. She was nervous about getting everything we'd bought for Christmas wrapped in time, but I reassured her the old ladies had been taking care of the things that came and had volunteered to help her wrap them in time. She was excited to be coming home tomorrow. That meant I had to finish my business with Alex tonight.

When I left the hospital at the end of visiting hours, I went to the compound and straight to the Hole. The guys were waiting for me. He had taken even more pain throughout the day. I could see he had more cuts and it looked like one of the guys had used electrical shock, if the burn marks were anything to go by. I stepped in front of him. His head was tilted back on his shoulders. His eyes were mere slits.

"Hello Alex. Time for this party to end. I wish I could keep this going for several more weeks, but my Precious comes home tomorrow. And I can't have you living on the same property as her. The final thing I want you to feel is what it must have been like for her all those times you raped her. Now, I have a couple things I think will mimic that for you." His eyes got a panicked look as I held up what I'd brought for him. It wasn't anything unusual. It was an empty beer bottle. It was what I was going to do with it he wasn't going to like.

He tried to kick and struggle as I walked around behind him. I had Ghost and Savage put on gloves. They helped to hold his ass cheeks apart. I proceeded to jam it up his ass hard. He screamed in agony and yelled, "no please" over and over as I raped him with the bottle. I gave it one final hard thrust and left it there as I faced him.

"You didn't stop all those times you raped her with those toys, did you?" He cried as he shook his head. I could see my brothers looking at each other in disgust. "She told me what you used to do to punish her. And I heard you threaten to do it to her again in that basement. How does it feel motherfucker?! Not so hot does it."

I knew he was reaching his end. His heart was likely to give out from the shock and trauma soon. I had another thing for him to experience. I pulled out a long, glass rod. I held it up. "Do you know what this is?" He shook his head. My brothers all looked at it in confusion.

"Well, it was funny. I went online looking for some toys and I found this. It is a male urethral stimulator. Personally, I don't know who in the hell would ever find this enjoyable, but supposedly some men do. I bought it not for me, but to add to our collection of tools. A special treat for rapists, I thought. You get to be our guinea pig. We want to see if this is sexually stimulating or just fucking painful. Lucky for you, it came in the mail today."

He was moaning in fear. I put on a pair of rubber gloves and grabbed his flaccid cock. Then without any lubrication, I began to "catheterize" him with it. He yelled out in pain. All the guys were wincing in pain. Hell, I even felt it. Once it was fully inserted, I left it like the bottle. He struggled and screamed until he passed out. I looked at the guys. They were shaking their heads.

"Man, that is some fucked up shit. Remind us not to piss you off. And really, men actually like that stuck up their cock?" I shrugged.

"From what I heard, yeah some do. No thanks, I'll pass. Now wake his ass up. I want to end this. Then we want his body to be found. How about his car going over the edge of the road into a deep ravine where it explodes and burns him beyond recognition? Think we can make that convincing?" They all nodded.

Ghost woke him up using smelling salts. When he was alert, I pulled out a knife. "Time to say goodbye, Alex. It hasn't been a pleasure knowing you. Hope you rot in hell for eternity you, sonofabitch." I stabbed the knife straight into the hollow at the base of his throat. He gagged and blood gushed onto the plastic we had on the floor. He bled out in under five minutes. I left him for the guys to take care of. I needed to sleep and get ready for Ash to come home tomorrow.

Epilogue: Ashlee

The day was finally here. Today, I will become Mrs. Ashlee Cannon. Jack and I had only grown closer over the last three months since the shooting. My recovery had been slow for me, but fast according to the doctors. Our baby was growing in my womb every day. I am now eighteen weeks. I'd went to the doctor yesterday to have the ultrasound to find out the sex. We planned to tell everyone today at the wedding reception. We'd found a place in Knoxville for the wedding and the reception. The ladies had been such a huge help in getting everything ordered and planned. My dress was perfect. It was what I'd pictured in my head every time I thought of a princess wedding dress. I was still not showing enough for it to affect the lines of it.

I'd asked Harlow to be my maid of honor and then Harper and Brielle. Devil has asked Terror to be his best man and Viper and Sniper to be his other groomsmen. Angel was excited because she was going to get to wear a princess dress too and walk Mommy down the aisle. Bull had agreed to walk me down the aisle as the father of the bride like he did with almost all the other Warrior Brides. The guys had moaned because like Harper, I had them dress in real wedding clothes.

For the groomsmen, all were in suits in midnight blue with white dress shirts. Their ties were sapphire blue to go with the wedding colors of sapphire blue, midnight blue and fuchsia. They tried to rebel when I told them they had to wear pink then I took pity and let them know the only fuchsia was in the boutonniere. Devil Dog was going to be in a white suit with midnight blue shirt and sapphire blue tie to contrast with the other guys.

Harlow had found a beautiful long form fitting dress in fuchsia and the other brides' maids were the same dress only in sapphire blue. Angel's dress was also in fuchsia.

My dress was long with a ten-foot train and made of tulle, satin and lace. The entire bodice was encrusted with rhinestones. The bodice formed cap sleeves and dipped low between my breasts with clear netting between it and the neck where more of the rhinestones wrapped around creating a faux necklace. The sleeves were of the same netting and then around the wrists were bands of the rhinestones as well as a few scattered up the arms. The back was completely open to the hips except for the necklace part that came around from the front. I wore clear glass slippers. The bouquet was made up of fuchsia-colored roses with baby's breath and some greenery. My earrings were long chandelier type ones made of blue sapphires and diamonds.

The girls had done up my makeup to really bring out my eyes. My hair had grown out more and it was pulled back at the nape of my neck where they curled and pinned it into a chignon. I had forgone a veil since I didn't want anything to cover the dress. My nails were painted fuchsia on my hands and feet. I was putting on the finishing touches when there was a knock. Harlow answered the door letting in Bull. He was dressed like the groomsmen. Even at fifty-two he looked handsome and fit. He came over to me.

"Well, sweetheart, the day is here. Like I tried to tell all of these ones, you can still run." I laughed and shook my head no. He sighed. "Well since you're not going to take my advice, then I need you to take this." He handed me a small box. I opened it and inside was a gorgeous tiara. It was made of what looked like diamonds and sapphires, like what was in my earrings. I looked at Bull. "I give all of my girls a gift to wear. Since your theme is princess, it seemed a tiara was best. Harlow told me the colors, and I was able to get it matched to your earrings."

I tried to protest, it was too much, but he insisted. They helped me to put it on. Now, I knew why they had vetoed me wearing a tiara. Everyone left to get in their places. I could hear music starting. I gave Bull a kiss which only made him blush. We got Angel situated and waited for our cue. When the wedding march started, we left and walked down to the ceremony site. It was on the grounds at the top of some steps which had the woods as a backdrop. Now, since it was only March, the trees were without leaves, but we'd decided to do it at dusk and all the trees were wrapped in white fairy lights. An arbor wrapped in lights and flowers had been erected. Bear, the club's official minister, was the officiant.

The groomsmen and brides' maids stood one per step, so they were staggered up to the top of the step area. At the top stood Devil. He looked so handsome in his suit, that he took my breath away. He was staring at me as I carefully walked up the steps. When I reached him, Angel laughed as she handed me to him and then she ran to stand with Harlow. Devil chuckled and then took my hand when Bull answered he was the one giving me away. Devil pulled me close to whisper to me.

"You look like a dream, Precious. You take my breath away." I smiled and tried to not cry. The rest of the ceremony passed quickly and before I knew it, we'd exchanged rings. My band had diamonds and sapphires around it to match my engagement ring. His was a platinum band with a single sapphire in the middle.

He escorted me down the steps. Once we reached it, we walked back up the aisle between the chairs where the guests were sitting. There we were met by the photographer to take photos. An hour later I was tired and couldn't wait to sit down and eat. I had Harlow go with me to help me with the dress, so I could use the bathroom. The reception was set up under the tent pavilion, which had chandelier lighting, and was surrounded by stone walkways.

We'd added to the bistro lighting and added miles of white fabric and more lights which stretched across the ceiling and hung in swoops overhead and down to the floor on the sides. The tables were set in midnight blue tablecloths, sapphire blue toppers, and the linens were fuchsia. Centerpieces were more of the flowers matching my bouquet, candles, and glass stones in the two different blues as well as clear. We had dinner catered and had an extensive Italian menu for everyone to enjoy.

The four-tiered wedding cake had been done by Alannah. It was white with fuchsia flowers and scalloping and scrollwork done in the two blues with silver beads scattered around it. We'd picked out a lemon-blackberry cake. It had cassis-spiked blackberry jam and the buttercream frosting was lemon flavored.

The reception was a hit. Everyone was having a great time. For us, we'd decided to take our honeymoon away after the baby came. Instead, we were going to spend a couple of nights in a private cabin near Sevierville. Before we cut the cake, we got everyone's attention. Devil addressed the group.

"As you all know, Ashlee and I are having a baby in August," everyone cheered. "Well, we wanted to share some news we got yesterday. We had an ultrasound done and we wanted all of you sharing this special day to know we're going to have a- son." Everyone was yelling and cheering for us. After everyone settled down, we shared our wonderful cake with them.

Not long after we finished eating the cake, Devil whisked me off so we could get time alone. He said he'd waited long enough. When we pulled into the cabin, he carried me inside. It had been prepared by someone. There were candles lit all over with rose petals scattered in a path to the bed and on it. A huge king-sized bed sat on a raised platform in the middle of the room. I barely had a chance to look around because Devil was devouring my mouth as he worked to undo my dress. I laughed.

"In a hurry for something, Jack," I teased? He growled.

"Yes, I want to make love to my wife. I've been in agony ever since I saw you in this dress. Now get naked while I get these damn clothes off." I eased off the dress as he started to tear his off, He watched my every move with hungry eyes. When I was down to my panties and heels, he stopped me.

"Leave those on and keep on the jewelry." I had to laugh again. When he was naked, he scooped me up in his arms and carried me up to the bed and deposited me there. Then he slowly worked my panties off and crawled up on the bed with me. "Babe, I want to go slow but this first time, it's gonna be quicker than I wanted. I want you too much. I'll make it up to you."

Then he was kissing me over and over sucking on my tongue, biting my lip, and licking my lips. Whether he went fast or slow, he never failed to make it perfect for me. When he was done with my mouth, he worked down to my breasts, where he gently played with them and sucked on my nipples. Since I'd gotten pregnant, I couldn't handle as much rough play as I'd liked before. He still made it super pleasurable. Once he'd paid enough attention to my breasts, he kissed down to my stomach where he nuzzled and whispered nonsense to the baby.

I was now almost mindless. I pushed his head toward my core. He laughed and then sank down to devour my pussy. He licked and sucked me until I was almost ready to blow. Then he sank his fingers into my pussy and my ass. It took no time for me to come screaming. I'd come to love his playing with my ass.   Once I came down from the high, he had me get on my back with him standing on the platform.

"Wrap those legs and sexy heels around my waist. I want to fuck my princess." I wrapped my legs around him and he slid into me hard and fast. I gasped and moaned. He was thrusting in and out like he hadn't had me in months rather than a day. He was rubbing my clit and sucking on my breasts as he powered in and out. I was moaning and he was groaning when he finally got me off. I felt almost faint from the pleasure. My pussy clamped down hard on his rock-hard cock. He jerked and spilled his cum deep inside while he groaned out his pleasure.

After we regained our senses, he took me to the bathroom, and we got in the huge tub together. He leisurely washed me as we soaked in the warm water. I'd have preferred hot, but I couldn't enjoy that again until after the baby was born. When we were done, he gently dried me and carried me out to the bedroom again. He pulled chocolate strawberries and sparkling cider out of the fridge, since I couldn't have alcohol. We laid in front of the fire enjoying them. We laughed and teased and just talked for a while.

Suddenly, he got up and grabbed something out of his luggage and came back to lie down. I tried to see what it was, but he hid it under the rug we were laying on. Then he crawled up my body to start kissing me. I could feel his hard cock pressing into my leg. I guess he was ready for round two. This time he teased and tortured me for what felt like forever. I'd gotten off twice before he decided to end my torture.

"Get on your hands and knees, Precious." I eagerly did so. He kneeled behind me and slid into me slowly. Once he was fully inside, he started to slide in and out going slow but deep. The sensation was wonderful. He kept this up for a while until I begged him to do it faster and harder.

Devil started thrusting faster and deeper. I could feel myself tingling and I hoped it meant my orgasm was coming soon. As it built more and more, I pushed back on his cock. He groaned, and I felt his fingers bite into my hips. Suddenly, he stopped. I looked over my shoulder at him in confusion. He bit my shoulder lightly.

"Do you trust me, babe?" I nodded yes. "I want to try something. Stay there and look forward. Don't look." I looked back away and fought not to peek at what he was doing. He'd pulled out of me.

I jumped as I felt something cold and wet touch my ass. Then I realized he was putting lube on it. Over the last few months, we'd increased our anal play to include not just his fingers. He'd used dildos and butt plugs, as well as anal beads on me. The only thing he hadn't fucked me with was his cock. As I thought of this, I felt him pressing inward. I relaxed and that's when I realized it wasn't a toy or his fingers, it was bigger than any of those. It was his cock! I moaned and tried to relax more.

I hissed as the burning and pain increased. He went slow and worked himself in and out progressing a little deeper each time. By the time he was buried fully in my ass, I was ready to cry. The burning had slowly subsided, and it was beginning to feel kind of good. Then he started thrusting. My whole body lit up. This was indescribable.

He worked in and out of my ass increasing the speed and how hard he was thrusting, when I started to moan more. I began to thrust back to meet his cock every time he withdrew. He was panting and I knew I was moaning in constant pleasure. "Harder, Jack. I need to come." He powered into me harder and faster.

Suddenly, he smacked both my ass cheeks. It lit me up. I clamped down on his cock and came yelling his name, as I thrust back into him over and over. He grunted and growled then I felt his warm cum bathing the inside of my tender ass. When I was done milking him dry and he was done coming, we collapsed down on the rug. He kissed and rubbed my back until he slowly withdrew and rolled me into his arms.

"Babe, are you alright? Did it hurt a lot?" I shook my head.

"Not after you got all the way inside. Then it was perfect. Why'd we wait so long?" He chuckled.

"I wanted you prepared and then I decided I wanted to do it on our wedding night. I love you, Ashlee Cannon. Thank you for loving me and giving me a family." I kissed him.

"I love you, Jack Cannon and thank you for loving me and my kids and making us a family." We kissed. Then he helped me up. After we cleaned off, he tucked me into bed in his arms.

"Now, take a nap, babe. I have plans and that includes round three in an hour or so." I laughed as I drifted off to sleep. Jack Cannon was perfect for me. I couldn't wait to see what the rest of our lives would be like.

The End until Book 9: Blaze's Spitfire

About The Author

Ciara St James

I'm a sassy Libra bookaholic who has been reading since I was six years old. I love the written word and numerous genres, but romance has always been my favorite!

I grew up in Rural southeastern Ohio in a village of 4000 people. Then I married and went to Sand Diego where the population was several million, quite the change I can tell you!

Today, I live in beautiful TN. And I'm ruled by two pugs who try to get me to stop writing and be their sofa. If I don't read every day, I become antsy.

2019 I took the plunge and quit my nursing job to dedicate my time to writing. It had been a life long dream.I find I like all romance but have a particular love for steamy romances in all its forms. My biggest dream would be to have others read and receive joy from my books as I have from several of my favorite authors! Please let me know what you think of my works.

Books In This Series

Dublin Falls Archangel's Warriors MC

Terror's Temptress

Savage's Princess

Steel & Hammer's Hellcat

Menace's Siren

Ranger's Enchantress

Ghost's Beauty

Viper's Vixen

Devil Dog's Precious

Printed in Great Britain
by Amazon